Praise for 7

In this luminous and deeply engaging novel, a gifted psychotherapist and her introspective but wary young client embark on a journey through the terrain of dreams, uncovering truths that ripple into their waking lives. Most of *The Owl and the Dreamcatcher* unfolds in the therapy room, where sessions pulse with authentic detail and emotional resonance, while scenes from each woman's home life refract and amplify the dream work in surprising ways. As the therapist's own relationships—with her mother, her husband, and her children—quietly echo the struggles her client faces with her parents, the reader is drawn into parallel arcs of self-discovery and transformation. Richly characterized and beautifully written, Clara Hill offers readers both an absorbing work of fiction and an illuminating window into the art of psychotherapy.

    DEIRDRE BARRETT, PHD   Author of *The Committee of Sleep*; Dream researcher, Harvard University

Clara Hill's new book, her first novel after writing some of the most important and widely read texts for practicing psychotherapists, is an absolute delight: a psychologically rich depiction of therapist and patient engaging in smart and thoughtful therapy sessions, including a complex and astute dream analysis. Like Lori Gottlieb's *Maybe You Should Talk to Someone* or Judith Rossner's *August*, we're privy to and fascinated by the inner worlds and conflicting emotions of both therapist and patient. It's about time we had another great, authentic-sounding novel about psychotherapy and Clara Hill has come through with the real goods.

    BARRY FARBER, PHD   Professor, Teachers College, Columbia University; Author of *Positive Regard in Psychotherapy: Carl Rogers and Beyond*, *Secrets and Lies in Psychotherapy*, *Self-Disclosure in Psychotherapy*, *The Psychotherapy of Carl Rogers: Cases and Commentary*, and *Rock 'n Roll Wisdom: What Psychologically Astute Lyrics Can Teach About Life and Love*

Using a story format, rather than a textbook or manual, preeminent dream researcher, author, psychotherapist, and mentor to many, Dr. Clara Hill provides a compelling inside look at how dreams are used in therapy and the simultaneous impact of dream-oriented therapy on a young woman coming of age and her therapist who is facing a midlife crisis. Clara Hill's engaging style will bring you into the consulting room and the thoughts and dreams of both patient and therapist. Examples of many common dreams and nightmares such as falling, being chased, and abandonment may stimulate your own dream life and lead to important personal insights. Of general interest, but especially relevant for therapists and students at every level of training who want to better understand both dreams and the process of therapy.

> ALAN SIEGEL, PHD   Author of *Dream Wisdom: Uncovering Life's Answers in Your Dreams*

The Owl and the Dreamcatcher gracefully weaves together Clara's decades of experience as a professor and practicing psychologist with her deep fascination with people's internal life stories. In Christina and Dr. Esther, Clara shows us therapy from the inside out, allowing us to witness the process of transformation for both client and therapist. If you've ever wondered what therapy might look like, this book is for you. If you've been in therapy and were curious about what your therapist might have been experiencing during the work, this book is for you. If you're intrigued by the process of human growth and healing, this book is for you.

> SARAH KNOX, PHD   Professor, Marquette University; Co-Editor-in-Chief, *Counselling Psychology Quarterly*

Dr. Clara Hill brings her lifelong passions as a dreamer, healer, and writer to bear on an exciting new creative project with *The Owl and the Dreamcatcher*. Although a work of fiction, the novel shines with the living truth of the healing dynamics between actual clients and therapists. Among its many virtues, the book presents what amounts to a brilliant case study of dream interpretation as an ally in psychotherapy. Highly recommended.

> DR. KELLY BULKELEY   Director, The Sleep and Dream Database

An absorbing tale of the parallel and intertwined lives of psychotherapist and patient. Following the enshrined principle of "Show, don't tell," master psychologist Clara Hill illustrates the inner workings of intensive psychotherapy. *The Owl and the Dreamcatcher* is a riveting, frank story bred from decades of clinical seasoning and personal development. A must-read for all those fascinated by the talking cure.

> JOHN C. NORCROSS, PHD, ABPP   Distinguished Professor of Psychology, University of Scranton

Therapy in fiction is often sensationalized or contrived. In *The Owl and the Dreamcatcher*, an internationally recognized psychotherapy researcher gives readers a unique window into what therapy sessions with compassionate and skilled practitioners can be like. The intersecting stories of Christina and Esther highlight how therapy can foster meaningful change for both patients and therapists.

> CATHERINE F. EUBANKS, PHD   Professor, Gordon F. Derner School of Psychology, Adelphi University

THE OWL AND THE DREAMCATCHER

a novel

THE OWL AND THE DREAM CATCHER

Clara E. Hill

BOLD STORY PRESS

CHEVY CHASE, MARYLAND

Bold Story Press
Chevy Chase, MD 20815
www.boldstorypress.com

Copyright © 2025 by Clara E. Hill

All rights reserved. No part of this book may be reproduced or used in any manner without written permission of the copyright owner except for the use of quotations in a book review. Requests for permission or furtheinformation should be submitted through info@boldstorypress.com.

First edition: 2025
Library of Congress Control Number: 2025917187
ISBN: 978-1-954805-88-0 (paperback)
ISBN: 978-1-954805-89-7 (e-book)

Cover and interior design by KP Books

Printed in the United States of America
10 9 8 7 6 5 4 3 2 1

I dedicate this book to
my therapist Dr. Rona Eisner,
who taught me about therapy,
and to my husband Jim Gormally,
my best friend and partner in life.

CONTENTS

PART I Summer 2023 . . . 1

1 Christina: Lost in the Forest . . . 3
2 Christina and Her Parents . . . 15
3 Christina: Lost in the Jungle . . . 17
4 Esther and Her Family . . . 27
5 Christina: Setting Goals . . . 29
6 Christina at Work . . . 39
7 Christina: Mother Crying . . . 41
8 Esther's Memories . . . 51
9 Christina: Chair Work with Mother . . . 53
10 Esther and Parents . . . 59
11 Christina: Jumping Out of a Plane with No Parachute . . . 61
12 Christina and Chendu . . . 69
13 Christina: Sitting on My Shoulder . . . 73
14 Christina and Mother . . . 81
15 Christina: Mother's Family . . . 85

PART II Fall 2023 . . . 93

16 Esther: The Muddy Pit . . . 95
17 Christina: Barbie . . . 105
18 Esther: Husband Beaching It . . . 113
19 Christina and Mother . . . 121
20 Christina: Career . . . 123
21 Esther: My Dream about Barbie . . . 131
22 Christina: Angry at You . . . 139
23 Esther: Strangled . . . 147
24 Christina: Shooting for the Stars . . . 157

25 Esther: Exam Dream, Part 1 ... 165
26 Christina with Grandma ... 175
27 Christina: Scared of Men ... 177
28 Esther: Exam Dream, Part 2 ... 185
29 Christina: Sexuality ... 193
30 Esther: Gone Husband ... 203
31 Christina: Death ... 209
32 Esther: Adjustment ... 217
33 Christina: Fear of Competing with Mother ... 225
34 Esther: My Mother ... 231
35 Christina: I Want to Be Your Daughter ... 239
36 Esther: Out of the Muddy Pit ... 247
37 Christina: Fired ... 255
38 Esther: Final Session with Paul ... 263

PART III Two Years Later ... 271
39 Christina: Go West, Young Woman ... 273
40 Esther and Sunday Family Dinner ... 281
41 Christina: Dreaming About You ... 285
42 Esther and Her Mother ... 291
43 Christina: A Little Gift for You ... 293

Acknowledgements ... 307
About the Author ... 309
About Bold Story Press ... 311

PART I

SUMMER 2023

1

CHRISTINA:
LOST IN THE FOREST

As the clock struck the hour, I heard the doorbell ring at the private entrance to my home office in suburban Maryland. I opened the door to see a frightened-looking young woman. "Hello," I said warmly, "You must be Christina?"

"Yes, hi, Dr. Shapiro," she said so quietly I had to strain to hear her. She didn't look directly at me but stood waiting to see what to do next.

I asked, "Are you okay with dogs? Star is a therapy dog, but not everyone is comfortable with dogs."

"I love dogs," she said petting Star, who docilely followed Christina into my office. "Where should I sit?" she asked timidly.

"This is my chair," I said, pointing. "Any of the other seats are fine," I responded.

She chose the chair farthest away from mine. With Star seated next to her, Christina didn't look around the office but sat waiting.

I observed Christina as she settled in. She looked to be about eighteen, was average height, and had mousy, brown hair hanging down, almost hiding her eyes. She was dressed neatly in clean blue jeans and a t-shirt. I wouldn't have noticed her if I passed her on the street. She looked like a small, wounded child all tightly knotted up into herself. My maternal instincts kicked in, and I wanted to rescue and protect her. "What led you to seek therapy at this time?"

She responded haltingly without looking directly at me, "I'm, uh, I guess, at a loss about what to do with my life." She started crying softly.

After a pause to give her some space, I said quietly, "Tell me more about what's going on in your life."

She sighed, "I'm, well, waitressing but don't know what I want to do in the future."

Feeling her ambivalence and desperation, I asked, "How are you feeling as we talk?"

Christina paused, looking uncomfortable. "I don't know exactly. My head kind of feels hazy and full of cotton."

Hoping to encourage her to talk more, I asked, "When did you start feeling bad?"

"Um, that's hard to say." She looked away from me and didn't say anything for a while. "It seems like it's been forever."

She stopped talking and seemed more interested in petting Star. I wanted to help her feel safe. She was hurting, and I could feel her pain. Somehow, I needed to help her feel that she could trust me enough to open up. I tentatively asked, "Have you ever been to therapy before?"

"No."

"For many people it's difficult to meet with a therapist. How does it feel for you?"

Christina sighed. "I'm, maybe, a little scared. I don't know what to expect or what to talk about. I've only known about therapy from stuff I see on TV. It looks artificial, like the therapist has all the answers."

"Well, I certainly don't have all the answers, but I hope we can work together to come up with some."

Silence.

I asked, "What was your childhood like?"

"Fine," she replied almost reluctantly.

Trying again, I asked, "Tell me more about your family."

After what looked like an anxiety-filled moment, Christina said blandly, peering at me through her hair, "Everything is fine. I'm an only child. We're just a normal American family."

"*Normal*," I said, emphasizing the word. "What does *normal* mean?"

"Um, no fighting. We're just average I guess," she responded vaguely, making me wonder what was underneath the veneer of this *normal* family.

She hesitated for a long time, so I circled back looking for an opening. "You mentioned not knowing what you want to do in the future. Tell me about that."

"I don't have any particular talents or interests. I am just average in everything. I had no motivation to apply for college, so I didn't, and now I'm stuck living at home with no future."

I guessed that there was more going on that Christina wasn't in touch with or able to tell me about in a first meeting. I decided to try a different strategy and see if I could spark some curiosity. "We can work on career goals, but I'd like to get to know you a little better first. What's your earliest memory?"

She briefly perked up as if not expecting this question but then mumbled, "I can't remember anything about my early childhood. It's all kind of a blank." After a pause, Christina continued slowly, "When I was maybe five,

I vaguely remember something about my mother leaving, or being gone, or not being there." Her voice drifted off, making me wonder what happened.

Feeling encouraged that she responded to the early-memories question, I asked, "What about dreams?"

She glanced at me questioningly, "I dream a lot and have vivid dreams, but I never know what they mean. In our psychology class in high school we learned that dreams are just random bursts of the brain, so I didn't think I would be able to talk about them here."

"It can be helpful to look at your dreams, because they say a lot about you. Did you by any chance have a dream before coming into this session?"

"I had a dream last night. It's been a recurrent dream. Do you want me to tell it?" She sounded eager.

"Yes, that would be great," I responded, relieved that she seemed more engaged.

> I am in a forest. It is starting to get dark, and I am cold and scared. I shimmy up the trunk of a big tree. There is no place to sit in the tree, though, so I slowly make my way back down to the ground and sit against the trunk. I can feel my bones shaking because it's so cold. I hear animals moving around and an owl hooting. I am hungry but have nothing to eat and don't know how to forage for food. What if I ate something poisonous? Suddenly I hear sounds like someone is after me. I wake up, and my heart is pounding.

I'm intrigued with the vividness of the dream and how fully Christina immerses herself in it. "Describe the forest for me so I can imagine being there with you."

She looked up toward the ceiling and said thoughtfully, "A lot of big, old trees, dark, cold."

"What's going on inside as you picture yourself in this forest?"

"Beyond scared. Kind of frozen and not knowing what to do. Helpless, I guess."

Hoping to trace back to past experiences, I queried, "When you think of a forest, what comes to mind?"

"Hansel and Gretel getting lost and leaving bread crumbs to find their way back and then having birds eat up the crumbs and not being able to find their way out of the woods. Little Red Riding Hood getting tricked by the big bad wolf. Bad things happen in forests. I shouldn't be alone in the woods. What was I thinking?" she berated herself.

She's hard on herself. I wonder where she learned that? I thought. Wanting to keep the focus on the dream for now though, I asked, "Any memories of forests?"

"A vague memory of going hiking with my parents. They would get impatient with me when I couldn't keep up. They never brought snacks and just wanted to keep going even when I was tired. The other memory is of a place like Central Park where people go out at night, and it can be dangerous, especially for women. I could be attacked. I remember hearing about a strangler who attacked women at night while they were running."

Struck by all her negative associations, I continued, "Pretend I'm from Mars and have never heard of a forest. What is the first thing that comes to mind when you think of a forest."

"It's wild. Lots of trees. Animals live there. There could be snakes, deer, birds. It's not a jungle but more like something you would see in New England. There are no houses, and people don't live in this forest. You're not supposed to go off the trails because that could damage the ecosystem. It would be better to have a guide rather than being on your own. I shouldn't be there, especially at night. I also think of the phrase *can't see the forest for the trees*, and I can't see beyond my face."

I loved how freely Christina could associate, albeit with the tendency to berate herself. The dream suggests so many hypotheses about Christina: there's a lack of attunement with her parents, life-and-death danger that she feels ill-equipped to handle or survive, and existential issues of death anxiety and isolation.

"What memories do you have of what your parents told you about going into the forest when you went on these family hikes?"

"Just that I had to go. I didn't have a choice. They didn't like me talking back to them. I was supposed to be seen and not heard." I could hear the annoyance in her voice and briefly flashed on hearing my own mother's critical, bossy voice. She continued, "Oh, I just remembered getting lost on one of those hikes. I looked around and didn't see my parents anywhere. I was so scared. I couldn't stop crying, and I didn't know how to get help. Eventually they came back looking for me and yelled at me because I hadn't followed them. They didn't help me at all and didn't even seem worried about where I was." Star looked up startled as Christina's voice got louder but settled back down to snooze when she petted him. I noted that she could be reassuring with Star.

"Wow. Being alone and lost sounds painful."

"I did feel alone. But it was a familiar feeling."

"I'm also wondering about your parents not only not being worried but being angry at you. I wonder if you felt any anger at them?"

"No," she said strongly. "I blamed myself for not keeping up. I *should* have been paying better attention. Maybe I was lost in my thoughts and spacing out. I do that a lot, and they get annoyed with me when they I'm not paying attention."

Tying it back to what Christina had talked about before, I queried, "I'm remembering that you talked about how your family was *normal* and never fought. Sounds a little different here."

She nodded, looking a little chagrinned, "Well, maybe I portrayed the family a little too positively. I feel like I'm betraying them if I say anything negative about them. There is a cloak of secrecy within our family. We aren't supposed to air our dirty linen in public."

"So," I said to bring it closer to our relationship, "you might have a little difficulty here in therapy if you feel pressured to break the family code of secrecy?"

Christina looked down, "But I guess I have to be honest if I want to get better."

"It's hard to go against the rules in your family." After a pause with no response, I asked, "Is it okay to keep going?"

"Yes," she sounded a little resistant and whiny, "although I must say this is harder than I thought it would be."

"Thank you for letting me know that. Therapy can be hard work. We can go as slowly as you need," I responded. After a pause to give her some space, I pressed on, "Are there any situations in your current waking life where you feel lost and on your own?"

"Well, that's why I wanted to start therapy. I feel alone a lot of the time. I hadn't made the connection between the dream and seeking out therapy until now, but it makes sense to me."

"I also hear that you want to be seen and heard."

"Yeah, that's for sure. It feels good to have someone listen to me."

"Tell me more about feeling alone in your family," I changed the topic slightly to learn more about her family history.

With more confidence, perhaps because she had an idea of what to say, Christina answered, "I'm an only child, and my parents were older when I was born, and they are set in their ways. They are both quiet; you'd probably call them introverts. They don't have many, if any, friends. They work, and they're stoic, solitary, Norwegian types who keep to themselves. They don't show any affection to each other or to me. They don't seem particularly unhappy, just reserved. I feel like I don't know them, and they don't know me. As a child, I wondered if I was adopted; I wanted to have siblings. I remember reading about families that were so alive with lots of kids and fights and fun. I didn't have many friends either, so I was by myself a lot. I read a lot and mostly kept to myself."

"I can feel the sadness wafting off you."

"Yeah, I feel like crying just thinking about it."

I saw the hint of tears in her eyes and felt her pain. "Imagine yourself right now sitting under the tree crying."

Christina quickly inhibited her tears, as if crying made her feel too vulnerable. I decided not to push her in that moment.

"Yeah," Christina said shakily, still looking down and petting Star, "I realize how lonely I must have been and am. Being lost in a forest with no way out and not knowing if there's something that's going to get me makes me feel desperate."

Trying to help her build some coping skills, I suggested, "What might you say to yourself now, looking back with some compassion?"

"I don't know."

"I think you do know what that little girl would like to hear."

After a long silence, she muttered softly, "It's okay. Take a deep breath. We'll figure this out."

"Great!" I reassured her for the big step. "How did that feel?"

"I feel calmer. I guess I do know," she said with a wry smile.

Wanting to get back to the dream, I gently steered her, "Let's take a look at another image. Can you pick one of the kind animals or creatures who was in the forest?"

"Maybe the owl. Do you want me to describe it more?" She sounded unsure and wanting to please me.

"Yes, what does it look like?"

"I can't see it, only hear it. It has a mournful hooting. I think of the owl in *Winnie the Pooh*, kind of wise, far off, distant. At first it seemed a little scary, but now when I think of it, it seems more friendly. Maybe it is keeping me company."

"Any feelings in your body as you talk about the owl? Pretend that you have a flashlight and turn it inwards."

Christina looked reflective. "I'm breathing a little more easily. My head feels lighter. I kind of like the owl. I picture it having big eyes, its feathers blending into the color of the tree as camouflage, coming out mostly at night, kind of like it's talking directly to me."

"Maybe like it's there to protect you?" I suggested.

"Yeah," Christina looked as though she liked that idea. "Maybe it's my spirit animal."

"What associations do you have to owls?"

"They come out at night, hunting for little animals; they are wise. I've only seen them in books, although our neighbors said they have seen an owl in their back yard, which is strange in the city."

"The owl seems like a friend."

"I like the owl." She smiled at the thought.

Again, trying to bolster her resilience, I offered, "Perhaps you can remember the owl next time you feel lonely or scared?"

She looked intrigued. "I'll try that. Maybe I'll get a picture of an owl."

Realizing that we were almost out of time and wanting to get to what might be an important image, I moved along, "Finally, the someone behind you at the end. Tell me about that."

"It is so scary; I feel like someone is following me and is going to attack me and hurt me. I'm shaking even remembering it."

"That sounds awful, as if your very survival is at stake."

Christina drew a deep breath and admitted pensively, "It was awful."

Remembering that she said the dream was recurrent, I wondered aloud, "Is the feeling of being chased a familiar image for you?"

"Actually," Christina nodded appreciatively. "Now that you mention it, I've had many dreams about being chased and sometimes captured. I usually wake myself up before anything can happen, but I'm usually terrified."

I tentatively interpreted, wanting to help her make connections but not waiting to move too quickly and frighten her away "Almost as though something bad has happened to you and you're reliving it."

"Hmmm," she reflected. "That could be. I sometimes feel I could explode. There are so many feelings bottled up inside me with no place to go. The world feels like a dangerous place."

Not wanting to leave her with the danger as the last memory, I suggested, "I wonder if there's any image from the dream that you could use to calm yourself down?"

She mused for a moment, "I like the idea of the owl being there."

"So, maybe good to remember that one when you need a friend."

To check in with how she felt about the session, I said, "I'm aware that our time is almost up for today. What was this like for you talking about your dream?"

"It helps to tell you about it." Christina emphatically said. "It seems strange to say how upset I've been by the dream, but every time I have it, it's hard to function the whole next day. I know it must be an important dream if I keep having it."

"It does feel important and may help us unravel what's going on for you."

Christna added, "I've never been able to figure out what my dreams mean, so this is great. I guess they always felt a little silly. Do they mean something, or is there a message? What should I do with them? But somehow it feels like we uncovered some important things here, and it feels a little easier than talking about my current boring life. Will we be spending a lot of time on dreams?"

"That's up to you. If it feels helpful, we certainly can. I like to work with dreams because it's a safe way to get to deep things. It's like the dream is a mirror that you hold up and can use it to see yourself more clearly. And I help you polish the mirror so that you can remove the distortions and see what's actually there. Thank you for sharing your dream with me and trusting me with it. If you feel like it, you might start a journal. Write down dreams and ideas that come to you that you might like to talk about in therapy. Maybe draw a picture of the trees and forest and owl if that appeals to you. We can start with that next time if you want. Is the same time next week good for you?"

"Yes, this works for me." She halted for a second and then added, "Can you tell me how long you think I'll need to be in therapy?"

I sensed that feeling trapped might be a big anxiety for her. Not wanting to give false assurances, I noted, "That's hard to say because it differs for each person. Let's check in with each other as we go to make sure we're working well together. Please be as honest as you can so that I can figure out how best to help you. See you next week."

I reflected that Christina had seemed more open once she started talking about her dream. It seemed easier for her to work with dream images than deal with real life. The dream itself was powerful. I'm worried about the image of the person behind her who could attack her. She seems so defenseless and alone. Given that there are no other people in this dream, it seems she has trouble trusting others.

I need to be careful about jumping in and trying to rescue her, given her anxieties. I feel a pull to fix her and make everything better and to be her friend since she seems to have so few of them. My wanting to fix my clients is something I've worked on a lot as a therapist. It's so compelling to want to fix everything, but I want to restrain myself and empower her to fix herself. I'm also interested in how she blamed herself when she got lost in the woods. I've worked a lot on not blaming myself when things go wrong, so I'll be interested to see how that plays out, and I wonder what issues it will bring up for me. Her asking how long therapy could last probably reflects some anxiety—we need to talk about that. I wonder how much reluctance she has about working with me in therapy.

2

CHRISTINA AND HER PARENTS

Christina drove home slowly, thinking about the therapy session. On the one hand, she had enjoyed talking about her dream, but on the other hand she had some doubts about how helpful talking would be: How would that change anything? And she didn't know if she clicked enough with Dr. Shapiro. She couldn't put her finger on anything, but maybe it just wasn't what she expected from therapy. Her image of a therapist was of someone younger and maybe more sophisticated. She had hoped to get some answers, but she felt worse instead of better. She was still halfway into her dream and feeling vulnerable.

She hesitated before turning into the driveway. She didn't want to see her parents and answer questions about therapy. She wished she hadn't had to tell them, but she needed them to pay for her sessions through their insurance because she couldn't afford it on her own. Reluctantly, she went into the house to get ready for work, opening the door as quietly as she could.

Her parents were in the kitchen getting dinner ready. Her mother, Kristin, called out, "How did it go?"

Christina knew that her mother was worried about her, but she didn't want to talk. "Fine," she said, and walked quickly up the steps.

She overheard her father, Harold, talking to her mother. "I'm not sure Christina going to therapy is such a good idea. She'll grow out of this. People should solve problems on their own."

Her mother replied angrily, "Like we solved all our problems, eh?" and stalked out. She headed for the stairway, wanting to connect with Christina. But then she hesitated. Christina had been so prickly for the last few months. She sank down on the stairs, feeling sad and lonely. She wished she had been the one to go to therapy but felt she was too old to change.

3

CHRISTINA:
LOST IN THE JUNGLE

Christina looked harried as she rushed into my office ten minutes late. I wondered if her lateness reflected possible ambivalence about being in therapy, but she started talking as soon as she sat down.

"I had another dream last night," she said hesitantly, as if wanting to know if it was okay to tell me her dream.

> I am lost in a deep jungle. I hear drums and lots of sounds. Suddenly, my high school teacher appears and says that I am going to flunk English because I didn't do my homework. I wake up and feel a deep sense of shame and fear.

"Take a minute and breathe deeply," I said gently. When she looked like she was settling in, I asked, "What image from the dream comes to mind as the most important or salient?"

She answered promptly as if ready for this question. "The teacher. She was dressed in jungle clothing—you know, a pith helmet and safari jacket and pants. Actually," she said with a surprised tone, "she reminds me of you."

"How so?"

"Well," Christina reflected. "She's nice, soft-spoken, and kind. I always wanted to please her. I worked hard in that class, but she never seemed to notice me. I liked the way she talked about books in class. She seemed interested in her students. I wished that I could go and talk to her like other students did, but I never got up the nerve."

Curious about the connection Christina made to me, I asked, "I wonder if you worry that I won't notice when you're working hard?"

"Oh no, no, you definitely notice me," she replied a little too quickly, as if trying to reassure me or perhaps herself. She stopped and thought more. "But I guess I do worry that you will be bored or will like your other clients more."

Impressed that she recognized the transference from her teacher to me, I pressed, "Is there anything I'm doing that makes you think I'm bored or that I prefer my other clients?"

She took a minute before answering and then mused, "I think it's my fear based on my parents not being very attentive."

I nodded in agreement. "Please let me know, though, if there are any specific times you feel a need for more attention than I'm giving you."

"Thanks," she said and then added with some effort. "Maybe I'm feeling extra needy right now and worried that my neediness will push you away."

I leaned forward and made eye contact with her. "Thank you for your honesty. I promise to let you know if you are asking for more than I can give. Right now I feel that you've been very appropriate in not pushing boundaries. If anything, I want you to ask me for more when you need it."

"That's interesting," Christina looked down, "because I feel like I'm asking for too much."

"That's not too surprising, given that you felt you couldn't ask for anything from your parents for fear they would get annoyed." After a pause, I asked, "What about the homework?"

"OMG," she replied talking rapidly and looking at me with fear in her widened eyes, "I just remembered you told me to work more on my dream from last week. I was supposed to write about it and maybe draw it, and I didn't. I can't believe I forgot. My bad. I'm supposed to be trying to get better, but I didn't even do my assignment. I failed again." Christina cringed as if awaiting punishment.

"No problem. Take a minute again and breathe." After Christina took a few deep breaths, I added, "Tell me more about how you're feeling right now."

Looking down, Christina said, "I'm scared you'll kick me out of therapy. I was excited about writing about the dream after the session and then it slipped my mind. I started playing my video game, and I guess I just got swept away and forgot."

"Perhaps it felt too hard at the time, and you needed to avoid working on it. That's okay. My suggestion was just that, a suggestion. If it works for you, great. If not, we can revise and figure out what works better. We're in this together," I said reassuringly.

"Whew," she sighed, looking visibly relieved but still a little shaky.

"What's going on inside? What are you thinking?" I wanted her to verbalize her anxiety and fears, which often takes the sting out of them.

"Actually, I'm not thinking too much," Christina admitted. "I'm just kind of blocked. I guess I'm back to the shame," she winced. "I'm embarrassed that my dream was so obvious and that I didn't even connect it to forgetting to do the homework. Part of me wants to be here, but it's hard work, and I'm not very good at it."

I wondered to myself if this blockage was why she was late for the session. "Can you remember other instances when you felt ashamed?" I asked. "What's the first time that comes to mind?"

"Oh, here's a good one. I was staying with my relatives for a summer when I was ten, and my uncle was very strict and scary. We went to a fair, and I had to go to the bathroom badly. I ended up pooping in my pants. What a mess! When we got back to the house, I hid the panties in the basement hoping no one would find them. My uncle found them and was furious, wanting to know whose they were. I had to admit that they were mine. I can't remember what happened after that, but I remember being incredibly ashamed, especially in front of my perfect, prissy cousins who never did anything wrong."

"That's a difficult situation to handle when you're at someone else's house!" I noted to myself that here was yet another situation where she was distressed and the adult was angry instead of supportive.

"I've always wondered if he told my parents. I don't know what they would have done, but they never said anything to me. To this day, I still get anxious about finding a bathroom in time. And even saying it makes me have to go to the bathroom. Is it okay if I go now?"

"Of course. It's right down the hall to your left."

I used the brief respite to think about Christina's avoidance and ambivalence on the one hand and her eagerness and insightfulness on the other. I am warming up to her.

After she returned and sat down, this time remembering to pet Star, I asked. "How about the teacher in the dream? Can you remember any situations in your real classes with her that bothered you?"

"Well, there was, um, this time when we were supposed to turn in a paper on *The Great Gatsby*. I had been sick with mono and couldn't focus on writing the assignment. I asked her for an extension. She said I could have another week but she would have to lower my grade one level. She had her rules and wouldn't budge. I finished the paper, but I was upset with her for giving me a lower grade when I had been sick and had a doctor's note. I had never asked for any special considerations before that." She bristled, with a hint of anger in her voice.

"I can see how her decision felt unfair," I reinforced her being in tune with her feelings, but I also wanted to test the reality of the situation. "Did she treat you any differently than other students in the class?"

"No, come to think of it, she was generally fair. But it just took so much effort for me even to ask, so I don't know, I guess I wanted her to give me special treatment. It didn't seem like an unreasonable request."

"So, we've kind of been talking about how you felt about my suggestion to work on your dream. Would it be okay to talk about that more directly?"

"Um, I guess so, although I feel a little nervous." Christina looked at me warily.

"Nervous about . . . ?"

"That you'll be angry at me for not doing my homework. I'll be in trouble. You won't like me," she whispered, grimacing slightly.

"The fear of disappointing is deep," I said quietly to mirror her whisper.

"Yeah, I guess. Are you angry?" She looked at me with worried, widened eyes.

"No, I'm not angry; it's your therapy. It's up to you to choose whether you want to do the homework. I'm more interested in hearing your thoughts about why you didn't do it, because that can lead us to some important stuff. But," I paused, "let's step back and reflect for a minute about why you might have projected anger onto me?"

"I'm sure it goes back to my parents exploding at me if I did anything they perceived as wrong. I feel strange saying it, but I lived in fear," she said, turning inward with some puzzlement.

"That's similar to the fear in your first dream!"

"Yeah, you're right." She seemed interested in the connection.

Wanting to encourage her further, I tried to offer a different perspective. "I want to note that you said you *did* think about the dream after you left the office. So, in effect you did do your homework, just not in writing."

"Hmmm, I like that!" She smiled but added nothing more, so I wasn't sure whether the new perspective registered.

"What were your thoughts about our session after you left last week?"

Christina sighed. "I was surprised about how alone I felt in the dream. It's so obvious, right? I was on my own in that forest, and no one came to help me. That feeling of aloneness is what really made me seek out therapy. I get anxious about being alone. I can't depend on my parents. They don't even seem to notice me. I was afraid that's what you would be like. I like when you ask me questions because then I have a better idea about what I should be doing here. But I still sometimes worry I'm boring you. My problems feel so mundane. It's not like I've had big traumas. I can't imagine why you'd want to listen to me."

I smiled at her. "Actually, it makes sense to me that you'd be scared about my being bored when you feel like your parents don't listen to you. But when a client voices this kind of concern—and I actually begin to feel a bit bored—it's interesting and helpful to me, because it tells me they are feeling defensive and scared. It tells me something about what the client might be experiencing. That said, I have to say that when we work on your dreams, I feel very engaged. You have such rich and interesting dreams, and you're working hard to understand them."

Silence. Christina intently studied the pattern in the carpet and absently petted Star. I realized that I had moved into my professorial mode and lost her. "I apologize. I went off on a tangent about boredom in general rather than talking specifically about you. As I reflect, I wasn't bored with you. At first, I was feeling frustration that I might not be able to help you because you seemed so frightened."

Silence.

"Once you started talking about your dreams, though, you became quite engaging and seemed less timid," I added, given that she seemed to have withdrawn and I wanted to reestablish a connection.

"I like talking about my dreams. But it's hard to hear anything negative."

Thank you for telling me your feelings. I can only know what's going on if you tell me."

"Okay, I'll try," she murmured.

"That didn't sound very convincing," I gently challenged.

"Well, I am anxious right now. Because my parents got so angry at me, I assume everyone is angry at me."

"I'm curious. How do you react when you think others are angry at you?"

"I shut down," she admitted with a shrug.

"Ah, yes, it looked like you shut down. Let's come back to the homework idea. How do you feel about whether you want me to assign you homework?"

"Maybe not right now. I focus too much on what I *should* be doing."

"Well, as they say, *shit on the shoulds*. Let's pay attention to that because we might discover more about when you *should* yourself."

"Oh, I like that idea," she said, and we both laughed. That's something I can say to myself, 'shit on the shoulds!' Feels liberating."

"Great! Now, how are you feeling about our work today?"

"I'm relieved you're not angry with me for not doing the homework. I still wonder though about how long therapy will last. I'm nervous making a commitment for a long time and not having control."

"You seem to have some ambivalence about being in therapy with me."

Silence.

"Let's talk next time about goals. That might help you figure out whether you want to be in therapy. Maybe you can think about what specifically you would like to focus on in therapy so that you have more of a sense of control. Would that be okay?"

"Sure"

"See you next week?"

"Sure. Thanks."

Christina's anxiety and fear of judgment are affecting me—and not in a good way. This relationship feels rocky. She's testing whether she can trust me. There were several awkward moments in the session, and I don't think I handled her concern about being boring very well.

Christina reminds me of myself at her age, particularly her social anxiety, insecure attachments, difficulties with her parents, tendency to isolate, and lack of life goals. We were both miserable but handled it differently; she is more isolated, cautious, pliant, and eager to please, whereas I was angrier and more rebellious. We come from different backgrounds (mine being Jewish from Eastern Europe, whereas she's White Norwegian). We are different ages now and at different stages in life. I'm forty-five, have a PhD in clinical psychology, am married with two children, and have a meaningful career. She is eighteen, without a career or social relationships—at least any she's talked about. Given how similar we are in some ways, I have to be careful not to over-identify with her. I must see her for herself.

4

ESTHER AND HER FAMILY

As Esther was ruminating after the session with Christina, her children—Josh, twelve years old and Jess, nine years old—stumbled into her office after walking home from camp. "Mom," Jess yelled, punching Josh, "he was so mean to me today at camp! He said bad things about me to the other kids."

Josh retorted, "Well you shouldn't be such a dork, hanging around me all the time. Get your own friends. Oh, I forgot," he smirked, "you don't *have* any friends!"

"Mom, there he goes again," Jess whined. "I have friends, just none of them are at this camp. It's not fair that I had to go to this camp just because Josh wanted to."

Esther sighed, her hopes for a nice, peaceful evening disappearing. "Well, how about suiting up and going down to the pool before dinner?"

"But, Mom, can't you make her stop hanging around me at camp?" complained Josh.

"We can talk about it over dinner," Esther said, hoping that she could get Steve to help with the continual scrapping between the two.

"Okay, I bet I can beat you to the pool," yelled Jess, once again making it a contest.

"Steve," Esther called into his office, "are you going to the pool with us?"

"No," he said, putting his hand over the phone. "I've got to go out tonight. I've got a meeting with Henry and won't be home until late."

Esther stood stunned for a minute. When had they started passing each other like ships in the night? Why was he meeting yet again with Henry? Why was it up to her to solve all the problems with the kids and to make dinner all the time? "Well, that's just great. Thanks for helping out!" she muttered to herself as he continued to talk on the phone.

5

CHRISTINA:
SETTING GOALS

After Christina sat down in the same chair, she looked around as if it were her first visit, which indeed it might have felt like since she had avoided looking around before. She glanced at the Georgia O'Keefe pictures of flowers, the Hummel figurines from Germany, and a wooden Buddha statue.

"Who's the artist of those flower pictures?" she wanted to know.

"Georgia O'Keefe," I said, interested to see that she related to the O'Keefe prints more than the other things. "Do you like them?"

"I really do, especially that one of the apple blossoms."

"What do you like about it?" I asked, thinking about how useful it can be to associate to anything—a dream, story, movie, picture.

"It makes me think of spring and hope."

"And maybe you're feeling a little more hopeful now?"

"Hmm. I guess I am," she said sounding surprised.

"So," I brought up the agenda, "what are your goals for therapy?"

"Well, I feel a little unsure about how to phrase my thoughts. I want to understand myself more and figure out who I am. Now that I've been working on my dreams, I can see how little I know about myself. I feel so dead inside. I want to understand why, where that comes from, and what I can do about it. Until starting therapy, I never thought much about my motivations or understood why I do what I do. My family discouraged talking about feelings or asking questions. You know, *children should be seen and not heard*. I feel like I'm beginning to think for myself more, and I like that."

I made a mental note to come back to the idea of children being seen and not heard. "It does seem like you're getting more curious about yourself. Other goals?"

"I also want to work on my relationship with my parents because I have a lot of anger at them," she continued. "From the things you've alluded to already, a lot of what I'm going through seems to be related to childhood.

"Absolutely. Parents have a lot to do with how we develop," I confirmed. "Any thoughts about which parent you need to work on most?"

"It's slightly easier with my mother than my father because she seems more open to having a relationship with me. It's hard to get close to my father because he is so withdrawn. Sometimes I'm not even sure I want to bother. And his anger terrifies me."

"Say more about feeling terrified."

"I just retreat into myself. I freeze. I guess I'm afraid of being punished."

"Where are you feeling that in your body?"

"I'm having a hard time breathing and want to run away."

"I can hear the anxiety. Take a deep breath." Pause. "We can work on that so that you can figure out how to cope more effectively."

Christina continued, "As I said before, I want to figure out what to do with my life. I feel uncertain about what I want to do in the future. I beat myself up for not going to college this fall, but I wouldn't have known what to major in if I had gone. I am at a loss for how to find a direction. I have no talents or real interests. I don't know where to start talking about it, but I feel an urgency to make decisions and start living my life."

"Sounds like a good goal for us to work on here. Anything else come to mind?"

"Hmm, well, maybe friends. I've been alone and lonely too much. It's hard to see everyone else with friends. Maybe not as pressing a concern, but something I want to get to soon. Oh, and something I forgot to bring up before. Weight. As you can see, I'm about thirty pounds overweight. I eat when I'm happy, sad, angry, or bored. Really, anything triggers my eating. I feel out of control, especially at work where I can snack nonstop. It's something I'm upset about because I don't like being overweight. I guess that's about it for now."

I probed, "Do you get into anorexia or binging and purging?"

"No. Anorexia has looked appealing sometimes when I look at social media. But that's not me. It's mostly obsessing about eating and being overweight. I think about it all the time."

"Perhaps," I posed tentatively, "you obsess about food as a distraction from other more important concerns, like career and death?"

Looking intrigued, Christina paused and reflected, "That hits home. You might be right. Eating is definitely an obsession, and I do avoid thinking about other things."

"Many people do. Avoidance can be reinforcing." After a pause, I noted, "You haven't said anything about romantic relationships?"

She quickly looked away and said abruptly. "I don't think I'm ready to work on that."

I wondered about her strong response but sensed it was too early to press her about it.

"So we've got self-understanding, your mother and your father, career, friends, and weight. What would you like to start on?"

"Maybe first my mother, then maybe career concerns so I can move forward. And the weight is right up there too. I'm not sure about the order of the other things right now, but they are less important."

"Sounds good." Realizing that we had not talked much about fees and logistics, I also wanted to assess how that was going for her, so added, "and what about how often we meet and the fee? I've been seeing you weekly through your parents' insurance. How has that been for you?"

"Weekly is fine. I can fit it into my schedule easily. In terms of the fee, I hated telling my parents I wanted to go to therapy, but I had to because I need to use their insurance. I don't make a lot of money, so there's no way I could afford it otherwise."

"What was it like telling them you wanted to go to therapy?"

"It took me a long time to work up the nerve. They aren't therapy-type people. But I knew I needed help. Actually, my school counselor suggested I go to therapy because of not having any plan for college or the future. She was worried about me. It took me a few months before I did anything about it, but I eventually did."

"I'm glad you did. It took a lot of courage. Sometimes the hardest part is taking the first step and making the appointment."

"I was scared for sure. While we're talking about this, can we come back to how long you think I'll have to be in therapy?"

Noting that length of therapy was a theme, I said, "It really depends on you. I would imagine we could go anywhere from six months to a few years. But it's up to you to determine how long you want to keep working."

"That sounds good. I don't want to feel like it's going to last forever."

"Why do you suppose you're concerned about the length of treatment?

"Hmm, I don't know exactly," she said hesitantly. "Maybe I just don't like feeling out of control or being trapped. And I don't like feeling beholden to my parents since it's their insurance. But I also think I just want to feel better soon."

"I can hear the fear of being trapped. I suggest we reevaluate your goals and progress every few sessions. If you want to do it more often or if you have concerns, please tell me."

"That makes sense."

"Okay let's try that." After a pause, I noted that it looked like she was stuck, waiting for further direction. "How would you like to spend the rest of our time today?"

"Maybe talk about my mother." Breaking eye contact and looking into the distance, Christina added, "As I said, she's distant and uncommunicative. I sense she's sad, but I don't know why. I hardly know anything about her background. When I was little, I thought I had disappointed her, that she would have liked to have a different child. But I don't know what's going on with her."

"Close your eyes and visualize her. Tell me what you see."

"She's tall and thin. Average looking. Maybe even a little mousy looking. She never stands up for herself. She's quiet."

She could be describing herself, I thought to myself. Like mother, like daughter.

Christina continued, "She acts scared around my father. I guess that's not surprising because he can be critical and has that underlying explosive anger. I wish I could ask her about herself, but I just sense that it's not okay to ask about anything." Looking inward, Christina quietly admitted, "All of a sudden I feel like crying."

"I can feel the tears," I said soothingly, noticing that she again inhibited her tears. "Be the tears. What would your tears say if they could talk?"

Christina said pensively, "I feel sad. People say I look like my mother, and I want to be close to her, but I just don't know what to say to make her feel better. I wonder why she's so sad. What she was like at my age. What did she want out of her life?"

"What would you like to say to her?"

"I don't know if I could say anything to her. It feels like she pushes me away. It's so quiet in the house. Why doesn't she want to have a connection with me?"

"Could you try saying, 'Mom, I wonder if we could talk?'"

"Well, I would never say *mom*. It's always been *mother*."

"Okay, *mother* it is. Pretend your mother is over there in that chair right now." I pointed to a nearby empty chair. "What would you say to her?"

Taking time to get in touch with her feelings, Christina asserted weakly, "Mother, I'd like to talk to you. I'd like to know you better and for you to know me better." After another short silence, Christina added, "I feel so lonely, and I wonder if you feel lonely too?"

Very gently and softly, I brought her back from talking to her mother so that she could process the work, "How was that for you?"

"Wow," Christina said, looking directly at me for a change. "All of a sudden, I had this powerful feeling that she was so depressed, just a well of sadness. I don't know why she's sad, but it seemed like a dark cloud hanging over her. And I felt sorry for her. I wanted to find out what's underneath all that sadness."

"Sounds like you want to get to know her better." She nodded. After a few seconds I added, "You said that people say you look alike. Can you tell me more about that?"

"We both look a little mousy, like we are trying to shrink away from being noticed. When you asked me to visualize her earlier, though, I thought she looked kind of pretty. I've seen pictures of her when she was young, and she was attractive. She looks so old now."

"She sounds intriguing—what with her sadness and attractiveness. I can see why you would like to get to know her. I wonder if you can imagine during this week what she might have been like as a young woman? What it might have been like to meet her when she was your age?"

She asked warily, "Are you suggesting that I ask her?"

I shook my head. "Not necessarily. I was thinking more of your having an imaginary dialogue with her, just kind of pondering what she was like as a young woman. We don't want to move too fast here because these are long-standing patterns. Let's just play with this, maybe pay attention to your dreams this week and see what comes up."

Looking relieved, Christina ventured, "Oh, okay, that sounds good. I liked that I had a different feeling about her today in the session. It feels like there's something there that I want to learn more about."

I quickly supported her growing curiosity, "Yes, I'm also intrigued by the similarities and differences between you and your mother. And I noticed again the explosive anger you mentioned about your father. It reminds me of the fear in your forest dream. There's some stuff there to look into further."

"Hmmm. That is an interesting parallel about the fear," Christina agreed.

Coming back to the importance of getting Christina to voice what was going on inside her, I said, "We're just about out of time, but I wanted to check in with you about how you felt about our session today."

With some energy in her voice, she quickly replied, "I liked setting goals. It feels more like I know what we're doing and where we're going. It gives me a concrete sense of where I am and a sense of having some control over this process. I have hope that things can get better, that I can get better. Thank you," she said with a shy smile that gave me a glimpse of her nascent sense of self.

"Thank *you* for opening up and trusting me a little more. I'm enjoying getting to know you and look forward to our work together."

"Me, too," Christina said on her way out the door.

The session was easier today. I'm glad we were able to work through the rupture from last week. Christina was so nervous about being trapped. Slowing down and working on concrete goals seemed to make her more comfortable. I have to be careful not to push her too fast.

As I thought about Christina's relationship with her mother, I realized I had been triggered about unresolved issues with my mother. We fought like cats and dogs when I was a teenager. I hated her for a while. I thought I had worked through all those issues in my own therapy with Paul, but apparently there's more there. I don't feel as negatively about her as I did, but I need to do more work. I do miss having the time with Paul to sort out what was going on with me, and I worry that my unresolved issues will leak into my work with Christina. I have to think about how to handle the feelings that are coming up. I'll see if they persist. Maybe bring up the case in peer supervision? Maybe get back into therapy myself?

6

CHRISTINA AT WORK

Christina sneaked into work, hoping no one would notice her and start teasing her again. Her coworkers were okay but could be a little much. She wondered yet again what she was doing here and whether she was going to be stuck waitressing for the rest of her life.

"Hey, Christina," called out Joannie, "come hear the latest about Curt. I'm sure he likes you." Curt was the cook, and Christina well knew that he flirted with everyone and wasn't interested in her at all. Besides, he scared her because he was so cocky and self-assured.

"Can't now, sorry, Joannie. I've got to get to work. Mr. McGinnis told me I have to get all the salt and pepper shakers filled since I didn't do it last night." She scurried away quickly to avoid talking to any of them.

Curt came up behind Christina and said, "Boo!"

Christina jumped half out of her skin. "Go away. Can't you see I'm working?"

"Hey, chill out," he said. "You're so uptight. Mr. McGinnis isn't even here. He called in because he's going to be late. How about going out back and having a cigarette?"

"No thanks," Christina said primly and scooted around the table to get as far away from him as possible. Thankfully, he took the clue and left to flirt with another waitress.

"Christina, you have to be careful with Curt. He can be a real lech," said Darla, a middle-aged waitress who acted like everyone's mother.

"No worries there. I'm not at all interested in him," Christina replied curtly.

"You know we all worry about you, Christina," Darla persisted. "You seem so naïve; you have to toughen up to work at a place like this."

Christina sighed. This was going to be a long night.

7
CHRISTINA:
MOTHER CRYING

Christina started our next session eagerly, like a proud kid with a present, "I had a dream a couple nights ago about my mother. It was only an image, but it was so vivid I thought it was real and had to remind myself it was a dream." She paused and then began,

> My mother is sitting very still and quietly weeping, like she has lost something important. Then there are these ghosts floating above her head and drifting away.

"That was it, but I could almost reach out and touch her. It was the middle of the night, and I woke up and rehearsed it a couple times so I could tell you."

"Such a rich dream," I said, delighted that Christina had dreamed about her mother after talking about her last week. "Describe more about your mother in the dream. How old was she? What was she wearing? Where was she sitting? Close your eyes and try to focus on her.

Say whatever you can visualize as you put yourself back into the dream."

Turning inward, Christina began, "She is wearing a printed flannel nightgown tied with a pale, yellow ribbon right up to her neckline, so it must be nighttime. It is cold, and she is shivering and crying. She's in a bedroom I think, but I can't see any furniture except the bed, and it is dark outside."

"What are you feeling as you see her sitting there?"

"I feel this profound sadness that she's weeping. I want to talk to her, but I don't want to intrude on her privacy. I feel like a voyeur observing something I shouldn't see. My parents are so private and would be ashamed if I saw them undone or in crisis."

"What associations do you have to your mother sitting there? The first thing that comes to mind when you picture this image?"

"She's by herself in total anguish. She could be a portrait in a gallery, *Mother Crying*. She's lost in her grief as though she's lost something monumentally important to her."

"Interesting that she's alone in this dream, just as you were alone in your forest and jungle dreams," I say to draw the parallel between her and her mother.

"Yeah, I guess we're alike that way," Christina murmured thoughtfully.

"Can you place her age in the dream?"

"I don't know. She looks young and vulnerable."

"Any other feelings?"

"I'm angry that my father isn't there comforting her. Maybe he's working, or maybe he doesn't even know she is upset. Like I said before, they don't talk much. She's just sitting there crying, like the world is ending."

"Do you have any memories of times when she cried like that?"

"I can't remember ever seeing her cry," Christina said, shaking her head.

"How about you? What are your memories of crying unconsolably?"

"I don't usually cry, especially around others. Sometimes when I'm by myself. Nothing specific. Just times when I have felt lonely and like nothing will ever get better. I got into some despair during high school and had fantasies about suicide."

I quickly paid attention, given the need to do an assessment of lethality when suicide is mentioned in therapy. Clients often have a hard time admitting to suicidal thoughts because of the fear of judgment or worry that they will have to be hospitalized. But they often feel better if they can talk openly about such feelings, so I wanted to check if this was a hint. "Tell me more about those fantasies about suicide."

"I just thought how sad my parents would be if I died. I imagined them at my funeral, kind of like in the book *Tom Sawyer* where he's at his own funeral watching from the balcony. Maybe I thought they would finally pay attention to what was going on with me and recognize my unhappiness."

I made a mental note that this poor kid feels she would literally have to die to get her parents' attention. I wondered if there might be something more serious going on with her parents than just being private and reserved.

I asked, "Did you ever have any specific plans or means of committing suicide?"

"No, it was just a fantasy, I don't think I could ever actually do it. And there were never any weapons in the house and no sleeping pills."

"What kept you from killing yourself?"

"Strangely enough, even though I felt hopeless, I also wanted to see what life had to offer. And I didn't want to hurt my parents."

"If any such feelings come up while we're working together, please tell me, call me, or email or text me. I want to be there for you. Can you do that?"

"Okay."

"It's especially important to contact me if suicidal thoughts are persistent or if you are thinking about how, when, or where you would hurt yourself."

"Okay."

"If for some reason you can't reach me, can you promise to call 988 or go to the emergency room?"

"Okay."

Christina sat quietly, not looking at me. I guessed she was uncomfortable with this whole discussion about suicide and my insistence that she contact me or the hotline, or perhaps she had more feelings she wasn't revealing. But this was important information to relay to her, despite her discomfort.

"How was it for you talking about suicidal feelings?" I asked gently.

Slowly, Christina replied, "I don't like thinking about suicide or admitting even to myself that I've thought about it. But I guess it's important to talk about."

"Yes, it's crucial to talk about these things. Secrets often lose their power when you reveal them," I reassured her. After a pause to let the idea about secrets sink in and to see if she wanted to get back to the discomfort about airing dirty laundry, I asked, "Ready to go back to the dream?"

She nodded, looking relieved to be done talking about suicide.

"Any waking-life events that might have triggered this dream?"

"We talked last week about working on my relationship with my parents, and you suggested having a dream. So, I guess I did my homework," she said playfully.

Smiling, I said, "And how does that feel?"

"I'm relieved that I did what you suggested." She smiled back.

"I hear relief, like you're a good student and won't get punished. But I wonder if you're a little resentful too because you said you didn't want to be given any homework," I said, wanting to check about possible negative feelings.

"No, I think this was okay." She sounded sure of herself now. "I didn't have to actively sit down and do anything. It just happened."

"Any other waking-life triggers, any interactions with your mother this week?"

"Well, I observed her a little more closely than I had before. She does seem sad, like there's something hanging over her head. And I sense she doesn't want me to leave home. I don't think she would ever say it, but it's just a feeling I get."

"Hmmm, interesting. How about the ghosts? Tell me more about them. What did they look like? Paint the picture so I can see them."

"They are just kind of vague images floating above her head. Hmm, now that I go back, I think at the beginning of the dream they were near my mother and then they floated off and quietly disappeared. Maybe there were more than two. I can't quite remember that part."

"Any description of the ghosts as you look at them in your memory?"

"They're small, like little bundles, maybe the size of dolls, wrapped in white cloth. Oh geez, I wonder if they were dead babies? That's weird. My stomach just dropped a million miles. I don't know anything about miscarriages, but I know my parents were married a long time before I was born. I just assumed they couldn't have children. But now I wonder. Could that have been why she was crying? Maybe she lost babies. Maybe after I was born she was worried that I would die. She was always overprotective of me. Now that I think about it, it often felt like there was death hanging in the air. Maybe that's why I'm so obsessed with death."

"How are you feeling as you imagine these ghosts who might be babies?"

"I'm thinking of how much I would have liked a sibling, someone to talk to, someone to buffer me from my parents, someone to play with. But I'm also imagining what it would have been like for my mother to have miscarriages, something you want so badly and then poof they are gone to who knows where."

"Imagine what you'd like to say to your mother about this dream."

Quickly, Christina protested, "Oh, I could never say anything to her. Back to that secrecy thing; we're not supposed to intrude on others' privacy or talk about such things."

"I'm not suggesting that you actually say something, just that you imagine what you might say if you could."

She gave this some thought. "What comes into my mind is that I'd like to sit next to her, hold her and comfort her, although that is not something we do. I'd like to grieve with her, let her know that I am there." After an inward-looking pause, Christina continued, "I feel closer to her just thinking about this. I'm wondering about whether something did happen, whether they lost babies. Or maybe there were just ghosts in the house all along, and I never knew it," Christina said, trying to lighten the mood and making us both laugh.

"It is thought-provoking." I brought us back to the topic. "I certainly don't know if the ghosts were dead babies. But I am struck by how you feel closer to your mother now and want to comfort her. Let's try to imagine just a little more about your father, where he might be and what's going on with him."

"The thought that comes to mind is that he's in the living room watching sports on TV. It's like they live separate lives. He doesn't know she's upset. As I think about it, it's not as if he doesn't care, but maybe more that he just doesn't have a clue about what to do. Maybe he's on the autism spectrum, a nice guy but not great at relationships."

"What do you feel when you say that he might be on the autism spectrum?"

"Some disrespect and annoyance, like how can he be so dense? But also guilt, because I *shouldn't* think that. I guess I also maybe feel a little better about him. It's not that he's a bad guy, just that he's a bit inept and doesn't know how to respond. Also, if there was a baby who died, maybe he also felt grief, but they couldn't comfort each other. Whew," she hesitated, "I feel terrible thinking about this, invading their privacy. But I'm also curious about whether something like this actually happened."

"Well," I cautioned. "Let's go slow here and not make any assumptions. This was a dream; it could reflect that your parents lost babies, but it also may reveal feelings within you about yourself, maybe reflecting parts of you that identify with your mother and father."

"I've never heard of that idea," Christine countered. "What do you mean by parts of me?"

"Each part of the dream can reflect an inner part of you. The theory," I said, worrying that I was sounding too much like a professor, "is that we incorporate important people into our heads and they become a part of us, kind of like each of us has a community of voices inside our head, often reflecting deep inner conflicts. So perhaps your mother in your dream is reflecting a part of you, something you've lost. If that were the case, what might the ghosts represent?"

"Interesting. Hmm, let me think. The ghosts floating away. Maybe parts of me are floating away, like I'm losing myself. The other thing is that if it's me, I'm in a bedroom in a nightgown that looks very chaste and old-fashioned. Kind of prim and proper. And I'm alone and crying. I'm despondent. No partner. What does the future hold?" In a panicked voice, she said, "All of a sudden, I want to run away."

"I hear the fear in your voice. Take a few deep breaths and feel your body on the chair and your feet on the ground," I said reassuringly, noting that we had clearly hit on a wound that she wasn't ready to get to. Changing back to her father, I asked, "What part of you is like your father sitting in the living room oblivious to what's going on in the next room?"

"I am kind of oblivious to what's going on with my parents. We all live in the same house but don't know each other. Sad. Angry. Guilty. I'm also anxious because I'm aware that we're almost out of time for today." All of a sudden, Christina looked up and urgently asked, "How should I act around my parents? Should I say something? I feel like the rules don't quite fit, and I don't know how to relate to them anymore."

I pinged it back to her. "What sounds good to you? Let's think about tonight when you go home."

More calmly, Christina replied, "I go to my waitressing job from here and get home late, so I won't see them tonight. I mostly see them in the mornings. Um, maybe I'll just try to act normally and not say anything yet. Maybe

I'll try observing them and see if I notice anything about their relationship."

"Sounds great. Observe what you feel and use that to guide your decisions."

"Okay, thank you. This is really hard, but I feel like we're getting to something important."

"Terrific. What other feelings do you have about our work together?"

Pausing to reflect, Christina said, "I like coming here, but I don't want to burden you too much with my problems."

"Thanks for letting me know that. I will be sure to look out for feeling burdened, but I don't feel that way right now. I'm excited about working on your dreams and talking about your parents. It seems like a breakthrough that you're able to talk about them without feeling you've betrayed them."

"That's true," Christina concurred somewhat reluctantly. "I'll guess I'll have to think about that more." She rushed out the door.

Christina's dream helped her get to what might be a core secret about her mother, her anger at her father, and something else traumatic that she can't quite talk about yet. Noting how she rushed out the door at the end of the session, I'm reminded about how difficult it is for her to talk about her secrets. So much pain and shame.

8

ESTHER'S MEMORIES

All this talk about miscarriages brought up memories for Esther of her relationship with Steve. BK, or before kids, as they joked about it, were good years. They were good friends. They both had their work, they went for long hikes together, had great talks about politics and existential issues, and cooked together. Things were easy between them. She remembered a particular conversation about having kids. She had been reluctant to bring it up because Steve had been so hesitant about committing. He had a rocky relationship with his parents but hadn't wanted to go to therapy to try to resolve issues. She knew it was a tense subject, but she also had been talking a lot in her own therapy about how she had to speak up if she wanted to get her needs met.

"I've been thinking a lot about having children. I think I'm ready. What are your thoughts?" Esther began tentatively, as they were walking along Sligo Creek Parkway on a beautiful summer day.

"I'm not sure. I'm just not sure I'm ready. There's so much going on at work, and I feel so much pressure to get ahead," Steve said abruptly.

"I'm not sure we'll ever be ready completely. We've always talked about having a couple kids. And my biological clock is ticking away. I'm ready to make some changes so that I have time to take care of kids." Esther could feel the pleading in her voice.

"It would change everything." Steve said petulantly.

"Of course it would change things. But I think we have a strong enough relationship to handle it. I think you'd be a great dad."

Steve winced. "I'm not so sure about that. My father sure wasn't much of a role model."

Esther figured she had pushed as much as she could at the time. A couple weeks later, Steve had said, "Okay, we can try. I'm still reluctant, but I know it's something you want a lot."

"Are you sure?" Esther had a hard time not showing her excitement. "I don't want you to do something you don't want to do."

"There's probably never a good time. Why do people have children anyway? Is it just a biological imperative? But, okay, let's try," Steve said.

Looking back, Esther realized she should have paid attention to the red flags Steve was wildly waving. At the time, though, she had felt nothing but overwhelming happiness that he had conceded. She had immediately started planning. She had wanted kids for as long as she could remember. She thought at the time that once they had the kids, Steve would be happy, or at least she hoped so. Perhaps best not to think about it too much.

9

CHRISTINA: CHAIR WORK WITH MOTHER

Christina seemed unusually subdued when she walked into the office. She sat quietly waiting for me to begin.

"You're quiet," I probed. "What's going on?"

Sounding defensive, Christina began. "I don't know. I feel upset, but I can't pin down what's going on. I didn't feel like coming today. I don't know what to talk about."

Clients often shut down after a particularly powerful session, so I wanted to dig into what was happening with her without pushing her too far after her panic last week. "Let's try to unpack it. You talked a lot last week about your mother and your dream about the ghosts. What thoughts did you have during the week about that or about your mother?"

"I found myself getting all anxious around my mother again, so I kind of avoided her all week." Looking at me warily, she sighed, "I hope you're not angry at me."

Checking in with myself, I realized I was supportive rather than upset with her. "No, I'm not angry. So interesting, though, that you project anger onto me. What might be going on?"

"I don't know. I'm afraid of everyone being angry at me or disappointed in me."

"What's that about?"

"My dream about my mother felt so real, and I don't know what to do about it. I kind of feel like I've regressed to where I was before therapy."

"I'm sure that's frustrating after all the work you've done. Sounds like you are beating yourself up a bit."

"Yeah, for sure. I do that." She nodded.

"Tell me more about being worried that I'm angry at you."

"It's just something I keep thinking about and can't get out of my mind, especially when I'm trying to go to sleep," Christina said pensively.

I asked, "Is there anything I'm doing that might make you feel that I'm angry?"

"Hmmm, good question," she said, shaking her head. "No. If anything, it seems like you're attentive and asking good questions. Maybe I just don't trust you or anyone else."

"How does it feel to say that out loud?"

"Not good. I can't believe that anyone would be interested in me, so I'm not sure I trust that you really are." She looked like a hurt little girl.

"Well, I am not angry at you, and I am interested in you. I enjoy working with you. And my heart aches for how lonely and anxious you feel."

Christina sat looking down, petting Star.

"What's going on inside?" I probed.

Christina took a deep breath and looked up shyly, "Okay. I'm here."

"Where did you go?" I wondered if she had dissociated.

"I just kind of felt outside my body for a minute. I do that sometimes."

I asked, "I wonder if it was difficult for you to hear that my heart aches for you?"

"Yes," Christina said, looking down again, as if she was steadying herself. "I want to talk more about my mother, but I don't quite know what to say about her."

"You mentioned last week wanting to comfort her. I know the idea of being rejected by her is strong, but I'm wondering if we can do a little more in fantasy by having you talk to her as if she were here in the room with you right now."

"Uh, okay," Christina said reluctantly.

Pointing to the empty chair, I directed, "Imagine her over there in that chair and say what you might say to her."

After taking a deep breath, Christina faced the other chair and tentatively said, "Mother, I had a dream about you the other night." After another inward-looking pause, she sighed and continued, "You were sitting alone in your room crying. There were some ghosts the size of small babies over your head, and then they just kind of melted away and were gone. I didn't know what to make of the dream, but it felt real. I don't want to intrude if you don't want to talk about it, but I wondered if you had maybe lost babies when you were younger?"

"Good, now go over and sit in the other chair," I pointed, glad that she was able to get into the chair work, "and be your mother. How do you think she might respond?"

Chistina slowly moved to the other chair, thought, and then whispered, "Yes, I lost three babies to miscarriages before you were born. I have always wanted to tell you but never knew how. I was depressed for a long time and didn't think I could ever have a live baby. I was scared to death to try again. And your father could not understand why I was so sad."

I pointed for her to move, "Now go back to your chair. What would you say in response to your mother?"

After moving, Christina said, "I feel so bad for you."

"How did that feel?"

"My heart aches for her." I made a mental note to myself that Christina used the same phrase I had used a few minutes before. Maybe she's starting to use me as a model to figure out on her feelings?

Christina continued, "It's like she's been carrying around this pain for so long. I imagine she would have had a hard time allowing herself to get too close to me. Maybe she was afraid I might die or something would happen to me. And I feel awful that she couldn't rely on my father to help her. I'm guessing that, like I said last week, he was upset too but didn't know what to say to her."

"Could you speculate about why you might have had the dream about your mother and the ghosts?"

"I've been thinking about her a lot. I don't really know if any of this is true," she said, breaking eye contact. "I have no idea if my mother actually had miscarriages and if so, when they would have happened. That's just what came into my mind when you asked me."

"I can hear your hesitancy. You're right, we don't know." I paused to give her a chance to breathe and then asked, "Where would you like to go with this? How might you like to react around your mother this week in real life?"

"Maybe I'll just see what happens. I already feel closer to her. I understand more about her reasons for being hesitant to get close to me. We're alike in a lot of ways, being quiet and sensitive. I can't imagine what it would be like to lose a baby, let alone three babies. I'm sure it would be devastating. She was young and didn't have anyone to talk to." She lit up suddenly, "I would like to be closer to her." Then, she immediately backed away, "But I don't know, I'm cautious because there's so much history of our avoiding each other and keeping the code of secrecy. It's like trying to break down a brick wall."

"It will be hard to change. Maybe just be aware of your feelings when you're at home and see what happens. Just tune in to whatever emerges," I advised.

"That makes sense. I feel a lot better right now about my mother. I like the idea of taking it slowly and seeing how it goes rather than trying to push anything. Oh, if we have time, I wanted to tell you about something that came up at work."

"Go for it."

"I wanted to tell you about Curt, this guy at work. He flirts with me, but then again he flirts with all the waitresses, so I don't think I'm anything special to him. I overheard him making a nasty remark about me. He said he thought I was gullible and easily taken advantage of. I don't know what he could have been talking about, and I can't imagine asking him. It makes me a little anxious being around him. I feel naïve, I guess, but gullible?"

"Oh, my, that would hurt. Puzzling too. No context?"

"None that I know of."

"Any other situations where you have been naïve or gullible? Does this trigger any memories?"

I see a shadow crossing Christina's face, but she quickly turns away. "No, I don't think so," she says softly.

As it is close to the end of the hour, I choose not to comment but wondered what was behind the shadow. "Hmm, hard to figure out what might be going on, but good to keep your ears open." Bringing it back to her beginning concern so that we could wrap up for the session, I query, "How are you feeling now, given that you felt upset initially but didn't know why?"

"I feel better. I can see several reasons why I was upset: my mother, the job, starting therapy. I have been having a lot of sleepless nights where I worry about all this stuff. I'm glad I could talk to you today."

"Next week, I'd like to hear more about your thoughts when you're not able to sleep. Have a great week."

Christina seemed needier than usual, and I'm not sure we delved deeply enough into the real issues. The comment about being gullible and the shadow on her face; what were they about? I also need to pay attention to whatever feelings she has about me; her concern about my being angry with her has been a persistent theme. I have to be careful about pushing her too much and instead allow her to come to decisions on her own.

10

ESTHER AND PARENTS

The memory of her discussion with Steve about having kids made Esther go back further and think about her own childhood. She had spent considerable time in her therapy with Paul talking about her relationship with her parents. As a result, Esther was less angry at her father than she had been and more compassionate about his alcoholism and outbursts, given his own painful childhood. His death when she was in high school had been both traumatic and . . . relieving. She had lost an ally, but she didn't have to deal with his anger anymore. But her problems dealing with her mother's dominating and unpredictable personality had gotten worse. It still confused Esther that her mother tried to control her after having been controlled and abused herself. It helped when Paul had wondered if her mother had a personality disorder, but it also made Esther sad and then worried that she might have inherited her mother's borderline tendencies.

One episode stood out in Esther's memory. Her parents were having one of their violent fights, throwing dishes and swearing. Esther and her sister were crouching at the top of the stairs, listening and fearing what would happen next. Then they heard the front door slam, as their father left to go to the local bar and get drunk.

"What are you looking at?" shouted her mother when she saw them. "Never marry anyone like your father. I wish I had never met him."

She had another memory, this one of her mother interacting with Steve. She was so deferential to Steve in person, saying things like, "Oh thank you for being so good to Esther," and then when he wasn't around, denigrating him to Esther, "I don't know what you see in him." Sometimes it was exhausting thinking about her mother.

CHRISTINA:
JUMPING OUT OF A PLANE WITH NO PARACHUTE

Arriving at her next appointment, Christina was once again quiet. I wondered if she was still having doubts about being in therapy. Even though I generally like to let clients start the sessions, I wanted to help her out, "Any dreams this week?"

"No, I guess I'm feeling kind of stuck. I'm not sure what to talk about and how this all works. I didn't really have any thoughts about our session last week, just a bit of dread about coming today." I wondered if coming in stuck and depressed was becoming a pattern, and if so, why.

Hoping to help her become curious, I said, "Let's see if we can figure out what's going on. I wonder if we're moving too fast and you're a little scared?"

"I don't know," Christina looked down. "I thought I wanted to work on all these things, but I'm feeling more awkward at home, and I've been out of sorts at work. One person I've kind of been friendly with noticed it and asked if I was okay. So, I don't know, maybe it's just that a lot is getting stirred up."

"That makes sense. You've been trying to keep a lid on all these feelings for so long, and now they're leaking out. Maybe your defenses aren't as strong as they were before," I said. Wanting to name what might be underlying her anxiety, I asked, "Does that make you think about stopping therapy?"

"I have had thoughts like that, yeah, like, is it all worth it?" Christina admitted.

"It is scary to make changes and face the unknown, like the old saying, *the devil you know is better than the one you don't know*." When she didn't respond, I asked, "What would it be like to stop?"

With her arms crossed protectively over her middle, Christina murmured, "On the one hand, I'd be relieved. I gave it a try and maybe I'm not ready. On the other hand, I'd be disappointed that I gave up too quickly, that I failed yet again."

"Perhaps we could slow down a bit? What do you think?"

"Yeah, maybe." She looked down, crossed her legs, and said a bit defensively. "I guess I should stay and not run away like I always do."

"You know, it's a big deal that you can talk about your feelings about being here, given that you said you and your parents don't talk much about feelings and personal stuff. What's it like for you?"

"Hard!" she exclaimed. "It's all so new to me. And, like I said before, I never feel like people want to listen to me."

"Are you feeling that with me right now?"

"No. Actually you listen too much to what I say, and I feel vulnerable."

"I can understand that, given your background. But, even though it's scary, it's an important step," I offered, to reinforce her attempts to process the feelings. When she didn't respond after a moment, I gently asked, "What's on your mind now?"

"I think I want to stay and keep trying," she said apologetically looking down. "I feel bad for being so wimpy."

"I'm proud of you for being able to tell me what you are feeling. I feel hopeful that by working on our relationship, we can make it better and then you'll be able to apply what you learn to other relationships. Does that make sense to you?"

"Yeah. It's hard here, but it's even harder with other relationships. I know you have to be here, but others don't."

"Well," I pushed back. "I *don't* have to be here. I have a choice. I want to be here to work with you."

Christina was silent and focused on petting Star, who looked up expectantly at me as if waiting for instructions.

"What was that like to hear that I want to work with you."

"It's hard to hear. But thanks, I appreciate it," she mumbled unconvincingly. Suddenly, she perked up and said, "You know, I just remembered a fragment of a dream."

> I'm jumping out of an airplane, and I don't have a parachute. I stop it before anything bad happens.

"What are your memories of airplanes?"

"I've only been on an airplane one time. I remember being scared, but it was almost like being on a bus, just in the clouds. I made sure to sit in the aisle seat and didn't look out the window. It was a relatively short flight, and I was glad when it was over," she responded thoughtfully.

"What about jumping out of airplanes?"

"Not something I'd ever want to do," she said quickly, "even if I had a parachute."

"Any ideas about what the dream might mean?"

"Well, it sounds like a good description of how I felt today, being ambivalent about being here. I feel like I'm jumping into the unknown and don't have all the right equipment."

"And the feeling is . . . ?"

"I'm petrified," she said quietly.

"What do you suspect was going to happen in the dream?"

"Probably I was going to die. I've heard that when you die in a dream, that means you're really going to die. Is that true?"

"Not necessarily. I don't believe there are universal meanings of dream images," I said and worried that I was falling back into my professorial mode. "It depends on what the dream means for you. For some people it might mean death, for others it might reflect being scared, and for others it might reflect an exciting risk. I'm interested that you stopped the dream before anything bad happened."

"That's true. I did," Christina said, sounding relieved that it might not mean she was going to die. "I avoid bad situations or get out of them as quickly as possible. I tried calming myself down to get back to sleep."

"Good," I said to reinforce her resiliency. "What did you do to calm yourself down?"

"I did the deep breathing we've done in here. I also thought I could tell you the dream and felt pleased that I had done my homework by having a dream. And then I just tried thinking about something else and eventually fell asleep. I was tired and knew I had to get some sleep before going to work the next day."

I noted to myself the comment about having done her homework. She gets into her good-girl compliance and assigns me the uncomfortable role of being a demanding taskmaster.

"It's great to hear that you have some good coping strategies." Christina didn't respond, perhaps not being able to take in positive feedback or not believing me. I tried another tactic, "Would you like to focus on the dream a little more today?"

"I think not. It's a little too close to home. But I did have some thoughts about college. Can we talk about that?"

"Sure," I said, relieved that she had something she wanted to talk about.

Christina continued, "It's the end of July, and most of the kids I went to high school with are starting college next month. They are all moving away. Now granted, I wasn't great friends with any of them, but they are going ahead with their lives, whereas I am not going anywhere. I don't know how much longer I can put up with this waitressing job, especially after that nasty comment last week about being gullible."

"I hear you. September, when school starts, could be challenging. It's the first year in how long that you haven't gone back to school?"

"In a way I've always been in school. I was in day care from the time I was three months old and then school since then. It's given structure to my life, with deadlines and people telling me what to do. It always felt like I was working toward something: kindergarten, elementary, middle school, and now high school. Graduation each time was a big deal, the end of an era. But now it feels like there's a big void for me, with everyone else moving on to the expected next step."

"I wonder if you always expected you would go on to college?"

"That was the expectation. Everyone from our high school goes to college, lots of them to prestigious places. My parents keep hinting that I *should* be figuring things out."

"Hmm, there's that *should* again."

"Oh, yeah, shit on the shoulds," she said gleefully, and we both laughed.

"How would that feel to shit on the shoulds?"

"Delightful. It even feels good to say *shit*."

"I wonder if there's something you can do in the next couple months to remind yourself that you made a decision *not* to pursue going to college right now?"

"Well, you might be giving me more credit than I deserve. I wouldn't say I actively made a choice not to go. I just didn't do anything about going. I ignored the decision, and then it was too late to apply."

"Is it too late?"

"What do you mean?"

"Isn't it possible that you could take classes at a community college?"

"I don't know. It would be such a comedown to go to a community college when all the other kids are going to prestigious universities. There's quite a bit of snobbery here about where you go to college. If it's not Harvard or Yale, you're a piece of crap," she asserted testily.

"You sounded quite adamant when you said that. Can you say a bit more about the snobbery you've encountered."

"Well, we live in a pretty wealthy area. My parents don't have a lot of money, but many of the kids in high school had money. They had their own cars, went on big trips. I always felt like an outsider because I couldn't afford to do the things they did."

"What does being an outsider feel like?"

"It was, or maybe should I say is, painful. They look down on me for waitressing."

"And maybe you look down on it yourself?"

"Hmm, yeah, good call," she owned up. "Another one of those projection thingies. I do feel like I could do better than waitressing. And like I told you, there are people working there who have been there forever. They think it's an okay thing to do, which it is, of course, if you need money and have few other options. Clearly, I have some conflict around what I *should* be doing with my time."

"Yep, there's that *shoulding* again. We need to keep looking at that and help you figure out what *you* want to do, what you *choose* to do."

"Yes, please, I want to do that," she smiled. "I'm glad I came today, even if this is hard. I guess there really is a lot inside me that I have been hiding. In our psychology class, they called it *repression*. Do you think that's what I'm doing?"

"What do you think?" I lobbed it back to her.

"Yeah. Makes sense. This is hard work."

"But hopefully a bit fun too?" I queried.

"I do like working on my dreams. I think I'll get a notebook and start writing the dreams down so I can remember them better and keep track of them."

"Great. But make sure you're doing it because you want to rather than to please me."

"Oh, good point," she said ruefully. "Here I am, trying to be the good client again."

"You *are* a good client," I emphasized. "You're working hard. And if you choose to record your dreams, that's great. I just want you to think about the motivations for your choices, and only do what you truly choose to do."

"That makes sense. I'll think about that more."

"Terrific. See you next week."

There's starting to be a pattern here. Christina comes in feeling stuck and reluctant to talk, and I feel a pull to make her feel better and persuade her that therapy is going to help. I have to watch that. On the one hand, the motivation needs to come from her. On the other hand, given her avoidant-attachment style, she seems to need some initial encouragement to start the work. I think we need to have a more solid relationship before I confront the pattern directly.

I am painfully aware that, like Christina, I have a hard time with *shoulds*. It's so easy to do things because I'm supposed to. I rushed through college and graduate school. Did I truly choose to do that, or was it just expected? What were my motivations? Sometimes it's tiring trying to keep up with both a job and my family. I didn't get much sleep last night because the kids were sick. I feel guilty that I didn't cancel sessions so that I could stay home with them, but Steve took off today to take care of them. Every time I need to choose between my kids and my clients, I feel bad, whatever decision I make.

12

CHRISTINA AND CHENDU

Christina hadn't had a chance to work on her dream during the week. She had decided to go to Starbucks before the session to write about her parachute dream. She sat down, opened her laptop, and pulled up the dream. She immediately felt blocked. It was so much easier to work on her dreams in sessions with Dr. Esther. Falling out of a plane without a parachute just felt terrifying.

As Christina was sitting thinking about her dream, she saw Chendu, a friend from high school. Chendu looked up at the same time and came over to the table. "Hey, Christina, it's so good to see you. I was just thinking about you the other day, remembering the good times we had working on the newspaper."

Christina was stunned that Chendu remembered her. "Hey, it's good to see you too."

"Are you busy, or is it okay if I sit with you for a while?" asked Chendu.

"Absolutely, that would be great," Christina replied quickly. "You must be getting ready to go off to college.

Aren't you going to Harvard? I'm so jealous," she laughed, noticing that she was talking too fast.

Chendu sat and stirred her coffee. "I'm going off in a couple weeks. I'm excited to be going there, but honestly, I'm nervous about fitting in. I'm worried about the backlash against Asian students at Harvard and don't like being the model minority. But how are you doing? I was concerned about you at school because you seemed so distant during the last year."

"Well, actually, not so good. I ended up starting therapy to try to figure myself out," Christina responded hesitantly, deciding to be brave and try out what it would be like to say so openly that she was in therapy.

"Good for you," Chendu exclaimed. "I was in therapy for about three years during high school. It was a life saver. I was so angry all the time, and therapy helped me calm down."

"Wow. I never knew that. I thought you didn't have any problems. You always seemed so happy," Christina said.

"Yeah, interesting how looks can be so deceiving. I covered up a lot out of shame," Chendu reflected. "My parents weren't happy that I had to be in therapy but really wanted me to succeed. We kept having fights because they put so much pressure on me to get good grades. I wasn't doing well in school at the beginning, and they were terrified I wouldn't go to college. A colleague of my mother's suggested therapy."

"Well, maybe I should have gone to therapy earlier because I'm not going to college this fall. Actually, I was just sitting here working on a dream that I talked about last week in therapy where I felt like I was falling out of a plane and my parachute didn't open."

"I remember writing a story about dreams for the newspaper. My therapist didn't work with dreams, so I missed that. Tell me all about it," Chendu looked interested.

After telling her briefly about the dream, Christina looked at her watch, shocked that the time had flown by so quickly. "OMG, I better get out of here or I'll be late for my session. It was so good to see you, Chendu."

Chendu replied warmly, "So good to see you. Maybe we could get together again before I go, and I would love it if you came up to visit me this fall."

Rushing out the door, Christina realized that perhaps she had more friends than she believed. Her senior year of high school was just so miserable. She began to feel hopeful that she could understand what went wrong.

13

CHRISTINA:
SITTING ON
MY SHOULDER

Christina bounded in with uncharacteristic energy. "I have so many things to tell you—about a possible friend, a dream, and my mother. I'm not sure where to begin."

"It's good to hear you sounding and looking so cheerful. Can't wait to hear all about it. You choose what to start with." I was relieved that she didn't seem as stuck and depressed as she had been in the beginnings of past sessions.

She beamed. "I went to Starbucks on my way here. I was going to write about my dream for an hour before our session, but I ran into Chendu, someone from high school. We were on the student newspaper together. I always wanted to be her friend because she is so pretty and popular and smart. She came over to where I was sitting and asked if she could join me. We had this really nice chat. She's thrilled to be going to Harvard but nervous about fitting in. She asked how I was doing, and I told her about being in therapy. Turns out she had been in therapy because she had bad fights with her mother.

The best thing is that she suggested we stay in touch, and she invited me to come visit."

"Awesome! How did it feel to tell her that you're in therapy?"

"At first, I was apprehensive because I thought she'd be judgy, but she wasn't at all. I was surprised she had been in therapy and relieved that I'm not the only crazy one. It was good talking with her."

"Hmmm. You mentioned not having any friends. I wonder if you misinterpreted, and she already was a friend."

"Well, maybe, except that she's going away. She'll probably meet a lot of new people and might not have much energy for someone back home."

"I can see that you'd be a little nervous about where your relationship is going. Maybe you just need to not get too far ahead of yourself."

"For sure. I'll just take it slow and see what happens."

"You mentioned a dream?"

"Yeah, I had another dream about you a couple nights ago. I was worried about something, I can't remember quite what it was, but I remember being anxious." She looked at me, eyes wide. "All of a sudden, I felt your presence, but you were tiny and sitting on my shoulder. And you just said, 'Breathe.' After a minute, I calmed down."

"Glad I could be helpful." I smiled. "Take a second and reflect back. What might you have been nervous about? What image comes to your mind?"

"In the dream, I was going into a test and couldn't find the classroom. I've had that dream a lot. Either I'm lost and can't find the classroom, or I haven't studied, or I haven't been to class, or I don't have any clothes on, but it's typically about not being able to get to an exam on time. I usually wake up exhausted from rushing around."

"How did you feel when I appeared?"

"I felt reassured, like I don't have to do this on my own. You've got my back. Then I remembered in the dream that I *had* studied and was ready for the test. I breathed, then walked into the classroom and did okay on the test."

"You mentioned I was tiny and sitting on your shoulder. Any ideas about that?"

"Hmm. Just like a still, small voice in my ear. Maybe it was my unconscious speaking. I don't have an image exactly. I just sensed your presence."

"Any thoughts about the dream?"

"Well, like I said, I've had some version of this dream a lot, especially during high school." She looked at me quizzically, "What do you think it means?"

"What's important is what you think it means," I deferred. "Any ideas?"

Christina started speaking fast. "The first thing that comes to mind is being nervous about whether I'm doing the right things in therapy. Am I a good client? Maybe that's why I went to Starbucks to work on my dream. I want to be a good client. And then, wouldn't you know," she shook her head, "I got distracted and talked to Chendu instead of working on my dream!"

"Sounds to me like talking to Chendu was a wonderful experience."

"You're right; it was," she said slowing down to process.

"And you brought your dream here to work on it. So, you are doing both things."

"Yeah, you're right," said Christina thoughtfully. After looking down for a moment, she continued, "Another thing I wanted to talk about. My mother asked me to drive her to the airport on Friday. She's going to see her mother, who is eighty-five and dying of cancer."

CHRISTINA: SITTING ON MY SHOULDER

"Oh my," I said feeling protective and wanting to support Christina. "What are your thoughts about that?"

"I wasn't very close to my grandmother because they lived pretty far away, in Wisconsin. I don't think my mother is very close to her either. My grandfather died a few years ago, and I felt even less connected to him. But what I wanted to talk about is how I might use this opportunity to talk to my mother. Sometimes it's easier to talk when you're in a car. You know, no eye contact. And, because she's going to visit her mother, it seems like an ideal time to learn more about her background. But I don't have a clue how to go about it," she said with increasing tension in her voice.

"Interesting," I nodded. "I wonder if the dream was related?"

"Hmmm, that could be," Christina paused. "It does feel kind of like a test. Am I getting better? Am I ready to talk to my mother?"

I motioned with my hands to slow her down. "Of course, the more you make it a test, the more it's going to be difficult to do."

"Good point. I could build it up too much and put too much pressure on myself."

"What do you want from me?"

"Um, uh, maybe I'm hoping you can help me with how to go about talking to my mother. What should we talk about? Should I bring up the dream about the ghosts?"

"You're talking very fast. Do a body scan and tell me what you're feeling in your body."

After a pause, Christina said, "I'm feeling short of breath and dizzy."

"In your dream, you imagined me telling you to breathe. That's a good place to start."

Christina took some deep breaths and started again, "Okay, that's good. Thanks."

"I'm noticing a generational pattern here. You mother is not very close to her mother, and you're not very close to your mother. But there's distress there, perhaps a wish of all parties to be closer and more connected?"

"Hmmm, you might be on to something there. Maybe that's part of my mother's problems. I wonder, too, if it's connected to her culture. You know, Norwegians are stereotypically reserved and quiet. And Midwesterners are very polite and often don't reveal what they're thinking."

"That's an interesting connection." I love her insightfulness.

"Yeah, as I think about it, both of my parents are quiet. And they chose to work in fields where they each have a high-security clearance and can't talk about their jobs. It's not difficult for them to keep quiet about their work, though, because they never talk about anything. Their culture probably played into their choice of careers. We discussed culture in my psychology class, and I had to admit that I knew very little about the Norwegian culture. Of course, a lot of Norwegians live in Wisconsin, so maybe it's just the way everyone is there. It's very different here with people from so many different cultures, like Chendu."

"What would you like to know about your mother?"

"I was thinking about the chair thing we did a few sessions back, when I imagined telling her my dream about her. But I'm not sure I'm ready to do that. Maybe a first step is just learning more about what it was like growing up in Wisconsin with my grandparents. Hmm, as I talk about it, I'm starting to hyperventilate. It just feels wrong, like it goes against the norms of our family to bring up anything personal."

I studied her body language. "I can see you clutching your hands into fists. And your voice got quieter just now."

"Yeah." After looking away, Christina asked hesitantly, "I just had a thought, but I hope I'm not asking for too much. Is there any way I could have an extra session this week before taking my mother to the airport?"

"Say more about *asking for too much*." I probed, wanting to focus on the idea of her asserting herself.

"Well, I'm not sure what the rules are. We've been meeting once a week, and I don't want to intrude on your time."

"And what's it been like for you *asking for too much* in the past?"

"Hmmm, good question. Well, one example is that time I asked for an extension on the *Great Gatsby* paper, and my teacher wouldn't give it to me. I never asked for much from my parents, maybe because I learned early on it wasn't acceptable to ask."

"Makes sense. Yes, I do have a free hour on Wednesday at two in the afternoon and could meet then. Would that work for you?"

"Let me think. I work later that day, but I think two would work out well. Thanks."

"How was it asking?"

"I feel relieved," she said, giving me brief eye contact. "I like this opportunity to test out what I'm learning. I'm excited. Is there anything I need to do before then?"

"Hmm, interesting," I gently challenged. "We've talked about how you don't want any homework."

"That's true. I did say that. I guess I just feel that I *should* be doing more in between."

"There's that *should* again."

"Yeah, I guess I'll shit on the should," she said with an impish smile. We both laughed, mirroring a growing connection between us.

"See what comes up naturally and what you feel like doing. Trust yourself on this one. It seems to me that you do a lot of work on your own between sessions and don't particularly need me to tell you what to do."

"That's a relief. Thank you for that." Christina smiled. She paused for a minute looking thoughtful and then added, "You know, maybe I don't need another session. Maybe I can just talk to her. I think I might be ready to try."

"Tell me more," I asked encouragingly.

"Well, lately it feels like she has been trying to connect more, even by asking me to drive her to the airport. I think I have been apprehensive and holding myself back from her, so if I push myself, I think she might be open to talking more. Maybe if I can understand my mother better, I'll understand more about myself and not fall into the same patterns that she has, especially in terms of choosing a partner."

"That makes sense; I think you're onto something there. Let's take it one step at a time. I have a feeling your mother is eager to connect but is afraid of intruding on you."

"Hmm, interesting, both of us afraid of intruding. Yeah, that sounds right. And, perhaps I can imagine you sitting on my shoulder giving me confidence. Maybe I don't need an extra session."

"Sounds good. If you change your mind, I'm here at that time on Wednesday. Either way, it seems like you've made a lot of progress. You're so much more aware of what's going on inside and what you want," I encouraged.

"Thanks. I feel good."

"Absolutely. Take care now."

Interesting that after two weeks of being reluctant to talk, Christina seemed so eager today. Maybe we're beginning to forge a bond. But I have to be aware that she will still get scared and back away. So many ups and downs in therapy. So great that she had a nice interaction with Chendu and that she's feeling more confident about talking with her mother—a good spiraling upward.

    I thought more about the parallel I felt last week between her figuring out her path and my struggling to balance work and family. I do sometimes feel like a fraud, thinking I *should* have solved all my problems. Her struggles are triggering mine as I empathize with her. During graduate school I thought I would go on to an academic career but then decided to go into practice full time. There are some parts of practice I love, like working with clients, but other parts, like the billing and notes, are draining. Steve has been grumbling about not liking his job. If he quits his current job to look for another one, I might have to step up and take on more clients to up our income. I'm going to have to do more thinking about this.

14

CHRISTINA AND MOTHER

As they settled into the car to go the airport, Christina asked her mother, "So are you sure you have everything?"

"Yeah, and thanks so much for taking me. I suppose I could have gotten an Uber, but I never have figured out how to do that."

"No problem. I didn't have anything else to do this morning," Christina replied. "So how will you get from O'Hare airport up to Wisconsin?"

"There's a bus that goes there, so it should be easy."

Christina took a deep breath, imagined Dr. Esther sitting on her shoulder encouraging her, and pushed herself to practice what she had been working on in therapy. "So, tell me more about Grandma. I feel like I don't know much about her."

"I apologize for not telling you more. I'm realizing more and more that she is a special person. I wish you had known her better," Kristin said.

"When did she come over from Norway?"

Kristin started slowly and then warmed up as she talked. "My mother's grandparents came over from Norway. They were young and looking for a better life. They moved to a small town in Wisconsin, as did many other Norwegians. My mother couldn't wait to get away and see the world. Her two older sisters moved to other towns in Wisconsin and kept contact with my grandmother but not with my mother. My mother was kind of the black sheep of the family because she was more liberal. Apparently, my grandparents were very strict with the two older girls, and there was a gap of a few years before my mother was born. The two sisters got married young and had children but never did much career-wise. My grandmother was a kind person who took care of neighbors, but she was very quiet, so maybe the introversion thing runs down the generations. Apparently, my grandfather was something of a figure in the town. He might have been the mayor at one point. He was conservative and religious, whereas my grandmother was more open and questioning."

"How did you get along with your parents?" Christina asked, keeping her eyes on the road but amazed at how her mother was so open and talkative.

"This might be too much information, but I had a big fight with my father in high school. That's why I couldn't wait to get out of Wisconsin." Kristin quit talking and looked about to cry.

"What happened?

"I was rebellious for once in my life after having been such a good girl growing up. My father was racist and said I couldn't date anyone who wasn't White. So, I snuck out at night to see a Black guy. My father found out and restricted me to the house. At that point, I decided I was leaving home as soon as I could."

"Oh wow. He sounds like such a jerk," Christina said sympathetically, thinking to herself that her grandfather and father sounded similar. Realizing that they were getting close to the airport, Christina impulsively said, "How would you feel if I went out with you to visit Grandma next time?"

"Oh," Kristin sounded surprised. "I would like that, and I'm sure Grandma would love it. She always asks about you and how you're doing."

Warming to the idea, Christina suggested, "Maybe we could make it a road trip, and you can tell me more stories about your growing up."

"I would like that," Kristin responded. "I'll check in with Grandma and arrange for it."

"We're here," Chrstina said pulling into the departures area of Baltimore Washington International Airport. "Call me when you get into Wisconsin, and let me know when to pick you up. Can't wait for our road trip!"

As she was driving back, Christina felt pleased with how well it had gone. Her mother was a lot easier to talk to than she had built up in her head.

15

CHRISTINA: MOTHER'S FAMILY

Christina looked relaxed. She pointed to the O'Keefe flower pictures hanging on my walls, "You know, I liked those pictures so much, I looked them up. I hadn't seen her paintings before."

"Interesting that the pictures speak to you. You have an artistic streak?"

"Not really. But I like them. And I like Star," she said petting him. "Your office is so comfortable."

"So, tell me how it went on the car ride to the airport," I said, curious.

"It went really well. My mother was quiet at first, and then, as she saw I was interested, she opened up. At the end, she gave me a hug and said she felt closer to me. I'm glad I took the risk of knocking down the wall between us, or at least making a little opening in it."

"Terrific. I can see how excited you are. Maybe relieved too?"

"Definitely relieved. I wasn't sure how it would go, but it was as if she was bursting to talk. She told me that she had a big fight with her father when she was a teenager, and their relationship never got repaired. She was delighted when I asked if I could go out with her next time to see Grandma. We're going to make a road trip of it."

"Great." I noted to myself that I no longer had to do much probing to encourage Christina to talk. Words seemed to flow out of her.

"What is your reaction to hearing about your mother's fight with her father?"

"I feel bad for her having to sneak around. I can't believe what a jerk my grandfather was. So much rigidity. I also had the thought, although I didn't say it to my mother, that my father is like that. She ended up with someone like her father."

"What do you make of your mother being so open to talking?"

"She seemed eager to talk. It was like I turned on a spigot, and it all came pouring out. She thanked me for asking questions. I told her that I had been talking about her in therapy and wanted to have a better relationship with her. I couldn't quite see because I was driving, but I think she started to tear up a bit. I think she's been lonely and hasn't had anyone to talk to."

"I'm impressed you told your mother about what we've been talking about in therapy! Good on you."

"I hadn't planned to, but it just kind of came out. I guess I wanted her to know. And she had told me so much stuff that it felt safe. I think she's happy I'm working on myself. She has been worried about me. Yeah, I feel like she is supportive. And who knows, maybe it will help her get into therapy at some point."

"What do you make of her, and maybe your grandmother also, being more liberal whereas the rest of the family is so much more conservative?"

"It explains some of the tension. I can empathize with my mother wanting to get out of that small town. I have wanted to get away but feel paralyzed and unable to make a move or decide what I want to do."

"I wonder if part of you wants to stay around to protect your mother?"

"That's an interesting idea." She looked a little gobsmacked but intrigued. "Maybe I have a hard time leaving her there in that sterile house. Now that you mention it, I do feel connected to her. And there's this possibility that I could feel connected to my grandmother, too."

"Connection is a good thing."

"Can we talk about death?" Christina asked hesitantly. "I'm thinking about my grandmother dying, and the idea of death terrifies me."

I asked, "What are your religious beliefs about death?"

Christina's eyes widened with interest. "My father was raised as a Baptist, my mother as a Catholic, but we never went to church, so I don't honestly know what I believe. I'm not sure I believe in anything, but it feels like a big void."

"What do you suppose will happen to your grandmother when she dies?"

"I don't know. I suppose the same as what happens to plants and animals. They die and that's it. It doesn't make any sense that there would be a heaven and hell just for us and not them. But who knows! I think we went to church once with my father's mother when we were young. The preacher talking about sin and hell was a little too much, scary. I don't really know what my parents believe now. They haven't talked about it much. I suppose that coming from two different religions makes it difficult to negotiate a compromise."

"I'm thinking of a couple weeks ago when you mentioned some suicidal thoughts. How does that tie in with the death anxiety?" I queried.

"Well, probably it's why I wouldn't commit suicide because I'm, um, afraid of death," Christina said reluctantly. "I don't know what comes after. And I don't feel like I've lived much yet. Like, what's the meaning of life anyway?"

"I'm not sure there's a meaning *of* life or *truth* for everyone. What's important is that you construct your personal meaning *in* life."

"Yeah, easier said than done. I never was very good at that," Christina looked bleak.

"You know, I think of therapy almost like a college education. You're learning about yourself and your family."

Christina nodded in agreement. "I like the idea that therapy is education about me. It feels like there's a lot I don't know or understand about myself."

"True, people are very complicated," I agreed, glad that she was becoming more interested and less afraid of delving into the mysteries within.

"That's for sure."

"It's exciting to see you making so many changes," I said genuinely. After a pause, I asked, "How has it been with your father with your mother away?"

"Well, interestingly, I asked if he wanted to have dinner together last night. I said that I felt like making some tacos and wondered if he wanted to have some, too. He said sure. I can't remember the last time just the two of us had a meal together. It was awks at first, but then we chatted about politics, who's running for President, the fires in Hawaii, climate change. Nothing big or personal, but at least we had a relatively good conversation. It felt less tense than when all three of us have dinner. But then I have to admit, I usually zone out at those times and don't try. With just the two of us, it was like I had to talk. He's an intelligent guy and had lots of thoughts about current events. He asked my opinion too and listened to what I had to say. Maybe he's not as bad as I have made him out to be."

"Wait," I paused, "what's that word you used? *Awks?*"

"Oh," she laughed, "that's something the kids say now for *awkward*."

I smiled. "I was going to say awesome that you're sounding hip, but that's clearly shows my age. What would be the way to say that?"

Christina laughed. "They'd say I was *fire* or *bussin'*. But it's okay to talk regular here."

"Going back, you've learned a lot about both parents! Did you mention anything to your father about your chat with your mother?"

"No. I decided not to. It felt like gossiping, and he hates gossip."

"What do you make of the new things you're noticing about your parents?" I asked to see if she could reflect more deeply about what was going on.

"Hmmm," she pondered briefly. "Well, I had to initiate the conversations. Maybe there's something to that intrusiveness thing that none of us talk unless we think the other person demonstrates interest. Also, I was with each of them individually, and that makes it easier. And with my father, we kept it at a superficial level where nothing triggered his anger."

"I wonder how much your relationship with your father ties in with your concerns about sexuality and relationships?" I wondered if she could make the connection.

"Probably," she said looking a little wary about discussing sexuality.

"You seem a little uncomfortable at the mention of sexuality."

"Yeah, it's kind of a taboo topic at home. I've never felt comfortable talking about it."

"We can come back to that. As it is, it seems like you've made some real progress in your relationships with both parents. How do you feel about that?"

"It's all good. Thanks, I know we're almost out of time."

"We have a few minutes left. I wanted to check in with you about our relationship. I'm wondering how you're feeling about it?"

Hesitantly, Christina admitted, "One thought is that I really know very little about you. I've been a little curious now that I think of it."

"What would you like to know?" I asked, thinking that her curiosity seemed to reflect her growing ability to be interested in others.

"Are you married, do you have children, how old are you—all that kind of thing," she said, looking at me warily. "I feel nervous even asking, like I'm not supposed to be so intrusive."

"There's that *intrusive* word again. That's big. How about if I promise to tell you if there's something I don't want to reveal. You can ask, and I can say no. Clearly, I have boundaries, and I feel comfortable telling you if you cross them. But, so far, your questions seem fine." I paused and then continued after not seeing any obvious reactions, "I have been married for almost fifteen years. I have two children, both almost teenagers."

"Thank you for telling me."

"Any surprises?" I asked given her hesitance about seeming intrusive.

"I am a little surprised you've been married for so long. I thought you were younger."

"What difference would it make if I were younger?"

"You'd be closer in age to me, maybe understand more what my generation is going through, kind of like knowing the slang terms. On the other hand," she quickly added perhaps to balance saying anything even slightly negative, "you're kind of the good mother I never had, maybe my fairy godmother. That's kind of fun thinking about."

"Say more about that."

"I guess it's because I can talk to you. Maybe because you have kids you know how to talk to someone younger."

"Thanks. Anything else?"

"All good. Thanks. See you soon," she called out, already on her way out the door.

I learned so much about the family history today. Christina seemed to have breakthroughs with both parents. I was impressed that she was able to ask about me. I admire Christina's openness and reflectivity, especially in talking about our relationship. It feels like we've settled into a good routine.

I set up an appointment with Paul, my old therapist. There's so much I need to work on: my burnout, problems with Steve and the kids, anxieties about death, and regrets about my relationship with my father, resolving problems with my mother. I also want to talk about my relationship with Christina because I don't want my own conflicts to intrude on my work with her. It's hard to admit that I need to go back—one of my own *shoulds*, I guess, about needing to be the perfect, problem-free therapist. I'm glad Paul is available. I have been having many thoughts about the past therapy, what I want to get out of seeing Paul when we start again, and what's changed. I will start recording my dreams, given that Paul always asks for dreams.

PART II

FALL 2023

16

ESTHER:
THE MUDDY PIT

Esther had ruminated endlessly before calling Paul, her former therapist. *What do I want? Why am I going back now? Why go back to him rather than seek out someone new? What is it about this client, Christina, that triggers me so much?*

Driving up to Paul's office brought back a flood of memories of the years they had spent together in therapy. Esther remembered how hard it had been initially to feel comfortable with an older male therapist, how she didn't quite trust him. They had to work through a lot of problems in their relationship, but they ended in a good place. She got a lot out of therapy, and things were good for a long time. But life had been difficult lately, and Esther again needed an outside perspective.

Driving into the parking garage made Esther reflect about how much clients go through even getting to therapy sessions. It's not just the forty-five or fifty minutes of the session, it's the traveling to get there and then going back to the real world afterwards and all the time that takes and the mental preparation for the session and then thinking about the session after it's over.

Walking into the office building felt familiar, and Esther was excited to be back to work on herself again. At the same time, she felt like a failure for having to go back to therapy and being unable to do it all on her own. It was the old imposter syndrome. But then she comforted herself thinking about how therapists she respected openly talked about their therapy experiences and about being wounded healers.

Esther hoped Paul remembered her. She wanted to be special in his memory, his favorite client. Was she beginning to sound like Christina? Sitting in the waiting room, she had to remind myself to breathe, to take it all in.

Paul opened his door and smiled warmly, "Esther, it's good to see you. Do come in."

"I'm relieved to be here," I said, looking around his office to see what had changed. I noticed he had some good new art and a cluttered desk, but I especially remembered the comfortable chairs and headed right for the one I had always sat in. I had spent many hours in this office and this chair and felt that perhaps Paul understood me better than anyone else ever had. He was like the parent I wished I had had.

I started hesitantly, and then it all just spilled out, a dam bursting. "I need to be here but also am disappointed that I need to be back. When we terminated, I was doing great, but life has a way of kicking you down. Working with clients is tough because their problems remind me of my unresolved problems."

"Slow down," Paul admonished soothingly. "We have time to sort this all out. Start from the beginning, and tell me what's foremost on your mind and how I can help."

I took a deep breath. "To review, for myself, I started therapy with you when I was in grad school. Learning how to work with clients was difficult for me. I was in over my head and sympathizing too much with clients. The faculty recommended therapy for all of us, although it was not mandated. and I realized I needed help. We focused on the challenges I had getting through the doctoral program, particularly the statistics courses. I started to enjoy doing scholarly work and presenting at conferences, but I never felt quite good enough at it to be an academic. I had a writing phobia and procrastinated, so it was hard to get my dissertation done. I got all the clinical experience I could during graduate school, and supervision was helpful, but it exposed cracks in my family relationships that I knew I had to get into. That's when I started seeing you. We worked for several years, and I gradually began to understand my family more and felt more confident in my skills as a therapist. You helped me in my relationship with Steve and with my angst about having children. I stopped therapy when my kids were little because I felt stressed and crunched for time. I was generally in a good place and was ready to stop."

"What is it you want from our work now?" Paul said encouragingly.

"My marriage is not good; Steve and I hardly talk any more. And he seems to be off at mysterious meetings all the time. Our lives are in such a perpetual rush that we don't seem to have any time for each other. I'm not sure I even like him now. We've changed so much. He's in business and doesn't understand or care about the stresses I'm under as a therapist. He can be very critical sometimes about my appearance and what I say. On the one hand, he acts like he's smarter than me and puts me down. On the other hand, he gets defensive that I have a PhD when he only has a bachelor's degree, although that's all he needs in his field. I sometimes feel like I'm walking on eggshells around him. He indirectly threatened to leave me the other night, and I panicked."

"What was going on?"

"He said we don't communicate anymore."

"Ouch," he winced. "And you're such a good communicator. That must have hurt."

"Yeah. But the thing that pushed me over the edge to come back into therapy is my work with a client named Christina. Many of the things she's going through remind me of myself when I was her age. She has been struggling to find herself. It's hard for her to individuate from her parents."

"We can certainly talk about that and see what's going on," Paul reassured me. "Anything else that you want to focus on?"

"Yes. I know that the first dreams presented in therapy are important, so of course I had one last night. Is it okay to tell you?"

"Of course, you know I love dreams," he readily agreed. "Go ahead."

> I'm doing group therapy with all my clients, but I feel very small, and then I disappear. I fall down into a muddy pit and can't climb out. You throw a rope down, but the sides of the pit are muddy and slippery. I can't get a good hold on the rope. That's when I wake up. My heart is pounding, and I feel dizzy.

"I suspect you've thought about what this dream means and why you had it last night."

"Yes," I admitted, relieved that he didn't force an interpretation on me. "It feels obvious. I'm feeling diminished by my work with clients, as though I'm losing myself. I give and give, both with my clients and at home, and I'm not receiving much in return. I'm despairing, as if I am indeed stuck in a muddy pit. I ask you for help, and you throw me a rope, but I can't use it to get out of the pit. I'm worried about whether you can help me. I'm also thinking of the fable you told me long ago, where the person standing on a bridge throws a rope over to a drowning person. The drowning person doesn't try to pull herself up, and the person on top of the bridge gets tired and must decide about how much he can help the drowning person. He can't lift the person out and is in danger of falling in himself and drowning if he holds on any longer."

"So, I will be destroyed if I try to help you with your big, murky problems?" Paul says, making the dynamic between us clear.

I nodded. "That about summarizes it, yep. If you're destroyed, you can't help me. And I worry that I'll drag you over the edge."

"It reminds me of some of the battles we went through when you were in therapy before. You wanted me to prove that I wanted to and could help you."

"It does," I agreed. "On the way over, I wondered if you even remembered me and whether I mattered to you. You have so many other patients. And, of course, that goes back to my father, of never feeling special in his eyes."

"Sounds so painful."

Crying quietly, I looked down and studied my hands. "Yeah, it brings up old wounds. My father wasn't there for me and couldn't or wouldn't fill my needs. And now I'm feeling estranged from Steve. Somehow, what with careers and kids, we don't seem to have time for each other. And when we do, we don't have much to say to each other. It's as though we no longer have much in common. I wonder what I ever saw in him."

"As I recall," Paul challenged me, "you also had some mistrust of me at the beginning. Remind me again, wasn't your mother abused?"

"Yeah, my father was alcoholic. He'd be fine when he was sober, and then when he drank, he'd fly into rages, screaming at everyone. I had to hide and stay out of his sight. He died when I was in high school, so I never got a chance to work things out with him. My mother did not divorce him, maybe because she was a housewife with no real career and felt she didn't have options. She wanted me to have more in life and encouraged me to go for my PhD so I could have a career and security. Oh, but I still have issues with my mother being controlling, dominating, and inconsistent. You even wondered at one point whether she has a borderline personality. She also tries to act like she knows more than me about how to raise my kids."

"Right. So, all the issues with your father and mother transferred over into your fears about me—either not being interested in you, raging at you, or dominating you."

"That's about it," I nodded.

"And how do all your issues with your family interweave and get tangled up with your relationship with Chistina?" Paul probed.

"Well, I hadn't put the pieces together until now," I admitted sheepishly. "I've encouraged Chistina to talk about her relationship with her mother, and that's been helpful, and yet I haven't been working on the relationship with my mother. Also, I've neglected helping Christina work on her relationship with her father, probably because of my fear of men."

"I can see why it must have been so difficult for you to trust me. Why do you suppose you sought out a male therapist in the first place?"

I laughed and shook my head at the memory. "Actually, I wanted a female therapist but couldn't find one. I thought maybe I could learn something by having a male therapist. But I'm certain that a lot of my reluctance with you came from my fear of men. I just didn't know if you were trustworthy, but I also longed for a good relationship with a male authority figure."

"How do you feel talking with me today?" Paul asked, bringing it home.

"I was worried before I arrived," I admitted reluctantly but quickly added, perhaps to reassure him (or myself), "but now that we're talking, I feel reassured. Interesting, though, I couldn't hold onto the connection between us from before and worried that you wouldn't remember me or want to see me."

"Indeed, I do remember you, and of course I went back over my notes to remind myself of the major issues we talked about." Paul gave me a reassuring smile.

"Can we go back to the dream of where I disappeared? That's so reminiscent of how I feel a lot of times. Christina even called me out on it saying she doesn't know much about me. It seems that's how I've lived my life; I make myself small so I won't take up much space, and I try to help everyone else and make sure they have lots of space and feel comfortable."

"Yes, I remember when you first started therapy with me, you did seem small. Your voice was weak, and you could have disappeared into that chair. And it certainly makes sense, given all you've said about your parents and your survival strategies. Your voice seems stronger now, though, and I'm guessing you've retained a lot of what you learned in our previous work."

"That's so true," I responded, feeling gratified because of his praise. "At the end of our therapy, I felt so much better. I did well in grad school. I gained confidence, felt smarter, and felt I could handle myself. I guess the intervening years with dealing with family and clients have chipped away at that though."

"So, Dr. Esther, what's your prescription for yourself?" Paul said with a smile.

Liking that he was acting as a coach rather than being bossy, I said, "I don't know how many sessions I need, and I know I don't want to return to years of therapy, but I do want to talk through these concerns and hear your perspective. I'm grateful that you agreed to see..."

"Not wanting many sessions fits with what I want to tell you," Paul interrupted. "I am retiring soon. I agreed to see you given our long relationship and not knowing exactly what you needed, but I want to let you know that I can only see you for the next three months. My eightieth birthday is coming up, and it's time to give up my license and practice."

"Oh, my," I exclaimed. "I didn't realize that you were that close to retirement. I guess I assumed you'd by here forever whenever I needed you."

"It's a big decision for me. I was trying to think of the best way to let you know. So, if we can agree to however many sessions we can have in the next three months, I'm up for it."

"Okay, that fits for me. I'm glad I have a chance to connect with you before you retire," I said holding back some tears.

After a pause, Paul asked, "What are your tears saying?"

"I am feeling anxious thinking about you retiring."

"Terminations are hard. I feel some ambivalence too, because I love the work. But it's time. We can certainly talk about it as we go on."

I took a deep breath. "So many changes. And I'm not good with change."

"So," Paul came back to our previous topic, "what would you like to accomplish in our limited time together?"

"I want to feel strong again. I'm also not sure I want to keep seeing so many clients. That's a big thing I want to consider, to maybe scale back and do some other things. Again, with Christina, it's so exciting that she has opportunities in front of her. I want to explore more and maybe go in some new directions. And, of course, I need to talk about my relationship with Steve. Interesting that I put that last. Oh, and as my two kids are approaching their teenage years, I'm getting into more control issues with them, similar to what I went through with my mother. So, let's put that on the agenda, too."

Paul asked, "How are you feeling about our session today, especially after all your ambivalence about coming back and my retiring?"

Unsure how much I wanted to get into discussing our relationship right now, I initially demurred but then warmed up to talking about us. "I'm relieved. It was hard to contact you, but it feels right to be back. I know I need to talk to Steve and tell him how I'm feeling. I'm also aware of how much energy it has taken for me to see so many clients. I care about them, maybe too much, and I feel depleted at the end of the day. I worry that I'm losing myself. I also am intrigued by this idea that my fear of men has been holding me back from pursuing the topic of Christina's father and her possible romantic relationships. I liked that you asked me what my thoughts were and what I wanted to do. You are a good role model, more the guide on the side than the sage on the stage, like you don't have to prove yourself to me. That's a good lesson for me to remember. And it's good for me to remember again how vulnerable it makes me feel to be the client. I feel I'm taking up more space now than at the beginning of the session."

"Yes, you are, and it's a pleasure to see you again. Lots for us to work on."

"That sounds perfect. I need a kickstart to get unstuck and remember the resources I have within myself."

"I can't wait to see what dreams you bring in next week and where you are with the muddy pit," Paul said accompanying me to the door.

"Thanks. See you next week," I said, already beginning to feel the loss of a final ending with Paul.

CHRISTINA:
BARBIE

Full of energy, Christina burst out, "I saw the movie *Barbie* with Joannie, a friend from work, and I had so many reactions. Then I had a dream about it. Is it okay if we start with the dream?"

"Of course," I responded. I wondered why she wasn't talking about the trip to see her grandmother but reminded myself to let Christina take the lead in what we discussed. She started,

> I am in the forest under a big oak tree at night, just like in the dream I told you about at the beginning of therapy. I'm ordinary Barbie and not feeling special, and I'm lost and alone yet again. Then these five stereotypical Barbies come up and ask me if I want to join them in this "thing." I feel thrilled to be included because they are beautiful and I want to be part of their group. Then five weird Barbies come up and beg me to join their side of this "thing." I kind of relate

more to the weird Barbies because they are unique and interesting. I am so confused. I'm not sure who I am or what group I should belong to, and I don't even know what this "thing" is. The scene shifts and I go up to the kitchen in a tall corporate building where I see this nice, older woman. I ask her for advice about what to do. Should I be stereotypical, ordinary, or weird? She just smiles at me and gives me a cuppa tea, and I wake up.

"What a great dream!" I had recently seen the *Barbie* movie too and loved it. I thought the *thing* or conflict she was describing about stereotypical, ordinary, and weird Barbies was a terrific metaphor for her figuring out who she was. Secretly, I hoped she'd choose the weird Barbie group, probably given my own hang-ups about how plastic the stereotypical Barbies are. "Let's jump right into it. Describe the ordinary Barbie."

Christina closed her eyes, as if turning inward and watching the movie in her mind. "She's dressed in ordinary jeans and a t-shirt, maybe ten pounds overweight, okay looking but nothing special. She has no particular talents and feels pressured to be something special. It's as if being ordinary is not good enough, although most people are ordinary and deserve happiness too."

As I listened to her describing the ordinary Barbie, I noticed that Christina had started dressing more creatively. Compared to the jeans and white or black t-shirt she had worn in our first sessions, she's now choosing brighter colors.

"Any particular feelings at that moment in the dream? Try to put yourself back at the time when you were sitting under that big oak tree and night is falling."

"I am scared at first because I am alone and it is night. I am, like, here I go again, I am still lost in the stupid woods. Why can't I find my way out? What's wrong with me?"

"So you're feeling isolated and scared."

"Yeah," she said, looking down and not adding anything.

"What associations do you have to the Barbies?"

"The Barbie I had as a child was the stereotypical Barbie with the perfect shape. All the other girls had Barbies, and I wanted them, too. I didn't have all the Barbie dreamhouse stuff that was in the movie. My parents were far too practical for that and would never give me such frivolous plastic junk. I remember going into the toy store and wanting all that stuff. I guess I thought it would make me cool to have it. Looking back, all that plastic perfect stuff is icky. As for ordinary or weird Barbies, I'd never heard of them before. I loved that in the movie I could definitely relate to the ordinary ones. It's kind of who I am right now, having no special talents and not knowing what I want to be."

"So, the ordinary Barbie kind of fits your self-image?"

"Yeah, it does. I would love to be beautiful, skinny, and popular like the stereotypical Barbies, but it seems so unrealistic and surreal. I have a fantasy of being the stereotypical Barbie and happy all the time. But on the other hand, that seems boring."

"Feelings when you first saw the stereotypical Barbies in the dream?"

"I really wanted to be part of them. I felt envious of how they seemed to have everything. Always the perfect day. Everything pink. But not sure I could ever measure up. How could I fit in that group? I don't know that culture. It's like they're from a different planet and I don't even know the language."

"Associations?"

"Oh yeah," she nodded emphatically. "The cheerleaders in high school. They all hung out together, and the boys swarmed around them like bees around nectar. They dressed perfectly and had hair that swung out and around."

"Anyone like that in your life right now?"

"Hmmm, not that I can think of. The people I hung out with in high school were the brainy kids. I was never that brainy, but I was more like them than like the cheerleaders."

"And the weird Barbies in the dream. Tell me about them."

"Ah yes, the rebels. Their hair was chopped off, and they had tattoos and weird clothes. They seemed free and creative. It gives me a good feeling inside to think about being weird like that. I can just imagine, though, that my parents would totally freak if I went home with a tattoo. The Goth kids in school scared me, but I was fascinated by them. They seemed to thumb their noses at everything. So, again, some fear but also some longing to be part of them."

"Interesting that there were five stereotypical Barbies and five weird Barbies but only one ordinary Barbie. Where do you suppose the other ordinary Barbies are?"

"Good question!"

"And the *thing*. What was that about?"

"In the movie, there's a war among the male dolls, the Kens and Allans. No one seems to know what the war is about and who's on which side, and it is kind of a riff on the ridiculousness of war. I think that's what this *thing* is, a fake war between the stereotypicals and the weirds. But good point, where are the ordinaries and the regular men in my dream?"

"I'm aware of time and want to make sure we get to the image of the older woman up in the kitchen. Tell me more about her."

"Oh wow, I just realized that she might have been you. And now I remember that you suggested I have a dream about you. I think the older woman was you!"

I smiled. "Say more about that section of the dream."

"There's this nice replica in the movie of a homey kitchen, a place you'd want to hang out and talk. And the older woman was ordinary and accepting. With her in the movie, it didn't feel like you had to be anything special. You could just sit and have a cuppa tea."

"What's the role of this older woman in the movie?"

"Well, it turns out she was the creator of the original Barbie. But she doesn't look anything like the stereotypical Barbie. She's just a nice, older woman who seems very motherly or grandmotherly. Not trying to be special, just authentic. Reminds me of my mother, grandmother, and you, I guess."

I was a little put off by the description of me as older given that the woman in the dream was elderly, but I shrugged that off for the moment. "So older women—you put your mother, your grandmother, and me all together into that image. How are we alike and how different?"

"Alike in, well, you're all older than me. I don't feel competitive with you, more like you're there to support me and help me grow. Maybe there's some wisdom there. I like that she gives me a cuppa tea but doesn't seem to need anything from me and doesn't tell me what to do. That kind of reminds me of my not wanting you to give me homework. Although you did suggest that I go home and have a dream."

"Good point. Maybe I did get a little bossy. You didn't really need me to tell you to have a dream. You do it on your own now."

"I feel so mixed about that. Maybe the best thing is my getting to the point of saying I don't want you to make suggestions."

CHRISTINA: BARBIE

"So, try that. Tell me you don't want me to make suggestions."

"It feels really awkward, but if you suggested something, I might say, 'Thanks, but no thanks; right now, I don't need any suggestions. When I do, I'll ask, if that's okay.' Kind of like last session you said I could ask you things, but you could say you didn't want to answer. I think you called that setting boundaries.'"

"Yes. That's great. I may make a mistake and suggest something, and you can just say, 'no thanks.' And sometimes you might want me to suggest things, and some of what I suggest might be helpful and some not. You can tell me. Clear communication. How did it feel to say that out loud?"

"Good. Sometimes I say that to myself afterwards, but it's harder to say out loud directly to you in this room."

"It is hard, but you're getting so much better at doing so." I paused to give her a chance to react, but Christina didn't say anything. "Any other thoughts about the movie?"

"It made me think about the role of women and men in our society. How we get put into these impossible roles of being one thing and have a difficult time breaking out and becoming ourselves, whatever that is."

"Good point. And that's obviously what we're trying to do here—figure out who *you* want to be."

"Yeah, can't wait." We both laugh. "OMG, I just realized we didn't talk about my family. I got sidetracked talking too much about *Barbie*. I bet we're out of time, aren't we?"

"Sorry, but we are," I said. "I guess we got carried away because it was so much fun talking about *Barbie*. Can it wait until next time to talk about family, or should we set up another session?"

"I guess it will have to wait," she said, abruptly getting up and heading for the door.

"See you Monday?"

"Yep. Thanks."

That felt like a rupture at the end. Things were going so well, and then suddenly Christina seemed angry. Maybe I got carried away talking about the movie. Perhaps I should have asked about the grandmother. So many choice points! I need to remind myself to be aware of the possible rupture next week. I wonder if I was distracted by my own therapy. Suddenly, things seem to be moving very fast!

18

ESTHER: HUSBAND BEACHING IT

Paul began, "Any thoughts since last week about coming back to therapy with me?"

"It took a lot of effort to call you, but I'm glad I did," I said after a brief pause. "I felt energized right after the session, but then the next day I felt strangely down and discouraged. I had no energy to get up and go. I just wanted to stay in bed and eat ice cream all day. So, I guess, up and down, happy to be back, but feels kind of like a scab getting ripped off a wound."

"Sounds unpleasantly painful. As you know, that often happens in therapy. It's hard to face difficult things, especially when you've been out of the routine of being in therapy."

"But I didn't expect it to happen to me."

"Because you're special, right?" he teased, and we both laughed.

"You're right. I want this to be quick, easy, and painless. It's hard to get back to committing to working on myself."

Paul was silent, which felt like letting me stew in my poisonous juices for a minute.

I looked down and then reluctantly admitted, "It hit me harder than I expected when you said you're retiring. It's strange, but I feel abandoned."

"I feel sad, too. It's hard to say good-bye," Paul said quietly.

"At least we have a few sessions," I said, sighing.

"Any more feelings about my retiring?"

"Yeah, lots. I feel worried about you not being there when I hit my next crisis. I seem to have frequent crises. I guess I could find another therapist, but it feels exhausting even thinking about going through the process of starting a new relationship. I feel good for you, though, taking care of yourself. It also makes me wonder how I'll know when to retire."

"I can see that my retirement has brought up lots of feelings. Let's keep talking about it. But I also know there are a lot of other things on your mind. Any dreams this week?"

I took a breath and centered myself, "I had a dream a couple nights ago. I almost laughed because I knew you would think it was so transparent."

> I'm giving a speech in a big auditorium of psychologists. It is well received, and I bask in knowing that I can do a good job at public speaking when I know the topic well and am prepared. I look out into the audience where I expect to see Steve, but he isn't there. I go down to the beach and see him sitting by the pool with a bunch of people, having a good time. He is so intently involved that he doesn't even notice me.

"You said you laughed because it was so transparent. Tell me more."

"I've been feeling disconnected from Steve, as I told you last week. It just played out again in the dream. I was doing something important that I felt good about. I wanted his support, and he didn't show up. He was hanging out with other people having fun, and I was excluded."

"I see that," Paul said, "although it may not be all that transparent. Let's unpack it. I'm intrigued by your talk. What was that all about? And how did it feel to bask in the praise of a big audience of psychologists?"

"It felt great, like I had my game on. And, as I mentioned, I need to think about doing other things than just seeing clients. I need to stretch myself, but I'm not sure in what way. But I can remember a few times in grad school when I gave talks and got positive feedback. It was gratifying. I remember liking the rush of giving a good talk and having it well received."

"Feeling special, being noticed. You certainly weren't shrinking away and losing yourself in that scene," he challenged with an amused expression.

"True," I acknowledged. "People were noticing me. I did stand out. I guess I do have a need to be special, to be noticed by my peers. And it reminds me of how much I longed to be noticed in my family when I didn't feel seen at all. I'm not sure my parents ever knew the true me. They saw me more as an extension of themselves." After a silence, I crossed my arms protectively across my midriff and said, "Yeah, that feels powerful. I'm not sure that I want to give talks, but I do want to do something where I am seen for being or doing something special."

"And Steve wasn't there to cheer you on or even notice you being treated as special."

"Yeah, that was a bummer. I wanted him to be there. I looked around for him before the talk and didn't see him but thought maybe he was just late. The thought did cross my mind that he wasn't there because he didn't want to see me shine. Remember I told you last week that it seems like there's been competitiveness between us. I let it go while I got into the talk. But as I was leaving the room by myself I felt so alone."

"Ah, you felt abandoned by both Steve and me."

"Oh, that's an interesting parallel! You're leaving me and won't be here to praise me about my accomplishments. And Steve is acting competitive. That hits home."

"And you've said your father didn't pay attention to you. The men in your life are not very trustworthy."

"Seems like it," I said, feeling tears coming to my eyes. "I feel sad thinking about it. I certainly don't feel special."

"And now go to that scene on the beach where you see your husband talking with a lot of people. What's going on there?"

"Well, I think maybe he was trying to start a new business deal or he was using this opportunity to work on his business. He's into AI and developing something, I don't even know what. Or maybe it was more social and he'd just met these people. But he was supposed to be at my talk, and he didn't even show up. I can't see why he took this time to hang out with other people instead of coming to hear my talk. Ah, even as I say it, I see it goes back to my parents; they weren't there when I did anything special. Being the youngest, it just didn't seem they had time or energy for me. I felt hurt. It's like in *Alice in Wonderland*; during the talk I grew larger, then I got smaller and smaller when I saw Steve, similar to the last dream where I disappeared in the group therapy. Like I could have slid down the muddy rabbit hole."

"But you didn't," Paul noted.

"You're right; the dream ended there." I paused, reaching inward to see what was going on. "I worry that the dream foretells that Steve doesn't care about me anymore. I wonder if the dream is telling me I need to separate from him."

"Well, as you know, I don't think the dream *tells you anything*. It's up to you to *choose* what you make of the dream, what you're telling yourself."

"Of course you're right," I acknowledged. "And now I'm remembering that you suggested that I talk more with Steve, and I didn't do that."

"Hmm, as I recall, you were the one, not I, who said you thought you needed to talk with Steve. What do you suppose that's about, attributing the suggestion to me?"

I reflected, startled I had projected this onto Paul. "I suppose I feel like you're the authority figure and that's what you would tell me to do, even though I'm reluctant to talk to him. I'm clearly blocking. I don't feel ready yet. I don't feel strong enough," I observed, again noticing that I sounded whiny and defeated. "I worry he's going to ignore me, that he has other, more interesting things to pay attention to, like those people at the pool. I feel bad when I say that," I muttered through tears.

Comfortingly, Paul directed, "Be your tears. What are your tears saying right now?"

"Okay, I can do that." I took a deep breath. "My tears are saying that I feel sad and lonely. I want a partner. I don't want to go it alone. I want to matter to someone. I want to be special with my partner."

"Good awareness. But can you tell that to Steve? As I recall, we spent a long time in therapy before talking about how you want to speak up. You can't expect Steve or anyone else to read your mind. You have to tell him what your needs are."

"Yeah, you're right." I winced. "But what if he no longer cares enough to want to meet me halfway? What if it's over?"

"How would that feel if it were all over?"

Looking down and breaking eye contact, I timidly ventured, "I don't honestly know. I don't know what I want. Do I want to work it out with him or start over with someone new? Would starting over just be running away? I'd still have to work things out with someone else. As you have said, a geographical solution rarely works. I would be taking my communication problems with me."

"Let's reach back and think about how you felt when you first met your husband. What were your first reactions to him?"

"We met in a philosophy class. We were the two best students in the class, and we competed throughout. We had these great debates about Nietzsche and how much choice we have in our lives. Steve got very upset about Nietzsche being unreligious because Steve had strong religious beliefs. I am an atheist and totally agreed with Nietzsche that we each make our own choices in life. The differences in religious beliefs have been a source of contention in our marriage. We fight about how to raise the kids in terms of religion. Actually, it seems like right now we fight about most everything. Not the friendly debates of before, but fights in which no one wins. And we go our separate ways. I give my talk; he goes to the pool."

"That hurts," Paul said. "And it sounds like you're not sure what you want."

"You're right. I'm not seeing the answers. I know I can try to talk to him, but I'm not sure it will go anywhere. And I feel reluctant, like I'm holding on to anger and resentment about all the disagreements and I don't want to give it up," I said.

"I'm certainly not going to make you give it up. It's up to you to decide," he gently reminded me.

Getting into it a little more, I reflected, "I want to hang on to the resentment and anger. I remember when I was incredibly angry at a colleague, and the anger festered like a poison. Someone once said that it's as though anger invades your head, and you're the vessel that is poisoned rather than the other person. That stuck with me. Now that I think of it, I have fallen into these moments when I get paranoid and furious at another person. That deserves more thought, but it makes me tired just thinking of it," I said, again quickly descending into despair. "These issues never completely resolve. They just go underground and emerge when I'm under stress. So much for any fantasies of being cured and of being the perfect therapist."

"We're just about out of time for today, and I want to check in with you about how we're doing," Paul challenged gently.

I let out a long, deep breath. "On the one hand, I'm feeling discouraged about the situation with Steve, but at least I feel relieved that I can talk about it with you. I'm glad you're here to work with me, even if it's just for a few sessions. I was feeling stuck on my own, just ruminating and spinning my wheels," I admitted. Then I turned it back to him, "How about you? How are you feeling about us? I know I've been whining. Are you getting annoyed?"

"Hmm, no, I'm not annoyed. I'm feeling compassion for your pain. I'm engaged because you're working hard. And I'm glad you're bringing in your dreams. But I do have to admit that I also feel some guilt and pain that we only have a few sessions. This seems a tough time for you in your marriage and career, and I wish I could magically make it all better."

"Yeah, so do I," I said, with feeling.

"Let's continue talking about this next week." Paul said reassuringly, concluding our session.

"Yes, thank you. See you next week."

I walked slowly out of Paul's office and sat in the car crying. I had been keeping in all the bad feelings for so long that it felt like popping a big blister and a blob of pus running out. I had been planning to do some grocery shopping but instead went to a local lake and took a long walk to help myself get centered so that I could turn my focus to clients during the next few hours.

19

CHRISTINA AND MOTHER

As Christina pulled her car into the call-waiting area at the airport, her mother called and said she was walking to the arrivals area. When Christina pulled up, her mother put her suitcase in the trunk and jumped into the front seat.

"Thanks for picking me up," her mother said.

"So, tell me all about it. How's Grandma?"

"I'm glad I went. She's not doing well, but she was happy to see me. She was pleased to know that you're going out with me next time."

"What was it like to be with her?"

"I felt relieved to be there. It feels like I have my mother back. She's frail, but her mind is sharp. She wanted me to know how bad she felt when I left home when I was a teenager. She actually apologized. She told me about some of the difficulties she had getting along with my father and how she should have stood up for me more. We had such a good talk. I think she's made peace with her life. And I feel like I've made peace with her, finally."

"Wow! Sounds like you had a great talk!"

"I told her I loved her. And I wanted to tell you that I love you, and I'm so glad our relationship is getting better! I'm glad we don't have to wait until I'm on my deathbed before we have a good relationship."

Both of us were crying, "Me too!"

20

CHRISTINA:
CAREER

Christina sat down and stated in a business-like manner, "I'd like to talk about my mother's visit to see her mother and what happened there. If we have time, I'd like to talk about this friend at work. And if there's still time after that, maybe we can get started on career stuff."

Feeling a little chastened, I responded, "You have a lot on your agenda. I wonder how you feel about our not having talked about your mother and grandmother last session?"

"Well, to be honest," she hesitated, "a little annoyed. Talking about the movie was fun, but it seemed a little frivolous when there's all the big stuff going on in my life right now. And I did want to talk about my family stuff."

Feeling encouraged that Christina could state her feelings, I wanted to support her, despite feeling a bit rebuked. I also wondered if my own issues over feminism made me focus on *Barbie* more than necessary, but I bracketed that thought as something to bring up with Paul. "I can see that, and I apologize. I wish I had asked you at the beginning whether you wanted to talk about the dream or about your mother and grandmother. Thanks for bringing in a clear agenda today. How did it feel to tell me you were annoyed?"

"Good," she said, sounding more relaxed. "I like being able to express my feelings. It's a new thing for me. I guess sometimes I don't even know until later what I feel, and then I worry that I was too abrupt when I said what I was thinking."

"Hindsight is always clearer. But you did come back and bring it up. It's good to be aware that you were a bit abrupt. I was taken aback initially, but I liked that you spoke up about your needs. That's a big step. You'll get better at it with practice."

"Thanks," Christina admitted after a brief pause. "I practiced what to say. I was so anxious and worried I might fall apart at the beginning of the session."

"No wonder you sounded a bit abrupt. It's hard when you're sitting on so many feelings."

"It's a little hard to come down from the anxiety." She paused, took a minute to pet Star, and then said, "Let's go on."

"Where do you want to start?" I responded gently, allowing her to take the lead.

"Maybe with my mother, if that's okay?" Christina said.

"Sure. Tell me what's going on."

Sounding more confident, Christine began. "I picked her up at the airport. She was so different and easy to talk to. She was able to tell Grandma she loved her, and then she said she loved me. We had a moment of crying together. And we have kept talking since. My mother told me more about what happened when she left home. Grandma apologized for handling it all wrong. My mother had felt angry for so many years, and it turns out that my grandmother also felt terrible when my mother left."

"There's a lot there. How are you feeling about all this?"

"I'm glad my mother is opening up. It feels good to talk to her about all this. And I'm relieved I'll have a chance to see Grandma before she dies."

"What would you like to say to your grandma? Just say it as if she were right there in that chair, like you did with your mother."

Moving to face the empty chair, Christina began, "Grandma, I am going to make the trip to see you. I love you, and I'm glad you are my grandmother."

"How do you think she would respond?"

She nodded with a grin, "I think she would just smile and give me a big hug."

"You look so comforted," I affirmed. "How are plans progressing for the trip?"

"We set the date. I got off work. So, I think we're ready. I have to admit, though, I'm worried about seeing someone old and dying. I wonder if it will be creepy," she said frowning. "I've never seen someone near death."

Always looking for a chance to highlight death anxiety, I lightly said, "Nothing like reminding you of your own mortality!"

"That's for sure," Christina nodded vigorously. "As if a black cloud just hovered over my head, like the shadow of death!"

"It will be good to pay attention to those feelings when you're there with her. We too often segregate older people and don't have much contact. Maybe it's even good to reflect that you'll be old and dying one day and will want people to treat you as a human being," I said, thinking that I was talking to myself as much as to Christina. I had to make a quick decision about whether to focus on her reactions to my advice giving but decided it was more important to return to her agenda. "Anything more about that or are you ready to move on? You mentioned the friend at work?"

"Yeah, Joannie. She's the one I went to the *Barbie* movie with. She asked me if I want to go see *Oppenheimer*. I'm ambivalent about that movie because people say it's very long and a little hard to follow. I like having someone to go to movies with and wouldn't want to go by myself, but I feel a little uncomfortable around her, like she thinks I'm naïve or something. She's asked me to pick up packages for her when she's not in the restaurant, which is no big deal. I just put them in my locker, and she retrieves them the next day. But I feel funny about it. She's older and never went to college but has street smarts. She grew up on the streets of DC and is kind of a tough girl. She has bleached blond hair and a couple tattoos. Men are attracted to her. After the *Barbie* movie, we went for drinks and a couple men came up and hit on her. I kind of froze. Joannie noticed and blew them off. We talked about the movie for a while and went home. We don't have all that much in common, but it was fun going to the movie."

"It sounds like you're in that initial stage of friendship where you're each revealing a little and seeing how the other responds, then maybe testing the waters to see if it's safe to go deeper and reveal more."

Christina nodded in agreement. "Even if we're not friends for life, she could be a friend now. I don't know why I have the niggling feeling that something is off."

"Can you say more about that *off* feeling? You used the word *naïve?*"

"I don't know. I just wonder what she wants from me. I don't trust her completely, maybe because we're from such different backgrounds."

"Good to be aware of that feeling, like your radar is out."

"Yeah, but it feels silly on my part. She's never given me any reason not to trust her."

"Any problems trusting friends in the past?"

"No," she paused and looked away. "I can't think of any. I'll just keep my eyes open."

Hmm, that pause again; what's that about? "How are you feeling about maybe going to see *Oppenheimer*?"

"It sounds so different from *Barbie*, and people are definitely talking about it. Physics has never been my thing, but I am interested in history. So, it might be good to see it. Maybe I'll have a dream about the atomic bomb."

"More affirmation that the world is a dangerous place?" I ventured.

"Oh, that's interesting. Maybe that's why I'm reluctant to go. Hmm. I'll have to think about that more."

"It will be interesting to see what you do with that one in your imagination. I could see it going different ways. But you had one other item on your agenda," I probed, wanting to get to everything on her agenda so she wouldn't be angry at me at the end of this session.

"Yeah, it kind of fits in. I want to talk about careers and how to choose. I would love to take some kind of test that would tell me the *right* occupation for me. How does one even know how to decide?"

"Yeah, that's a big one. Our culture pushes us to pick the best career, the best partner, the best everything. The expectation is that everything has to be perfect and set off fireworks."

"Yeah, that's kind of what *Barbie* was about," Christina agreed.

"You mentioned that you want to take a test to give you the answer about the *right* occupation. That reminds me about your ambivalence over wanting advice. You want it, but it's the easy way out. My sense is that you'd rather struggle to figure it out on your own."

"That may be true," she crossed her arms and looked down. "Hmm. You had a reaction there. What went on inside?"

"It kind of felt like you were doing a *gotcha* kind of thing. Like I was caught doing something bad," Christina admitted.

I wondered if I had some residual upset about having felt chastised at the beginning of the session and was paying her back. She had struck a nerve for sure. I took a deep breath from my diaphragm and dragged myself back into the room to try to repair the rupture. "Sorry it struck you that way. What I meant to suggest was that you're more capable than you sometimes give yourself credit for."

"No problem," Christina quickly jumped in. "I know it's up to me. It's hard, though. How did you get into your career?"

I thought it was interesting that Christina asked me for a disclosure right after a rupture. Ordinarily I might not have revealed much about myself, but I wanted to honor her request by holding out a peace offering of a disclosure. "I had to struggle to figure it out. I took a lot of courses in college and crossed off the things I didn't like. That left psychology and sociology. I discovered that I loved psychology and haven't regretted that decision. You're facing the decision earlier than I did. I've worked with a lot of college students who change majors many times during college. I'm aware that we have only fifteen minutes left, though, and I wonder whether it might be better to hear more about *your* thoughts about *your* career choices?"

"Yeah, okay. Good point," Christina nodded looking more engaged. "Maybe I was trying to run away there from talking about myself. It's hard to talk about this career stuff."

"What makes it hard?"

"So many things. It's funny, I used to be so eager to go to college, and I had lots of ideas about what I could do. I couldn't wait, and then I just lost interest."

"What do you suppose happened to make you lose interest all of a sudden?"

"I don't know. It's weird, but my senior year was just depressing."

"Anything else going on related to career stuff?"

"My parents, probably because they're introverts in high-security jobs, never talk much about their work or themselves for that matter. They are certainly *not* passionate about their work. And it just seems like in high school there was this expectation that we *should* find something that we're passionate about, something that gives life meaning. And yet, I hear about people with midlife crises who have jobs they hate and people who just work so that they can live. I don't want to die in a boring job like the one I have now."

"What are some of the things you don't want to do?"

"I don't want to be a lawyer because I'm not good at debating and don't have confidence in my ideas. I'm not sure about teaching. I've never been drawn to it, never played school or anything like that."

"How about some of the things you like?"

"Journalism and psychology are still on the list. The other thing that's interested me lately is climate change. I'm worried about what's happening to the earth. I am upset about plastics and the lack of recycling and all the wasted food in restaurants. I think I want to do something where I'm around people and help people."

"Sounds to me like you have many interests and even some you're passionate about. You're right, there's a lot that needs to be done about climate change and social justice."

"Yeah, there was that young girl, I think her name was Greta something, who made a big difference in terms of raising awareness about climate change. She inspires me to want to do something so that we have a planet to live on."

"I'd like to hear more about your passion for making the world a better place. We're almost out of time for today, though. Any final words?"

"I'm glad we're talking about career stuff. Maybe I'll spend some time surfing the net to find out about different careers."

"Great idea. I'll see you next Monday."

Terrific that Christina stood up for herself a couple times today. I could see how hard it was for her. She gave a hint about being depressed in her senior year, but we didn't get very far with that. I wonder if something happened.

I wasn't happy, though, about how I intervened today. My baggage leaked out in the session with Christina, and I was a little off in some of my interventions, but I was mostly able to step back and get myself centered. I also noted that I let the session go overtime by a few minutes, probably because I felt responsible for being distracted. Time for another session with Paul.

21

ESTHER:
MY DREAM ABOUT BARBIE

I was aware ahead of the session that I wanted to work on my relationship with Christina, particularly since we had a couple ruptures last week. And I was also excited about having had a dream that I could tell because it was fun and paralleled Christina's Barbie dream. I sat down and blurted out, "I had a dream a couple nights ago about Christina and can't wait to hear your thoughts about what is going on in that relationship."

Paul shrugged amiably. "Go for it."

"Did you see *Barbie*?" I asked.

"Yeah. It was fun. It should get an Academy Award."

"Oh good, then I don't need to explain about the context." I settled back and said,

> In my dream, I am the mother bird and there are three baby birds that look like Barbie dolls: one an ordinary Barbie, one a weird Barbie, and one a stereotypical

Barbie. They are all fighting with one another and vying for my attention. Then, they suddenly gang up on me and start beating me up.

Paul raised his index finger and asked, "How exactly do you know the dream is about your client?"

In a rush to get it over with and onto the juicy stuff, I explained, "In one of my sessions with Christina we had a great discussion about the *Barbie* movie. She identified with the ordinary Barbie but was envious of the stereotypical Barbies and wanted to be a weird Barbie. The different Barbies seemed to represent different parts of herself, and she was struggling with which one she wanted to be. Then, in her dream, they got into a big fight with all the different Barbies wanting her to be on their side involving this *thing* and—"

"Hold on," Paul interrupted. "You said there was an ordinary Barbie bird, a stereotypical Barbie bird, and a weird Barbie bird. But you didn't describe yourself."

"Hmm. Strange. I was reminded of the mother bird in the book I read to my kids when they were little, *Are You My Mother?* In that book, when the baby bird is still in the shell, the mother bird goes off to forage for food to feed the baby bird. The mother is gone when the baby bird hatches, so the baby bird wanders off looking for its mother, mistaking everything, including a steam shovel, for its mother. Eventually, of course, the baby bird makes its way back to the nest and finds its mother, and they live happily ever after."

Paul brought us back. "Interesting that you're still not describing yourself in the dream. What exactly do you look like in the dream and what feelings are you having?"

"I guess I am kind of nondescript, just plain, not noticeable, not even ordinary, and that doesn't feel good. I feel competitive that the babies were all special in some way, but I wasn't."

"That *special* word again. You have a real hunger to be special," Paul observed.

"Yes." I nodded vigorously. "I can't seem to get enough, and that doesn't feel good. It's as though I need others to make me feel special. I wish I could turn inwards to get what I need."

"Don't we all!" Paul said smiling.

"Ah, yes, the human condition."

"And this *thing*, what is that?" Paul continued with another image.

"A *thing* in the Barbie movie is a fight, like a war about nothing. It's a commentary about how war is stupid. People are fighting but don't even know what they are fighting about. In my dream, the three baby birds are all fighting over nothing."

"What are your associations to fighting over nothing?"

"My first association is to all the wars going on in the world right now. What are they all about? I think of *War and Peace* and how war seemed like such a nonsensical thing and how boys like to play at war. On a more personal level, I didn't often fight with my siblings, but I didn't know how to get my mother's attention."

"Hmm. I wonder if there's a parallel to our relationship? Are you fighting to get attention from me?"

"Oh, that makes sense." I nodded appreciatively. "I did fear you wouldn't remember me among all your other patients. I'm ordinary and not as exciting as your other patients might be."

"Good insight. How am I doing today? Are you getting what you need from me?"

"Yes, all good so far," I brushed him off. "But I want to focus on Christina because I had a couple ruptures with her last week, and I feel off in being able to be present and help her."

ESTHER: MY DREAM ABOUT BARBIE

"Okay, let's go there." I realized that Paul was allowing me to avoid talking about us. "Sounds to me that perhaps Christina is angry at you."

"Oh, I didn't see that coming." I felt startled but had to consider. "Hmmm, yeah, maybe. But I have felt very positive about seeing her. She's getting so much better. She is now able to express her feelings. She's starting to know what she wants in different situations, has a better relationship with her mother, and is gaining insight into her family of origin. We've had several good discussions about our relationship, and she's expressed some things she doesn't like and things she wants. For example, she told me that she hadn't liked me focusing on the Barbie movie when she had wanted to talk about her mother. I felt a little hurt, but I didn't sense that she was angry. I wonder if I'm missing something, or maybe I have a hard time allowing her to be angry. I have trouble with anger expressed toward me. I shrink back and don't defend myself. I usually err on the side of wanting everyone to like me, and so I try to deflect anger."

"Everything seems a little too positive and calm in the relationship," Paul challenged. "Where's all the negative transference that should be emerging about now? I'm thinking of the Freudian bit about people being motivated by sex and aggression. How does that fit for this client?" he wondered.

"Good question," I agreed, feeling that we were onto something important. "The ganging up on me certainly seems like aggression. Maybe her anger is repressed. In terms of sexuality, it's interesting that she has never had a romantic relationship. If anything, she seems rather young and unformed, almost like her sexuality is also repressed. Come to think of it, it's not easy for me to talk about sexuality either."

"Good point," Paul affirmed, seeming happy that I had that awareness. "You rarely talk about sexuality. What do you make of that?"

"Sexuality is a tough subject right now," I responded. "Steve and I have been avoiding each other, and we haven't been sexually active for a while."

"So, maybe you're avoiding both anger and sexuality as topics because of the conflicts between you and Steve right now?" Paul summarized more clearly what I had been saying.

"Yeah," I confirmed. "I just don't know what's going on between us. It feels like we're roommates. Not a lot of animosity, but we're not talking either."

"Hmmm, a while ago, you mentioned wanting to talk to Steve. How'd that go?"

"Um," I looked down and shrugged. "I didn't do it."

Paul gently confronted, "What's that all about?"

"Um, I'm scared?"

"Are you asking or saying?" Paul softly wondered.

"Right you are. Okay, yes. I'm terrified. I have a hard time with change. What if something is going on? Like, he's having an affair or just no longer cares about me at all. But I have another thought about sexuality for Christina. It's interesting how she's in such a different spot than the typical high school or college student. So many kids of this generation are into being nonbinary or trans or LGTQA+. Maybe that goes along with her seeming very young."

Paul gently confronted me, "Do you want to talk about Christina or Steve?"

"Maybe we can focus on Christina today and come back to Steve next time?"

"Again, are you asking or stating?"

"Okay, okay, I'm stating," I grumbled.

ESTHER: MY DREAM ABOUT BARBIE

"Up to you, your dime and your time," he allowed. "But I do wonder what's going on between you and Steve."

"I'm feeling fragile," I said, "and my mind is fuzzy. I'm able mostly to keep it together with clients, but I often feel depleted after sessions. But, okay," I said breathing deeply, "let me try and focus. What would your reaction be to her as a client?" I wondered, hoping to get some insight into what I might be feeling.

"I can't know because I'm not in the room with her, but I feel a little bored when you talk about her," Paul immediately stated. "I don't see much trauma, and her problems are a little mundane. I'm not quite getting why you're getting into so much countertransference."

"Oh, that's interesting," I said, feeling a little hurt and surprised that he didn't like her as much as I do, making me wonder what I was missing and if he thought I was boring. "I am so into a positive thing with her. She is working hard. I can identify with her at that age."

"Okay, so maybe a bit of overidentification," Paul interpreted but then shifted the lens. "If we look at all the parts of a dream as being parts of yourself, what parts of your dream reflect parts of you?"

"I feel more like an ordinary Barbie than either a stereotypical or weird Barbie. But, as I reflect on my need to feel special, there's a part of me that feels like a special Barbie. My parents used to say, 'You're the best,' and in graduate school I certainly competed with the rest of my cohort to be the best. I guess there's a part of me that wants to be the best therapist. I know we're not supposed to want to be special, but I have to admit that I want to be considered an expert or master therapist. But then again, I know it's all about the client, so I tend to submerge my own needs to be responsive to what Christina, or any client, needs at the time."

"Hmm, the word *submerge* is interesting. I wonder if you're feeling resentful that you have to suppress your authentic self, and your needs aren't getting met," suggested Paul. "That's an issue you've talked about before. It's like the dream where you disappear down into the muddy pit when you're working in group therapy with all your clients. How you lose yourself in giving to others."

"Yep, that seems to be a theme. I give and give and don't find a way to replenish myself."

"Have you been doing much self-care lately?"

"Probably not enough," I responded. "I have to reflect more on why that is. I want to get back to walking and yoga. But back to the client, I think you're right that I need to dig deeper into anger and sexuality with Christina. Seems like a good direction."

"And maybe," Paul said bringing it back to me, "we need to get more into that for you as well. Maybe think more about what's going on for you to be avoiding so much. It's unlike you."

"Yeah," I said, feeling discouraged and defeated. At this point, I noticed Paul covertly looking at the clock and knew our time was about up. "Thank you for your input about both Christina and Steve. I have a lot to think about."

"I can see you're feeling down. It is hard when all these feeling erupt. I have confidence in your ability to figure out what you need."

"Funny, that song was going through my head about getting what you need but not what you want."

"Yeah, wouldn't it be nice if we got what we need. Maybe we need to learn to adjust to what we get handed in life? See you next week."

22

CHRISTINA:
ANGRY AT YOU

I'm so sorry I'm late. The beltway traffic was terrible," Christina said in a rush as she sat down. "I can't believe it. I had another dream about you last night. We were fighting over who had the right interpretation of a dream. I got angry at you and huffed out of the session. It felt real, as if it actually happened. I woke up and kept thinking about it. But it's strange that I've never consciously felt angry at you."

"Interesting! I had a feeling that you were angry at me," I responded. "I wonder if there's something going on between us?"

"Not that I know of."

"I wonder if perhaps you have some anger at me but have a hard time expressing it?"

"Hmm, maybe. As you know, I have never been able to express anger at my parents. I usually go to my room and seethe but don't say anything. Sometimes it's hard to even recognize that I might be angry."

"Let's just imagine," I pushed. "If you were angry at me, what might you be angry about?"

"Hmmm. Maybe I feel a bit trapped. Like I still don't know how long this therapy is supposed to last. It's not like you sign up for a semester. I feel a little out of control. And talking about my mother and grandmother has opened up pain about wasted time. I'm not comfortable with that pain, and maybe I blame you. If I weren't in therapy, I wouldn't feel it. Maybe bottom line, I just don't like having feelings," she said, sounding nervous about admitting something negative about our relationship.

"Yeah, I can see that," I wholeheartedly agreed. "Feelings suck sometimes. But I'm glad you told me. The other thing I wondered when I reflected on our relationship is it seems like we've just scratching the surface. I'm sensing that there's so much more that we haven't gotten to. For example, we haven't talked much about sexuality, and that seems like a big concern of yours."

Almost dismissively, Christina said, "I do feel confused about where I stand with sexuality. It makes me uncomfortable even to think about it. I hate to switch the topic, but I really want to talk about going out to visit my grandmother."

"That was a fast shift away from anger and sexuality," I noted, worried that we seemed to be missing each other. "Is that your choice?"

"I guess so," she said apologetically but firmly. "We're leaving next week to visit my grandmother, and I'll have to skip a session. I'm feeling nervous about not being able to see you. Will I have to pay if I miss a session?"

"No. My policy is that you don't have to pay if you tell me at least 48 hours in advance, and this fits within that time period."

"Maybe we can come back to anger and sexuality later?" she said apologetically.

"Sure, up to you," I affirmed, wanting to reinforce her for saying what she wanted. "And, yes, I can see that since the visit is coming up, we need to talk about it. But before that, I'm noticing the conflict. On the one hand, you bring up anger and then run away from it. You also brought up feeling trapped and out of control about being in therapy. but you're nervous about missing a session. Maybe you're a little anxious about becoming too dependent on therapy and on me?"

"Oh, wow," Christina looked caught off guard. "Such a good point! Trapped and wanting out, and yet worried about missing a session. Yikes! Yes, this is such a new thing, feeling that I can or *should* talk about my feelings. I'm digging up stuff that's uncomfortable. And spending time with my mother and grandmother is equally conflicting. I want a closer relationship with both of them, but I don't know if I can handle it. I don't even quite know how to do that. I feel like I don't have skills to pull it off."

"Okay, let's slow it down and take one thing at a time. How can I be most helpful to you? What do you most want to focus on today?"

"Let's talk about the trip. We have one more session after this one before my mother and I go to Wisconsin. I need to have some coping strategies for how to handle being around my mother for so long."

"Sounds good," I happily conceded. "You mentioned that you started to open up to her more. Maybe you feel some pressure to keep up the intensity of the relationship with your mother in ways similar to the pressure of keeping up our relationship?"

"Yeah, it feels like it's all or nothing. Either we tell all or we're closed off. Maybe we both have trouble knowing how to get close and how to handle the intensity."

"Just like you have trouble being open with me, right?" I again noted.

"True!" Christina conceded but didn't seem to want to go there. "Maybe I just have to set some boundaries at the beginning of the trip."

"Right." I nodded, going with her direction. "Imagine she's in the empty chair," I said pointing to the chair. "What could you say?"

Turning toward the other chair, Christina said, "I talked with my therapist about the trip because I am feeling a little nervous. She suggested we talk about the nervousness. So, I just want to let you know that sometimes I might get a little weird and retreat."

"That's great," I reinforced, "and such a good idea to talk about the nervousness right at the beginning. How did it feel?"

"Okay. Well, maybe a little awk. Sounds like *therapy-talk* rather than like how I would sound if I felt comfortable."

"Okay, how could you make it feel more comfortable, more like *you* talking? Direct it again to your mother in that chair."

As if to her mother, Christina said, "I just want to let you know I'm feeling nervous about the trip and being together and visiting Grandma and being away. I wonder how you feel?"

"Great. Go over to that chair and be your mother."

Moving over to the other chair and settling in, Christina said, "Yeah, I'm nervous too. I get nervous a lot, and I worry I'll push you away."

"Go back to your chair and respond."

Christina moved back and laughingly said to her "mother," "We're both a mess, aren't we? Maybe we can talk about it on the trip. We could plan for some quiet time so we don't have to communicate all the time." Then, turning to me, she said, "It's still a little uncomfortable talking to her, even in imagination."

"Well, you might not feel comfortable right off. It's hard to change established patterns and to figure out who you are and how you want to come across. Have you heard the phrase, 'Fake it until you make it?' That might help you out."

"I like that phrase. And I doubt that my mother will feel comfortable either. She's gone a lot more years than me being repressed. She might like to know that I want to have some quiet or alone time."

"Makes sense. How does it feel now that you think about it?"

"Good," Christina reflected. "I want to try to be more open with her. It worked on the trips to the airport. I think she's eager for a better relationship."

Given that she seemed talked out about the visit to her grandmother, I changed the focus. "Let's talk more next session about your feelings about the trip and your grandmother. If it's okay, though, could we come back for a minute to the anger between us that we talked about at the beginning of the session? I wanted to let you know that you're not the only one who has trouble expressing anger. It is hard for me to feel angry and to be the recipient of anger too, so I just want to let you know that's something we can work on together."

"That's interesting," Christina said. "I kind of thought therapists had to have it all together and have it all figured out. So, I'm surprised to hear that you would have any trouble with anger."

"Well, I don't have it all together," I said, wondering if I was disclosing too much." After a pause, I asked, "What's your reaction to hearing that I have trouble with anger and don't have it all together?"

CHRISTINA: ANGRY AT YOU

"I guess I worry that if you have trouble with anger, you won't be able to help me express my anger."

"Yeah, I can see that," I said swallowing and reminding myself that talking about the relationship is important even if hard. Wanting to educate her, I said, "I see therapy kind of like a journey, where we're fellow sojourners. I'm not better than you, just at a different spot in life. I'm more of a guide than a guru."

"I hadn't thought of that," Christina said. "I'll have to process that feeling. I guess I had put you on a bit of a pedestal, thinking you have it all together."

"No way I have it all figured out, "I declared. "But it's important for you to know that this space is for you, not for me, to work on my issues. I do that in my own therapy. To step back to your dream, how are you feeling about our relationship now?"

"I don't feel angry," Christina reflected. "I am starting to enjoy talking with you about feelings, and I'm liking that I can talk more openly with my mother. I think rather than scripting out what to say to my mother, though, I will try allowing for some silence but also push myself to say what I'm feeling in the moment."

"Yes! You're doing that here, and I think you can do it with your mother."

"Oh, and if we have a minute," Christina said. "I have one other thing to talk about."

"Sure, go ahead."

"Last session, you said I sounded abrupt when I expressed anger at you. That stuck with me. Could you say more about that?"

"Yes. Thanks for bringing that up. I should have said more. When you spoke last week, your voice had an edge to it; you spoke very quickly as if you were biting off the words.

Your voice is typically soft and gentle. I suspected that it was hard for you to be so open about negative feelings."

"It is hard. How about today? Was I abrupt when I talked about the anger in my dream?"

I thought back to that moment. "There was some tension between us, but you didn't seem abrupt as much as matter-of-factly telling me about the dream. How did you feel?"

"I guess I was a little worried about your reaction."

"I can see that," I said reflectively. "It's hard to talk about these negative feelings. Thank you for bringing it up. It seems like you find it hard to talk about both anger and sexuality," I put forth tentatively to set the stage for further discussions.

"I have a lot to think about this week. Let's talk more about the trip next session."

"Sounds good; you leave for Wisconsin the day after the next session, right?"

"Right. See you next time."

Whew! That session felt a bit like whiplash, the talk about anger and sexuality and then switching so rapidly to the visit with grandmother. And throughout the session, there was so much more to unpack about our relationship. It seemed to lack a clear focus. Clearly, we're in a rocky stage. All the feelings about anger and sexuality are stirring the pot.

I think Paul helped me get unstuck and face some things I had been avoiding. I do need to dig deeper into her anger and sexuality. I think I was protecting her a little. I keep worrying about pushing her too fast. Maybe I'm nervous about pushing myself, or maybe I am reacting to her conflicts about dependency, or maybe I'm just protecting myself.

23

ESTHER:
STRANGLED

"What's going on, Esther?" Paul wondered after waiting patiently for a minute. "You're unusually quiet."

I wasn't sure I could articulate my feelings but finally said, "I have a headache and feel defeated. I was so optimistic about coming back to therapy, but I'm reminded about how much work it is, kind of like Sisyphus endlessly pushing that goddam boulder up the hill."

Paul nodded, "It sure is shitty when we have those days. Do you want to wallow a while, or shall we get into it?"

"Thanks for the sympathy," I laughed. "Reminds me of the sign "No Whining" in my physical therapist's office. Okay, I'm ready. Go for it."

With uncanny perceptiveness, Paul asked, "What was your dream last night?"

I reluctantly reported:

Steve was strangling me and laughing. I pushed him away and left the house and walked past the house I grew up in. My father was out on the porch but didn't acknowledge seeing me, even though he was looking right at me.

Encouragingly, Paul probed, "And right now you're feeling?"

Turning inward, I said, "Scared, angry, resentful, isolated. I feel like screaming."

"So, scream, first at your husband," Paul said pointing to the empty chair.

Turning in that direction, I whispered weakly after a pause, "I feel hurt."

"Can you say that a little louder?" Paul coached.

Trying again, I said, "I am goddam angry with you. You're hurting me. You're a bully."

"Go over to that chair. How would he respond?"

I moved and then reflected and said looking down, "I'm sorry. I really didn't mean to hurt you. I'm so sorry. It's been hell. I don't know what I want."

"Come back to your chair. How would you respond?"

I turned to Paul, "I don't know what to say."

"Say that to him."

I moved and then hesitantly said, "I don't know how to fix us. What's gone wrong?"

Motioning me back to the other chair, Paul again coached, "What would he say back?"

As Steve, I said, "It's just something I'm going through. It will get better."

"Now back in your chair and be angry at your father," Paul prompted.

"You never paid attention to me. And I despise how you treated Mother. And I didn't respect you when you got so angry."

Pointing to the other chair, "Okay, be your father."

I paused for a minute. "I feel stuck. I just don't know what he'd say."

"And now at me," Paul pushed.

Directing my gaze away from him, I meekly admitted, "Yikes. I feel so lonely, and I don't know if you can help me. Should I have come back? Can you help me? Can I be helped?"

Paul responded compassionately, "That fear of men goes so deep."

"Yeah, it does," I nodded faintly. "I remember my mother talking about her father being abusive. And all my siblings were girls, so I never had much to do with boys or men. I avoided men. They always seemed so unruly, aggressive, and bold, like they owned the place."

"Where did you go to hide?"

"I went to my room. Sometimes I tried to listen to what was going on in the house, but mostly I buried myself in a book and escaped into another world."

"Did you ever have thoughts that you would like to be a boy?"

"No," I said adamantly.

"You sure said that quickly."

"I was afraid of boys and men. It wasn't until college that I started speaking to them at all. I think I told you that I met my husband in a class we were both taking. We debated a lot. I cared deeply about philosophy and was bursting to talk about ideas with someone who was into the topic. He listened at first and appreciated my ideas. He liked that I spoke up and that we had such good talks, at least back then."

"And then what happened?"

"Life happened, I guess. I got into my career; he got into his. We had kids, and they took up lots of time. He's been critical and hostile sometimes, but never came close to strangling me and laughing like in my dream. He's very gentle really. Oh, maybe I feel like he's strangling my talking, like I can't communicate with him. I guess I blame him for the problems we're having."

"It's interesting," Paul said thoughtfully. "You're such a good communicator, psychologist, and therapist. And yet you're avoiding the very person you're closest to. You hide in your room, absorbed in your clients' lives, instead of leading your life with your husband. You're letting this fear get the best of you."

I sat looking down at my knees.

"What just went on there?" Paul prodded.

"You called me out, and it hurt."

"So, I strangled you?"

"I guess so, yeah." I pulled myself back into the room. "No, I needed that. I needed to be confronted. I am avoiding. I can do better. Okay."

"I sense you're still angry at me," Paul invited.

"Yeah, I am. You call it like you see it. I have a hard time with that."

"Is *calling it like you see it* a masculine thing that strangles your being?"

"Maybe," I agreed, glad he understood. "It feels like men have more of a right to be bold and aggressive. I try to tamp everything down and keep peace everywhere."

"And how's that working for you?" Paul said, mimicking the famous Dr. Phil quote.

"Good point," I said, laughing along with him. "Yeah, I can stand up for myself. But I have to push myself to do it. I guess I wanted sympathy today."

"Sympathy," Paul challenged. "Is that what you want?"

"Whew. It reminds me of the *special* stuff. I want sympathy and to be special. Unfortunately, those are things I want from others. Looks like I have to dig more inside myself to feel good about myself. And I'm reminded of how I have to defend myself against my mother because she is so dominating," I said, feeling the tears welling up in my eyes.

"You really didn't have anyone to turn to when you were a child."

"In the dream, I went off on a walk to get away from Steve. And then I walked away from my father. Maybe I need to stay and deal with the bad things."

"Yes, you have the capacity to heal yourself, and that's great. But I also think you can ask more of a partner," Paul reminded me. "You know, I'm remembering a lot of things you said about Steve when you first met him, that he was sensitive, gentle, understanding, someone who treated you as an equal. Somehow you both have gotten away from that sweet spot. I wonder if and how you can get back to it?"

"Well, I have to quit waiting for him to step up and fix the problem. I have to let him know what's going on inside me. I think he's been so busy at work that he just hasn't noticed. But I'm guessing he's not happy either."

"How are you feeling right now?"

"A little chastened," I admitted. "But you're right. I will bring it up to him. I mentioned before to you the possibility of couples counseling. That's something we could try. Having a neutral party might help us get unstuck. I know you can't see us for couples counseling because that would be a conflict of interest, given how well you know me. And no way do I want to risk having you take his side."

"Hmm, still don't trust me completely, huh? Of course, you're right. I can't see you and your husband for couples counseling because of the ethical issues, but let's just ponder for a minute your anxiety about my not taking your side. It goes along with your thinking I wouldn't remember you or treat you as special or even be there for you. Your trust of me seems fragile," Paul commented gently.

"You're right. It's my skepticism about any man being trustworthy. When are you, or my husband, going to start strangling me? It's dangerous."

"Let's go back to your father."

I remembered back to childhood. "He was so big and powerful. His anger was overwhelming."

"He was big and powerful when you were little," Paul observed. "But are you still little?"

"No, and he's dead, so not much of a threat anymore," I nodded. "I regret never having worked out things with him."

"So maybe you're transferring your feelings about your father to your husband and not trusting him either?"

"Bingo. I think you're right," I said, nodding vigorously. "In the beginning, when I didn't expect anything because we were not involved, I could treat him neutrally. But as we got into the routine of married life, I became my mother and treated Steve like she treated my father, with fear and anxiety and maybe some hostility."

"So your parents didn't provide good role models for how to work on relationships. You're having to forge a new way on your own. You said before you wanted to try to talk with Steve. What happened with that?"

I equivocated. After a momentary break, I added, "Strangely enough, I'm feeling reluctant to talk to him."

"Maybe you're wanting to hold on to your anger and resentment?"

I realized how well Paul knew me. "Good point. I want him to be the one to apologize and make things better."

"Ah, yes, hurting yourself to prove a point. Is there a familiar feeling to being a martyr?"

Trying to go deeper and reflect, I admitted, "Well, my mother was a martyr. She didn't stand up for herself against my father and was steeped in resentment, but then she would be dominating and mean to us."

"That's one way to go," Paul challenged.

"Okay, I get the point," I conceded somewhat reluctantly. "But I'm going to have to sit on it for a while."

"Absolutely. You have to be ready. But I'm also wondering if you're sensing something going on, Steve beaching it, strangling you. Maybe your radar is tuned to danger."

"Hmmm. That's interesting. It might not be all about trying. Maybe that ship has already sailed. Maybe it's over," I said, beginning to cry. "I can't believe I even said that. I don't want to think it."

Paul was quiet for a minute, leaving me to my thoughts. Then, he said, "I can see how much pain that brings you, like a veil lifted from your eyes."

Still crying quietly, I said, "I just don't know what's real and what's not real. Is my radar on, or am I imagining things?"

"Good thing to observe this week." After a pause, Paul continued, "I wonder if we could try a parts-of-self interpretation of this dream?"

"Sure, but help me out," I sniffed trying to get hold of myself. "What are you thinking?"

"I'm wondering if there's a part of you that is strangling yourself and laughing or a part of you that's strangling Steve and laughing?"

"Oh," I winced. "Wow. I never think of myself as angry, so that feels really bad. But let me try it on. I feel distant from Steve, that's for sure."

"Go beyond distant. Try getting into strangling him because you're so angry."

Nodding, I turned inward and tried to imagine strangling Steve. "Okay, I can get in touch with it. I am angry. He's never there. He says it's work, but I'm not so sure. Why is he always having to meet with Henry? There's part of me that wonders if things started to fall apart when I went on to graduate school and got my PhD. He would make snippy comments about my getting uppity."

"Can you directly tell him in that empty chair that you're angry?"

Bolstering my courage, I turned to the empty chair. "Steve, I'm angry at you for not being around and not helping with the kids." After a pause, I continued, "Actually, Steve, I feel hurt that everything is falling apart. I'm angry that you won't fight for our relationship. It seems like you've changed from the person I knew."

"Go over to the other chair. What would he say?"

I just shook my head. "I don't know. I can't do it. It hurts too much." After another pause, I said, "I feel a need to run away from talking about Steve. Would that be okay?"

"It's up to you. Take your time."

I sat feeling empty, almost dissociated.

"What else is on your mind today?"

"I want to come back to the idea of cutting back on seeing so many clients. I think I need more time to work on myself."

"How would that feel?"

"Liberating, I think," I put out there with some hesitance. "I love seeing clients, but I think there's a limit to how many I want to see each week. I've always wanted to do other things and don't want to wait until I retire to find other opportunities."

"What might be some of the things you want to do?"

"Maybe more supervision of new therapists; maybe start my own clinic and have associates working under me."

"But isn't that just more of the same thing?"

"True," I paused again to reflect. "I'd like to pursue some art. Hmm. In high school, I acted in a couple plays. Maybe some community theater. Or a choral group. But something artistic. I like the idea of playing with what I might like to do in addition to seeing clients. Something artistic is appealing."

"You also mentioned that you enjoyed giving the speech and that when you were in grad school you wanted to do research. Anything scholarly you might want to do?"

"Yeah, I could contact my former mentor and classmates and see if there is any research I could get involved with. That's a good way to keep contact with people."

"One of the themes in the options you've mentioned is being around people. And you've said that you haven't had much time for friends. You know when you're doing therapy, you're around people and close with them, but there's a part of you that's not getting your own needs met. With a friend, you can have a fifty-fifty relationship rather than being the one who's giving all the time."

"That is so true. When the kids were little, we had a friend group of parents who had small children. But as the kids have grown, people have moved away, and we haven't replaced them."

'You haven't talked much about the kids since you've been back. How's that going?"

"Things are getting a little rocky; they are almost teenagers now. That's when things with my parents fell apart, and I'm having more trouble with them than I did when they were little. More eruptions too as they assert themselves and don't want me to set limits on them. They are starting to pull away more now, as they should, but I miss them being little and being so close. We used to read every night, and now they have their friends and lots of schoolwork. They're good kids, but I already feel like I am going to miss them when they go away to college and leave an empty nest. They don't seem to need me as much."

"Yeah, another loss."

"That's for sure. The time seems to go so quickly once they're past the toddler stage."

"Obviously, there's a lot going on in your head right now. Remember the old adage about baby steps and be as compassionate with yourself as you are with your clients."

"Sage advice, Paul! I am feeling better now that we're talking all this out. I really needed to come back to see you. I have renewed appreciation for the bravery it takes to be a client. I feel so raw and vulnerable. I need your challenges, but thank you for balancing the confrontations with caring and compassion. And thank you for the extra time today."

"Yes, I'm glad to see you. And to see you caring so much about what happens to you so that you take care of yourself. See you next week."

24

CHRISTINA: SHOOTING FOR THE STARS

I know I said I wanted to talk about the road trip and going to see my grandma," Christina said, sitting down and absently petting Star, who sat quietly next to her. "But before that, I have to tell you about the crazy dream I had last night."

"Okay. I'd love to hear it. And I'll keep track of time to make sure we have enough time to focus on your trip."

With enthusiasm in her voice, Christina began:

First, I am an astronaut flying a spaceship up into space to check out the Hubble telescope. Then we go down into a black hole, and it is awesome, swirling about and feeling that time is standing still or going backwards. Suddenly, we shoot out of the black hole and go down through the ocean to the center of the earth, where it's hot and molten. We come up in the ocean near the sunken Titanic, and I look around for the iceberg. And we end up on this lovely white sand beach in the Caribbean and go swimming and sailing. It was wild and exhilarating.

"Sounds like a big adventure and lots of fun, a different kind of dream for you," I responded, noting how she seemed to be enjoying the dream.

"It was a great adventure. I loved exploring all those different things, and I wasn't scared at all. The feeling of flying was so freeing. The image of the earth from space was stunning. I felt alive and free."

"I can picture it. I notice that you said *we* several times. In your early dreams, you were mostly alone, so this is an interesting development. Who was with you in the dream?"

"Oh, that is interesting. Hmmm. I don't exactly know who it was, but it felt like a group of us, and I was part of it all."

"What was the most salient image in the dream?" I asked.

"Being an astronaut. I loved navigating the spaceship and finding my way and exploring outer space and then the inner space of the earth."

"Well, you're certainly doing a lot of exploration of both yourself and the outside world in here," I said, with some awe at her newfound freedom in the dream.

"Yeah, instead of being scared like I have been in the past, I'm truly enjoying the freedom of exploring. And you're right, I like being with people and part of a group."

"I wonder if there are some ideas in there about your career choice?"

"Interesting that you bring it to career choice because I have been thinking a lot about what I want to do. You know, with all the kids from high school going off to college this month, it brings home that I need to make decisions. I loved exploring lots of different possibilities in the dream. I'm getting excited about the idea of going back to school. I looked up some courses at the community college, and I definitely want to take courses next semester."

"What courses struck your fancy?"

"There was a writing course that seemed appealing, a social psychology of evil course looked interesting, a course about canine cognition," she said, giving Star a stroke. "So, lots of different things looked appealing. I'm starting to like the idea of community college because it might be less pressure than a big university. Classes are smaller, and I will get more attention than in a 500-person lecture hall."

"Take a minute and picture yourself in ten years. Start from the beginning of the day and imagine how that will look, what you'll be doing, and what will happen."

Pausing to imagine the scene, Christina said, "I wake up early. I picture working on something important and ground-breaking. I'm excited about going to work and discovering things."

"*Important* and *ground-breaking* and *discovering things*. That does sound exciting. What about who you're living with, like a partner, kids?"

"I do want a partner, but I don't know what kind. I feel like I could go with either a man or a woman."

"Let's stay with this for a bit and get back to the dream later. Tell me more about how you could go with either a man or a woman."

"It's hard to say more. I just feel unsure of that. I want to think more about it."

"Kids?"

"No. I know I don't want kids."

"You sound very certain."

"I feel screwed up enough. I don't want to pass that on! I've sometimes thought people should have to get a license to have kids."

"Good point. You have lots of feelings about the way your parents raised you."

"Yeah, I guess they did the best they could, but I'm not ready to forgive them yet."

"So, back to the dream. What do you think it means?" I asked.

"Hmm. I like your point that I'm with people and exploring options. I loved the freedom of flying, of stretching my wings. I wonder, though, if it has something to do with this upcoming trip too."

"Say more about that."

"Well, we're going off tomorrow to visit my grandmother. I'm looking forward to spending time with my mother."

"Several sessions ago, we wondered if she might have had miscarriages. I wonder how you'd feel about asking whether there were any?"

"Hmmm." Christina looked away. "Yeah, now I'm nervous. I don't want to probe too much. It's so against the family culture to intrude so much."

"There's the *intrude* word again. Almost as if expressing interest in another person is intruding. I wonder if there's a way you could ask tentatively so as not to seem aggressive?"

"Yeah, I think that's a good idea." Christina perked up. "I can just try to see what comes up naturally. But mostly I want to see my grandma. I have already missed so much in terms of getting to know her."

"I can hear some disappointment in your voice."

"More anger, I think," Christina reflected. "Why has it taken so long to get to this point? What if I had never gotten into therapy? And sad that I've missed so much and that my mother has missed so much. It's so easy to get stuck in life."

"Yeah, I agree," I nodded. "But I come back to the image of your dream that you're shooting for the stars, you're going places, nothing is stopping you."

"That's a cool image. I like the feeling of shooting for something big and discovering something. I'm thinking of not going back to the waitressing job. It just seems like a dead end. There are other things I can do before I start school again. Money is an issue, of course. But maybe that's something I could talk about with my mother."

"Wow. Big, bold move. I love the idea of talking it over with your mother. What do you think you want from her?" I probed.

"Good question," Christina pondered. "I guess I want her approval. And I need to figure out something about money."

"Hmm. I wonder about the lab idea you mentioned. NIH is nearby, and there are several universities in the area. I wonder if you could get an entry-level job in a lab there since you mentioned seeing a lab in your future?"

"That's a great idea. Maybe work in a lab part time and still have time to take classes at a community college. But I have no idea how I would go about finding lab jobs."

"I have no idea either, but I bet it's something you could figure out. What comes to mind when you think about anyone who might work in a lab?"

"We have one neighbor who works at NIH, the high school counselor might have some ideas, and I can ask my mother."

Changing the topic so that we have time to talk about the trip, I queried, "Tell me more about how you're feeling before going off on this trip. Take a minute and collect your thoughts."

After looking down and going inward, Christina answered, "I'm excited, nervous, ambivalent, doubtful, and curious, a mix of things. But mostly, I'm looking forward to having an opportunity to talk more with my mother and grandma. And I remember that we talked last time about giving myself permission not to have to talk all the time. I'll

CHRISTINA: SHOOTING FOR THE STARS

try to pay attention to when my mother gets tired of talking to me, too. I love the idea of not going back to waitressing and of taking some community college courses and maybe getting a lab job. It feels great that I have made some decisions. I feel like I'm progressing and not as stuck as I was. I kind of beat myself up for not being able to do it on my own and earlier, but I'm grateful for being able to talk to you."

"You're doing lots of good work," I supported.

"I am a little nervous, though, about not being able to check in with you if something goes wrong. It's a long time to be away and be with my mother."

"How could you handle that anxiety?"

"Hmm. Take a deep breath, go off by myself for a while, and of course I could just tell my mother how I'm feeling."

"All great ideas. Any more final thoughts about the dream?"

"It's just nice to have a fun dream for a change."

"I love how you're exploring new worlds, shooting for the stars, and getting into the depths. What a dream! Have a great trip. I can't wait to hear about it."

"Yeah, me too. See you when I get back."

I loved Christina's dream and how different it was from her early dreams of being lost and alone. It seems like the dream reflects what's she'd doing in therapy. And I'm so proud of her going off to be with her extended family.

Christina's career exploration brings back memories of how I chose psychology. I really didn't know what I wanted to do with my life, but I had liked a psychology course in high school. I loved the psychology courses in college—well, most of them, except for statistics. I knew early on that

I wanted to be a therapist. But I like the science part of it too and miss doing research and scholarly work. I want to keep my options open. I'm glad I got a PhD because it opened up a lot of options for me. I do wonder how long I will want to stay in private practice. It was a good choice while the kids were young, but maybe I'll start exploring other options. Maybe I'll shoot for some stars myself.

25

ESTHER:
EXAM DREAM, PART 1

I eagerly asked, "Would it be okay if we were to work on one dream across two sessions? I had a vivid dream last night that may reflect a lot of the themes we're working on. I think it would help to go into greater depth in that dream."

Paul agreed, "Absolutely. You know how much I love talking about dreams."

I jumped right in:

> I'm frantically racing across the campus where I did my undergraduate studies to take the final exam in my calculus class after not having slept all night. I have been skipping classes and don't know the material. I'm late, but I can't find my way. Then I'm going through a dark forest and come to a pond. I keep running and am gasping for breath. I finally find the building but cannot figure out where the classroom is. Just as I get there, the professor, who looks like Steve, is

laughing and telling everyone to turn in their exams. I see my client, Christina, as she walks out of the room. She is exhilarated, high-fives me, and says she aced the exam.

"Ah, the old flunking-the-exam dream. I seem to remember that you had that dream a few times in our previous work," Paul noted.

I quickly said, "Yeah, it is a familiar dream, and funny thing, Christina had a dream recently about an exam. For images, let's do the calculus exam, being late, and maybe Christina. If we have time, maybe get to Steve."

"Okay, describe the calculus exam in as much detail as possible."

"An exam," I hesitantly started out, "is a test where you prove what you learned during the semester. I can't remember what a calculus exam would be like, which might be part of the problem. I know it is hard, with things I can't, or should I say won't, wrap my brain around. I don't have the kind of brain for math, or at least that's what I've been told. They have proofs of something, I don't even know; I just know calculus and statistics are not my thing. It's like a foreign language. It's evil."

"Your feelings seem right on the surface," said Paul. "But can you get into more of the experience about the image of the calculus exam in this dream?"

"I'm terrified I'm going to flunk the exam. I haven't been to class and haven't studied, I don't know how to do it, and I can't even find my way to the classroom where the exam is being held. I feel stupid and inadequate. Why can't I get it? I'm tired, and my future is in the toilet if I can't pass this exam. My stomach hurts; I have a sore throat. Fog is swirling around in my head. Far from feeling special or expert or even ordinary, I'm a failure. It's embarrassing and humiliating even to think about this test."

"Associations to calculus exams?"

"I am not good at math in general, and calculus was a particular downfall. When I took calculus as an undergrad, I skipped a lot of classes and never quite grasped the topic. Finally, the night before the final exam, I got a glimmer of what calculus was all about, but of course that was too late to pull out my grade. At least I got a D instead of flunking, but it was five credits of D, which did real damage to my grade-point average. Another association is that only smart people can understand calculus, so I must not be smart. The brainy kids in high school took calculus and physics. Thank goodness I don't have exams now. I made it through undergrad and grad school, and I would be happy never to take another exam. I remember being shamed by a male high school math teacher who hated girls. When I hadn't done my homework, he..."

Paul gently interrupted my diatribe, "If it were my dream, I might associate to how my wife is really good at math and how I get competitive with her. Does that fit at all for you?"

"Oh, yeah, it sure does," I readily admitted. "Both my mother and Steve are math whizzes. I feel inferior because I just don't get it. Competitiveness is something we haven't talked about a lot, but it goes along with the need to be special and better than others. It's not a good feeling. And I think a lot about grad school when I think about competitiveness, like there's limited resources."

"And how about childhood? Were there limited resources there?

"For sure. My parents didn't have much to give, and they had to spread it out among us kids. I used to be angry about that. Now, I just feel sad for them."

"Waking-life triggers?"

"Funny thing. I have a talk coming up, and I often have this recurrent dream about exams before giving a talk. It's not my natural strength, and I panic about standing in front of the audience and not being able to remember what I'm talking about. It's also a wake-up call, letting me know I need to prepare. If I prepare the talk and practice, I can usually get through it. In fact, when I'm passionate about the topic and know it well, I'm pretty good at it. But giving talks takes a toll on me."

"I can see that as a test. Any other triggers? I'm thinking it's interesting that your relationship with Steve doesn't come to mind, especially given that he was in the dream in a position of authority."

"Oh, that's an interesting association. Yes, the problems in our relationship are clearly a test, and I'm not doing so well. It feels like I'm running through quicksand there."

"You're so good at working on dreams," encouraged Paul. "Go ahead to the next image about being late. Describe that image."

"Being late is bad, at least in my mind. It's a sign of not being prepared. What's that saying: 'If you're early, you're anxious; if you're on time, you're neurotic; if you're late, you're angry'? Or something like that. It's a sign of disrespect to be late. You make everyone wait for you. It's like you are unable to organize your schedule. Psychotherapists in particular are time bound. Sessions start on the hour and finish at exactly fifty minutes if we have good boundaries. I have an internal clock and can feel exactly when fifty minutes is up."

"Okay, get into the feeling," prompted Paul. "What's going on inside you as you re-experience this image of being late for this calculus exam?"

"I'm anxious that I'm late. I have been up all night drinking a gallon of coffee, and I'm wired. I can't seem to make it to the classroom, like I'm running but my legs are not moving. I'm angry at myself for not going to class and not studying during the semester. I'm livid that I wasn't prepared during high school for calculus. And I never asked for help. I didn't have breakfast, and I'm hungry. My body hurts from running. I feel like a disaster about to happen. It's a familiar feeling, like here we go again."

"All good. Associations?"

"My mother was always, always annoyingly late. We would joke about it. We would tell her something was scheduled for an hour earlier than it was, but she would still be late. I remember standing on street corners waiting for her to pick me up from piano lessons. I would be angry because she didn't seem to care that I was standing outside in the freezing weather; I felt I was not important enough for her to be on time. Lots of people in the DC area blame being late on the Beltway traffic. Interestingly, Christina blamed the Beltway for being late a couple sessions ago. It gets to be a joke when someone is late. 'Oh, they got stuck on the Beltway.'"

"You sound pretty annoyed about time."

"Some people from other cultures don't care about time. Time is irrelevant. You show up when you do. But in our culture, showing up late is considered rude. Being late assumes that there is one right way to do things and that we should shape up and follow the rules. On one hand I hate rules, but on the other hand I follow them rigidly. Steve jokes that I am a routine junky. He's always exactly on time; I am always early. I like to have a cushion in case something goes wrong or I get lost. I don't want to inconvenience anyone as my mother did. It's a contract I feel compelled to keep."

"How would you like to do this?" Paul asked. "Do you want to just keep going, or would you like me to jump in with the *if it were my dream* idea to give you another perspective?"

"Oh, please, do. I love hearing your ideas."

"Okay. If it were my dream," Paul mused, "I might reflect on how annoyed I get when clients are late or miss sessions. On the one hand, it's nice to have the free time. On the other hand, I can't concentrate on anything else, because I'm wondering what's going on and thinking about the annoyance of having to charge for a missed session. Does that fit for you?"

"No kidding," I immediately agreed. "It almost always indicates that something is going on in the relationship. Interestingly, Christina has only been late once because of traffic, so she's more on the side of being on time. And, of course, in the dream, she was on time for the exam whereas I was late. So, I guess there's again my worry about fucking up and doing something wrong."

"Moving on to waking-life triggers. What's going on in your life right now that might be the trigger for this image of being late?"

"I have a pretty tight schedule," I noted, after thinking briefly. "Given that I have kids, I schedule my day so that I can spend as many hours with them as possible. When they are at school, every hour is scheduled. I am usually good with schedules, but last week I double-scheduled appointments with clients. It was embarrassing, and I felt incompetent. I was feeling frazzled and blew it. I apologized but felt bad. And the other waking-life trigger is that the kids' school drives me crazy. They have so many holidays, professional days, and other days off that it makes it hard to schedule around them. Then, I have to find something for my kids to do when they're off! I guess it was fine when women didn't work, but it's really a strain on the family. We don't have family nearby, so there's no one to lean on to help."

"Just go ahead to the image about your client Christina," Paul said, looking at the time and trying to keep us on track.

"Christina," I collected my thoughts. "In the dream, she's looking well put together. She's happy that she did well on the exam, she's dressed in cool clothes, she looks well rested. In fact, she looks great."

"What reactions do you have to her looks?"

"I hate to admit this, but I feel jealous and envious. I'm feeling like an absolute wreck, and she's sailing out of this really hard exam looking like it was a piece of cake. I kind of hate her for looking so perfect right now. And then of course I feel guilty for feeling that way. I *should* feel good for her doing well on this test. This is something she wants to do to get back into school. I *should* be totally supportive, so I feel like a bad therapist, like I'm flunking yet another test. Now I feel sad thinking about this because I truly do like her and am pleased that she's getting better. She's on the cusp of so many good things. She's young and attractive, and I'm feeling tired and old and like I'm running on a treadmill today."

"Associations?"

"Clients are asking for help, making themselves vulnerable, working hard to get better. It's hard to go to therapy. And then there's the associations to what we know about therapy. Is it an art or a science? Is the effectiveness due to clients, therapists, the approach, or something else? Associations about this particular client: she is young, bright, insightful, engaging. She is like me in some ways: White, middle-class, female, problems with parents, not knowing what she wants to do in life, eager to learn. She's also different from me in some ways: younger, from a family that is quiet and reserved rather than loud and dysfunctional. She's willing to take some time off to find out what she wants rather than just bulldozing through all the educational hurdles as I did."

"Good going. But you forgot waking-life triggers."

"Oh, right. Going back to my relationship with my mother, it's so complicated. There was the fear of doing better than she did and making her feel bad. There was anger at her for being inattentive to me and not really knowing me for who I am. There is guilt over not having resolved all my issues with her. Given that I'm a therapist, I *should* have my shit together. Instead, I feel like a mess. I'm aware, as I say all this, how much stress I'm under trying to balance work and family without much support from family. I have so little time for friends or self-care. I've tried to get more into a walking routine, but it's hard when I feel like others' needs have to come first. I also feel like I'm doing too many hours of clinical work. The intellectual side of my brain isn't being nourished."

"If it were my dream," Paul offered, "I would be thinking about what we talked about a couple weeks ago about sex and aggression. I would wonder why I'm not focusing on that."

"I should have known you'd figure out a way to fit that in," I jokingly complained. "Yeah, sex and aggression. Again, absent in the dream, which has to say something about both her and me. I'll keep thinking about that."

"Okay, and it's obvious we're running out of time and haven't yet focused on the image of Steve being the professor and laughing. Seems important, given that in your dream last time he was strangling you. Can you just take a minute and associate?"

"Yeah, interesting that I said last week that he was upset about me having more education than he did. Now here he is the professor, and I'm flunking out. A real role reversal. I know we're out of time. I'll keep pondering that."

"The hour went fast today," Paul said. "Any quick ideas about what the dream means as you ponder what you've talked about?"

"Certainly, the anxiety about this upcoming talk and needing to spend time preparing," I immediately stated. "And more about my mother and my anger toward her. And there's more going on in terms of my inferiority and competitive feelings. The jealousy and envy of Christina is palpable, and I feel so uncomfortable that I have negative feelings about her. I remember an article talking about therapists feeling hate in therapy. I mean, it's a normal reaction to have lots of feelings, and it's important to be aware of them so that they don't leak out. It's just that I feel like I should always be supportive and compassionate. And of course, the competitiveness with Steve is right there on the surface."

"Good points. Let's continue with trying to gain some insight into the dream next time."

"Yes. Thanks," I nodded on my way out the door.

CHRISTINA WITH GRANDMA

After a good but long road trip with her mother, Christina and her mother approached the simple midwestern farmhouse with a mixture of trepidation and excitement, wondering what it was going to be like. When they walked in, her two aunts gave big hugs and warned them that Grandma tired easily. They suggested being careful to leave if Grandma seemed stressed.

Christina and her mother headed into her grandmother's room together. Her mother said to Grandma, "Mother, look who I brought."

Grandma smiled and held out her arms, "Thanks for being bringing her, Kristin. How wonderful to see you, Christina. You're even more beautiful than your pictures. Give me a hug."

After giving her a big hug, Christina said, "Grandma, I'm so glad to be here. I want to hear all your stories, what it was like living in Wisconsin, raising my aunts and mother."

"We have plenty of time, girl. Sit down and have a cup of coffee," Grandma said, sounding weak but positive.

After settling in and taking a sip of coffee, Christina started off, "Tell me about the house, Grandma. What has it been like to live here?"

"This was your mother's room when she was growing up, but they moved me here to avoid the stairs. The big thing I want to tell you is how glad I am that your mother and I are talking again and how pleased I am to see you. Always remember how important family is and not to let little squabbles get in the way. I have regrets about how much time I wasted and not getting to see you grow up. But tell me more about you."

An hour later after trading stories, Christina and her mother noticed that Grandma was starting to drift off. Christina whispered softly, "See you later," and they went upstairs to put their things away.

27

CHRISTINA:
SCARED OF MEN

Christina jumped right in, "I have so many things to tell you. The road trip was fun. I learned a lot about my mother and got to hang out with my grandma. She tired easily but had lots of stories about her childhood and when my mother was growing up. But the main thing I want to focus on is that I came away realizing I'm scared of men."

"Tell me more."

"My grandmother talked about how she had to give up all her aspirations of being a scientist because my grandfather wanted her to stay home and raise their children. My mother talked about how angry my grandfather got when she wanted to date a Black man. That's when she had the rift with her parents and left home. She said it was difficult to communicate with her father after she left, and she basically gave up and had nothing to do with her parents for many years. And then I thought more about how dominating my father can be. He's more passive-aggressive except for when he blows his top. Everything has to be his way. And my mother gets quiet and doesn't stand up to him.

He called a couple times while we were gone and wanted to know when we'd be home. Hardly asked anything about my grandmother, just wanted my mother home, and—"

I interrupted to help her focus on her feelings, "You sound upset as you talk."

"I am pissed off about how badly my grandmother and mother were treated. It made me aware that I have a lot of anxiety around men. I feel scared of them. I was glad to hear that my mother left home to take care of herself, but it made me feel bad to hear how strained things were in her relationship with her parents. I heard things on this trip that had always been kept from me, perhaps because they thought I was not old enough to hear about them. I was glad to be included finally. My mother and grandmother resolved a lot of issues between them; there was a lot of talking and crying."

"Tell me your earliest memories of your father," I asked to channel her back to talking about her fear of men.

"In my first memory of him, he's angry at me. Maybe I didn't clean my room, or I didn't eat my dinner, or whatever. I can't remember what I did that was so terrible, but I remember him yelling at me and telling me I was bad."

"I can hear the tremor in your voice as you talk, as if you can still feel how awful it was when he yelled at you."

"For sure. I was scared. I really didn't know what I'd done to set him off."

"Where was your mother during this incident?"

"She must have been around, but I don't have a sense of where she was. What's weird is that usually my father is withdrawn. He only occasionally gets angry, but when he does, watch out. From the way he treated me, I really thought I was bad, an evil seed. I remember cowering in the corner to stay away from him. He didn't touch me or spank me, just yelled at me. I have another memory, maybe from around the same time, of him yelling at my mother when they were fighting, which they did so seldom it stood out. My mother tried to appease him, but he stayed angry for a long time. I don't know what they were fighting about."

"Your early memories are of him being angry, your being scared, and your mother not helping you. You must have felt very alone and little."

"Yeah, *little* is a good word. I wanted never again to do anything to make him that angry. I didn't know how to defend myself, and it was not okay to talk back to him. He wanted his peace and quiet. I don't think he liked having a kid around. He was used to everything being peaceful and calm. I learned early on to stay out of his way and not ask for anything. The house was always quiet, except, of course, when he blew up."

"I feel so sad for the younger you."

Softly crying, Christina agreed, "Me, too. It explains some things, like why everything is always so controlled and silent, sort of muffled. It's interesting that my father and grandfather were alike in terms of temper and being controlling."

"Seems like your mother picked a partner similar to her father."

"True. And it makes me aware that I need to be careful and not pick someone who has a lot of rage. But how would I know?"

"Good point. You don't always know, but you can be aware of how you feel around the other person."

"What do you mean?"

"If you feel you have to restrain yourself or feel anxious, that's a clue."

"Oh yeah, like I feel I have to be careful and tread lightly around him now. But maybe I'm so used to being cautious that I would be with anyone and so wouldn't be able to tell."

"Another good point. A reason to practice being bold so you can see how people react."

"I like that."

"Tell me more about your mother," I suggested to shift the discussion back to what occurred during the trip.

"What's interesting is she seems to be speaking up more now. Ever since she came back from that first trip to see Grandma, she's been more open and talking about her feelings. And my father is starting to talk more too, like the icy wall of silence is beginning to thaw."

"What did you learn about your mother?"

"She works in a high-security job for the government. She got into it because she's good with computers. She liked her job at first but isn't sure she wants to keep doing it. She wants to make some changes. So, maybe we're kind of in the same place, thinking of what we want to do when we grow up. I wonder why she married my father. I'll have to ask her about that. I wish I could have found out something about the little ghosts in my dream, but I didn't have the nerve to ask her. Other than that, I feel that she and I can talk more now."

She paused and stroked the dog's head as if to gather her thoughts. "I told her about the different career possibilities I'd been considering, and she was enthusiastic about my taking courses at the local community college next semester. She said that they would pay for them. And since I'll be living at home, I won't have many expenses. That gives me time to think about where I want to go and what I want to major in."

"You did a lot of thinking while you were away."

"Yeah, it's good to step out of my routine. I could hear your gentle voice in my head, asking me questions and encouraging me to talk to my mother and grandmother."

"I'm so glad that you're getting closer to them. All good. And great that you can use my voice. What was that like for you?"

"Comforting and reassuring."

"Good. Let's talk more about this fear of men because that's a great awareness."

Christina nodded in agreement. "Men just seem so big and angry. I shut down and make myself small so that I don't get noticed. But then I do that around girls and women too if they are loud and aggressive. Maybe I'm afraid of getting close to anyone who's aggressive, and it's easier to hide than show up. Oh, and I guess I should think more about sexuality too. There's just a wall of fear about relationships in general."

"The image of your father yelling at you and you cowering in the corner sticks in my head. It's hard to explore your feelings if you think you're terrified you're going to get yelled at."

"True that! I get anxious just thinking about friendships and romantic relationships. It's easier to avoid them, stay at a superficial level, talk about the weather and books."

"Sounds like a good focus for the next few sessions. We could talk about different relationships you've had and what they were like. Maybe have some fantasies about what you'd like in the future?"

"That sounds scary," Christina rolled her eyes and weakly protested. "I'm not sure I'm ready for that."

"No problem," I said trying to assuage her fear. "We can take it at your pace. Anything else that you want to discuss about the trip?"

"It's going to be hard to go back to waitressing. I know now that I'm not going to keep doing it forever, and I'm a little impatient to be done with it. But I do want the money that waitressing brings in."

"Hmm. Weren't you going to think about other options?" I challenged.

Petting Star and looking away, Christina said dispiritedly, "I did think of volunteering at an animal shelter. I love animals, and maybe that would lead to some opportunities."

"Sounds interesting. You relate so well to Star. He always sits right next to you, and he doesn't do that with everyone. He seems to know that you like him."

"Yeah, Star is the best," Christina said with more energy. "I do have time before the next semester begins, so I can try out some new things. Also, remember that Chendu invited me to visit her at Harvard. She texted me about it again."

"So, you now have two new things to experience—the possibilities of going to the animal shelter and Harvard. Super! How was it being in the car with your mother for the whole trip?"

"Surprisingly easy. We seem to have reached a new level in our relationship. It's beginning to feel like she's a good friend."

"And you were worried about your grandmother looking old and close to death. How was that for you?"

"Again, surprisingly okay. I think I was prepared for it. But it did start some thoughts in my head about death. I'm scared of dying."

"Scared of dying or of being dead?"

"That's a good distinction. I'm not sure. Just thinking about death is like suffocating under an ominous cloud."

Looking at the time, I concluded, "I'm looking forward to hearing more about those ideas and to hearing more about the discussions with your mother and grandmother. If you're able and feel comfortable bringing in fantasies about your sexuality and death, I'd love to hear about them too. Seems like we have lots to catch up on."

28

ESTHER:
EXAM DREAM, PART 2

As we settled in, Paul helpfully summarized, "To recollect, we're working on your dream about being late to the calculus exam after getting stuck in the quicksand. Your client Christina finished the exam brilliantly and in record time, and Steve appeared in the dream as a laughing professor. You've had time to let it all sink in and mush together. Why do you think you had this dream when you did?"

"Well," I said, trying to get back into it, "there's stuff going on in my life that I haven't been dealing with. There are themes of feeling overwhelmed with work and family, a sense of inferiority, competition, and being alone. I'm tired, like I'm running on a treadmill and not getting anywhere. And things are bad with Steve."

Paul asked, "How about thinking about how each part of the dream is a part of you? Maybe take the easier ones first."

"Yes," I nodded in agreement with this strategy. "Part of me is like Christina. I'm at a turning point and need to make some decisions about how I want to lead my life. Part of me feels like the calculus exam; my life is so complicated and hard to manage right now. I also feel like part of me is late, trying to get everything done but being behind. Oh, and the quicksand reminds me of the mess I'm in with Steve and not knowing how to get through that, another kind of muddy pit. And, much as I hate to admit it, part of me is like Steve—arrogant, laughing, strangling the life out of our marriage."

"You went through that quickly. Which part resonates most or least as a part of you?"

"Well, I'm stuck a little on the Christina part because I don't feel like I'm doing anything well right now, certainly not acing an exam. And I don't feel like the arrogant, laughing Steve. Maybe those are parts of me, but I don't recognize them."

"Hmm," Paul offered. "Maybe we can think of Freud's wish fulfilment. Maybe part of you would like to be like Christina and Steve, brilliant and arrogant. Maybe that's your competitiveness leaking out."

"Oh!" I felt stunned. "I hadn't thought of it that way. I guess it's that wish-fear thing of feelings being the opposite of what you think."

"All good," Paul agreed. "And how might the dream be related to childhood, given all your conflicts with your parents?"

"School was not a priority for my family growing up, so they didn't prepare me to succeed in school. My mother wanted to show off for others. My parents fought. I felt like I was running to keep up with other kids. I've worked through a lot of these things in our previous therapy, and I'm beginning to recognize the trigger points more, but I need to keep an eye on these things."

Paul urged me to go deeper, "What about all the competitiveness in the dream in relation to childhood? Can you reflect on that more?"

I considered, "Interesting. I didn't feel much competitiveness during childhood. Maybe, being the youngest, I felt jealous of my siblings and scared I couldn't catch up. But you're right; the dream is filled with competitiveness. The ugly reality is that I try hard to repress my competitiveness. I first became competitive in grad school. But when I'm doing therapy I'm working to help clients, so I try not to be competitive with them. That's why it stands out in this dream that I feel competitive with Christina. I must feel a need to prove myself, to be a great therapist. It's hard to see her grow when I'm having such difficulties. Yuck, that's hard to admit."

"Sounds like you hit a nugget," Paul agreed.

"Seems like it's related to this perfection thing I get into, having to be the best and then failing miserably. I have to remind myself to accept myself as I am."

"Yeah, always difficult for us mortals," Paul said compassionately. "Going off on a slightly different track, you don't talk about it much, but could this dream also be related to the future and existential concerns, like where you are headed and death anxiety?"

"Good question," I nodded. "What are the bigger values in life? I'm not sure what I believe any more. Why am I doing all the things that I do? We got a lot of education in our doc program about social justice and giving back to the community. I also remember doing research on meaning in life and thinking about religion and what I believe. That's a work in progress. Right now, I'm just trying to muddle through." Wanting more from Paul, though, I asked, "But what thoughts do you have about what the dream might mean?"

"Thought you'd never ask." Paul wagged his eyebrows and laughed. "I didn't want to interrupt your thought process. Hmm. I'm going to go out on a big limb here and speculate that it might be related to your relationship with Steve. You keep alluding to problems in the relationship, but you're far more willing to talk about your client than to discuss your problems at home," Paul gently but persuasively challenged.

"Oh." I choked back sudden protest tears. "I can see where you're coming from with all the competitiveness and loneliness and Steve laughing and feeling superior."

"We need to talk about it when you're ready," Paul prodded.

I nodded but looked away.

"Am I sensing just the teeniest bit of resistance?" Paul teased.

"Yeah, more than a teeny bit. I don't want to touch it with a ten-foot pole! I know I *should*, but even thinking about it makes me immediately feel tired."

"Ah, there's the tiredness and being overwhelmed," Paul confirmed. "What clues come to you from the dream about what you want to do about Steve?"

"Hmm," I pondered, "that's a good way to look at it. I have a test in our relationship. What am I going to do about it? I guess I'm trying to catch up and get there, even if I'm late out of the gate. It certainly feels like I'm in quicksand. I feel competitive with younger women that he could be involved with. I'll keep thinking on this aspect. It doesn't quite fit for me, but thanks for pushing me to deal more with Steve."

"What do *you* want in the relationship?" Paul didn't let me run away.

"I don't know." I winced at the whiny sound of my voice. "It feels like Steve has all the power of deciding whether we stay together or not."

"You're big on choice, so what's your choice in the relationship?"

"Okay, okay, I'm blocking, but I'll think about it."

Looking at the clock, Paul suggested, "If you could change the dream in any way you want, what would you do?"

"That's easy," I added quickly and enthusiastically, happy to get away from talking about Steve. "I am not taking a stupid calculus class. I respect that I hate math and do not want to do something so repellent to me. I have choices. I take an English literature or philosophy class where I have an opportunity to study important things in life. I loved learning in those classes so much that it wouldn't be hard to do. I go to a different college where learning is more important than drinking and friends and hook-ups. I am better prepared for college. And after taking and acing the exam in literature or philosophy, I go to a beach and enjoy the sun and friends. I can almost feel the sun on my face on this cold day."

"Okay, all lovely. And that seemed to get you unstuck. But," Paul quietly pointed out, "I notice there was nothing in there about changing anything with Christina or Steve!"

"Oh, right, I do seem to run away. Okay, let's think. I don't think I want to change them. That's just who they are. I want to change how I react to them. I want to be happy for Christina, and I want to confront Steve when he laughs at me."

"Good. Now on to the harder part of bridging the fantasied changes to actual changes you could make in your waking life," Paul prompted.

I contemplated briefly and set out resolutely, "I have some ideas, but I don't know which ones will stick. Maybe I'll slow down and not take on any new clients right now, maybe set aside an hour a day for doing things that are just for me like walking, yoga, reading, maybe prioritize time with my kids or set aside a day each week to do some scholarly work. We can afford for me not to see so many clients, and I'll feel more relaxed and eager to be with my current clients if I don't have so many clients."

"Makes sense. What else?"

"I'm excited about getting back to working with Christina. I will use what I've learned here to be aware of my feelings toward her, especially related to anger and sexuality. If I'm doing more of what I want in my life, I will be able to help her make better choices in her life. It's important to figure out what I'm feeling toward her and what's coming from her and what's coming from me. Clearly, my feelings of competitiveness and envy are coming from my own history, and I don't want that spilling over into work with Christina."

"Anything else?"

"Oh yeah, and I need to think more about how to work on my relationship with my mother. I wonder if she feels competitive with me. I know that I can't do it all at once, but that's certainly a growth edge for me. As they say, it's an fgo, a fucking growth opportunity."

"All great. But I can't help noticing how you are again avoiding talking about Steve." Paul raised his eyebrows and looked at me.

"Yeah, yeah, once again you're right," I admitted sheepishly. "Well, he's been gone for a few days. I feel at a standstill, but I guess I'm having a hard time focusing on my feelings, whatever they are. But yes, I want to get up the nerve to talk to Steve about what's going on."

"You've said vaguely that you're unhappy being with Steve. Can you be more specific about what's making *you* unhappy?"

"I can try. Let me think," I paused. "I want a soulmate, a best friend, someone I can confide in and can have deep discussions with, someone I can share the parenting with. He's been so distant lately, like he's not really present. I want a real relationship."

"So, you brought this dream in and wanted to spend two sessions on it. Clearly, it was important in your mind. What's the take-home message for you?"

"The easiest messages are related to taking better care of myself and looking at the competitiveness with Christina, and I feel ready to do those things. The harder one is the relationship with Steve," I sighed. "Your question about what I want is good and makes me aware of what's missing. But perhaps if I do better at taking care of myself and worry less about clients, I will have more headspace for working out problems with Steve."

"It's great that you're doing such good work related to yourself and your client," Paul congratulated me. "I would challenge you, though, to think more about what's going on with Steve and what the distance is about. And on that cheery note, we must stop for today."

Tearing up, I agreed. "You're right, of course. I will think on it."

I walked out feeling apprehensive about my future with Steve. For as much as I didn't want to think about it, I'm now thinking about it a lot. What to do? What's going to happen? Who's in control? What do I *want*? What do *I* want? *What* do *I* want?

29

CHRISTINA:
SEXUALITY

"I don't quite know how to start," Christina said dejectedly, as she sat down and focused on petting Star. "My mind feels blank."

"Take a moment to breathe and see what images pop into your head," I encouraged her.

After a minute, Chrisina said, "I'm wondering about the sexuality stuff we talked about the last couple of times. It's strange that I'm so ambivalent about getting into a romantic relationship and don't even know if I'm attracted to men or women."

"*Strange*, you say. What's that feeling about?" I wanted to help her become curious about what conflicts she might be feeling.

"People seem to know early on if they're gay or trans or whatever. I don't know what I feel or don't even seem to have any sexual feelings," she hesitantly said, avoiding eye contact.

"You mentioned last week being scared of men. Could that have anything to do with this ambivalence about sexuality?"

"Yeah, probably," she said, seeming more engaged and making eye contact. "I am afraid of my father's anger. What if I ended up with someone like him or my grandfather and had to repress all my own interests like my mother and grandmother did? Men in general are a bit frightening. But I don't know if I'm attracted to women either," she said. "I'm kind of afraid of relationships in general, getting too close to anyone."

"Well, your parents certainly set the tone of not getting close to anyone," I reminded her, hoping to help her make connections between the present and past.

"True. The iciness between them was difficult to witness," she responded reflectively. "I definitely don't want that."

"And you don't have a very good model for how relationships can be different."

"Yeah, it's sad to me that my parents stayed together when they clearly didn't communicate much with each other. But like I said, it's getting better. They are talking more, and our dinner conversations are better now. Maybe there's hope. My mother seems more energized. I guess they must at least *like* each other to stay together."

"Tell me about some relationships you've had."

"Hmmm. Let's see. I told you about Chendu. When I was younger in elementary school, there was a girl, Hannah, who lived next door. We played all the time, we had sleepovers, we were in and out of each other's house. She got into sports, though, and started playing soccer and then they moved away. I felt bad for a long time that she was gone."

"What did you like about her?"

"She was very creative. I remember she had an imaginary friend. We played school sometimes, and she taught her imaginary friend to read. She had a lot more toys than I did. Oh, she had some Barbies, and we had fun dressing them.

Her mom was really nice and would make us cookies so that we could have tea parties. I miss her."

"It sounds like you had a good and easy relationship with her."

"Yeah, that's true. We never had any fights. She felt kind of like a sister. I was seriously bummed out when she moved."

"Did you ever feel sexually attracted to her?"

She paused to reflect, "No, I don't think so."

"How about friends after elementary school?"

"In middle school, Krystal was my friend. She was a Black girl who lived across town. Her mom was a professor, and they lived in a nice big house. She was a good student, and we studied together. She knew a lot about computers and video games. That's probably where I got my love of video games. We had fun playing Minecraft. Then she went off to a different high school. And I think I told you that I was on the school newspaper in high school. I guess that's where I made the most friends. I remember hanging out and talking about the meaning of life, death, religion—the easy topics," she said wistfully. I noted that it was a good diagnostic sign that she had friends growing up.

"You have had some friends in your life. And I think you mentioned the friend from work who you went to see the Barbie movie with, and wasn't there a guy that you were kind of interested in or flirted with?"

"Yeah, work is a happening place. There are some good, down-to-earth people who know how to have fun."

"Have you been hanging out with them more?"

"More being friendly at work. I did go out with Joannie for drinks last weekend after work. She's the one I went to the Barbie movie with. She's more a friend rather than a potential partner. And a guy I was kind of interested in quit. So, I don't know." Again, she sounded hopeless.

"What do you suppose it would mean to be attracted to someone? Have you ever had a crush on anyone?"

"I had a crush on my history teacher in tenth grade. I used to have dreams about him but never even talked to him. I also had a crush on the female faculty advisor for the newspaper. She was friendly and encouraging, told me I had potential and should go to college. I think she was disappointed when I told her I was taking a gap year."

"What does it mean to be attracted to someone or have a crush on them? What does it feel like?" I probed.

Christina looked away briefly, pondering, "A lot of thinking about them, wondering about their lives outside of school, wondering what it would be like to be married to them." After a pause, "Um, I remember writing their names in my notebook and being worried that someone would see it. I never told anyone about the crushes, but I did listen to see if anyone said anything about them."

"Did you ever fantasize what it would be like to be sexually involved with any of them?"

Christina pondered the question, "No, I can't say I did."

"What about people more your own age that you might have been attracted to?"

"No one really. I just studied and played a lot of video games. And, of course, the COVID pandemic happened during high school, so that limited the amount of in-person time for two years. That affected a lot of kids my age and made us withdraw. I heard of kids who had mental health crises. It was a tough time."

"Yeah, COVID was bad. Let me probe you a bit more about sexuality. Do you get into pleasuring yourself sexually?"

"Not really. I've always had a vague feeling that it's sinful. I do sometimes have sexual dreams, though."

"Is that pleasurable?"

"Yes, but I can't remember any specifics right now."

"How are you feeling as we talk about sexuality?"

Suddenly, Christina took a deep breath and look panicked, as if she had been burned with a hot iron. She curled up in her chair, pushing Star off and started breathing shallowly. "Do I have to talk about this?" she asked plaintively.

"Not unless you want to. You have control of what you talk about," I reassured her quietly and calmly, wondering what was distressing her so much and what I had missed.

After a long minute, Christina whispered, "I have something I haven't told you."

A chill went down my back. I waited, trying to exude as much supportiveness as I could. I could feel her pent-up anxiety in my body.

After another long minute, she said, "I just can't talk about it. I feel like I'm outside my body even thinking about it."

After another pause, I said gently, "You know, I'm remembering your early dream in the forest where you said someone or something was following you, and you panicked. I'm wondering if something like that actually happened to you?"

"Yes," Christina murmured, looking down and withdrawing into herself.

"Maybe it would help to talk about it," I suggested. "It's so hard keeping such traumas all locked up inside."

Not looking at me, Christina said in a very small voice, "I had an abortion, and I'm probably going to hell."

Wanting to go very slowly, especially as I was painfully aware that past traumas had knocked me out so much I couldn't function, I gave Christina time to regroup. I then suggested, "Sounds like you've been through hell already.

You've gotten through the worst part of admitting out loud that something really bad happened. Would you like to tell me about it?"

Shakily and slowly, Christina started: "There was a boy last fall. He lived a block away. He's good-looking, but I thought he hadn't noticed me. As I was walking home from somewhere right after my eighteenth birthday, he suddenly appeared and started walking with me. We talked about all kinds of stuff—well to be honest, he talked, and I asked questions. The next day, he showed up again. We were talking about video games, and he asked if I wanted to go over to his house and play a video game. I said yes, since I love video games. No one was home at his house, and we went downstairs. We played video games. He gave me some wine. I'd never had wine, and I didn't know what to say, so I drank it. I probably drank it too quickly because it was nice and sweet. Next thing I know, I must have passed out, and when I came to, he was on top of me, and I couldn't move. When he got off, I grabbed my clothes and got out as soon as I could. I never told anybody. Then my period was late, and I got a test from the drug store and found out I was pregnant. I took some money that I had been saving up for college and used it to get an abortion. It was over quickly, and I put it out of my mind completely. All your questions about sexuality must have brought it back. I feel so ashamed. I guess *naïve* is a good word for me. I never would have thought something like that would happen."

"I'm so sorry that happened to you," I said, my voice catching because I felt so badly for her. "And you didn't have anyone to turn to."

"No, I didn't have anyone. And then I withdrew into myself. I think before that I was a relatively happy person, but I bottomed out. At some point, I finally realized I couldn't keep going on my own. Now that I think about it, I'm guessing my indecision about college was related to that experience. I got depressed."

"I'm glad you finally reached out."

"I thought I had shoved it far away. I haven't thought about it for a while. I quit watching the news because all the talk about Roe v. Wade getting overturned was so upsetting. I'm so lucky to be living in a state where abortion is legal. I just can't imagine what it would have been like if abortion was illegal here."

"Sorry, I didn't mean to push you further than you wanted to go."

"No, I'm relieved to finally be able to talk about it." After a few seconds, she asked hesitantly, "I guess I do wonder if you're judging me though."

"No judgment here. We've all had to make hard decisions, and it sounds like you did what was right for you at the time."

"Whew. I feel relieved."

"Just sounds so painful, especially going through it alone."

"For sure. It's so easy to get stuck in bad situations and not know what to do."

"Well, I'm impressed that you got out as quickly as you did, and that you were able to get an abortion."

"Yeah, I don't quite know how I managed all that. I think I was kind of on autopilot. But then after it was all over, I shut down."

"How are you feeling about it now, thinking back on it?"

"It was probably the hardest thing I ever did in my life, but it was the right thing." She began tentatively and then started getting more adamant. "It makes me so angry to hear people talking about women not having the right to decide what to do with their own bodies."

"It's especially uncomfortable being forced to do something you didn't agree to do. Did you ever consider reporting it?"

"No. I just wanted to get it over with. I've heard that reporting can sometimes be worse than the actual situation, that you sometimes end up feeling it was your own fault."

"I want to come back to another topic that you brought up and might be related. What about eating and obsessing about eating?"

"Hmm," she looked intrigued. "Obsessing about eating does occupy a lot of my head space and probably keeps me from thinking about other things. But it's kind of comforting, not having to think," Christina acknowledged. "Come to think about it, I started gaining weight after that."

"Makes sense; maybe eating became a way of soothing yourself."

"You're right. Eating is definitely comforting."

Admitting briefly to myself that I did not want to deal with all my issues either, I sympathetically added. "Once you avoid things, it becomes easier and easier to avoid them. Unfortunately, though, the problems don't go away." Wanting to give her something concrete to do, I added, "One thing you can try is to be mindful about eating. Be aware of each urge to put something in your mouth. Don't necessarily change what you do but try to heighten your awareness of what's going on in the moment. Then you'll be better able to make choices about what you want to eat," I said, knowing how much I hated it when anyone tried to make me follow a specific rule.

"I like the idea of being mindful about eating. I'll try it for a while and see how it feels. Sexuality and eating are both tough topics. I want to run away, but I guess I also want to resolve them. Thanks. I know our time is up."

I smiled, thinking about how aware of time she becomes when we're talking about tough topics. Then again, she allowed herself to focus on them for a while, which is a big step for her. And I reminded myself how difficult it is for me to tend to my difficult issues. "Great. See you next week."

Avoidance. Something Christina and I have in common, along with fear of men, anger, and sexuality. I'm reminded of how hard life is. Someone once said that no one has a monopoly on suffering. Even people who grow up in secure childhoods struggle to find themselves.

30

ESTHER:
GONE HUSBAND

I knew I looked disheveled and distraught when I arrived at Paul's office. Sitting down, I blurted out, "OMG, Steve left. When I finished work last night, he was packing his bags and said he needed time away to think and might want a divorce. I am blown away. I can't believe he just up and left. After all these years! I don't know what I'm going to do."

"Oh, wow, that hurts," Paul said sympathetically.

"That's for sure." I began sobbing and couldn't talk.

After letting me cry, Paul asked gently, "What's going on inside? You seem more angry than sad."

"I am beyond angry," I struggled to continue. "I don't know what I did wrong. Being a wife and mother has always been important to me. I can't trace back to the time when things went off the rails. It just seems like it all happened gradually, and now he's gone. I keep thinking of that book *Gone Girl*. It's *Gone Husband*. Poof! He's gone."

Paul let me cry for a minute, and then said compassionately, "Sounds like you're hurt and stunned. It's hard even to compute."

"That's for sure," I said, sniffling and then wiping the accumulated snot off my nose.

"Let's go back to this idea that there was no warning," Paul challenged. "Is that true? I'm remembering your dreams about him where he didn't show up for your talk because he was beaching it, him strangling you, and him laughing at you. And you've assiduously avoided talking about your relationship. Those seem like pretty big red flags. I wonder if, at an unconscious level, you've known for some time that this was coming?"

"That's true," I conceded. "Yeah, you're right. And I have felt so often lately that we're missing each other, that we have nothing to talk about anymore. Now that you mention the beach dream, I think back to the other people he was hanging out with on the beach. I wonder if he's having an affair. That could be why he's so disengaged."

"You went to the idea of an affair quickly. Any evidence, or is that old stuff from your parents replaying?"

"I don't think my parents ever had affairs, but my father was mean to my mother when he was drunk. I know I often wished she would leave him. Hmm, I wonder if she was passive like me and feeling that it was all up to my father."

"That's an interesting association. Say more about your passivity and how you might be like your mother."

"On the one hand, she's dominating and bossy. But on the other hand, she stayed with my father when she should have left him because he was abusive."

"So maybe there's something to staying in a bad situation instead of doing something about it that you picked up from your mother?"

"I never thought of it quite like that, but it makes sense."

"You know, I hear you're upset over him leaving, but I'm not hearing you missing him or saying how you actually feel about him," Paul challenged.

"I don't know how I feel. I'm not sure I've processed it all yet. Maybe I'm just trying not to think about it. In my last session with Christina, I realized that I tend to repress difficult things. But," I checked inside, "you're right, other than the shock, I'm not sure if I still love him. It seems we've grown apart, and he's supposedly been having a lot of meetings for work. So maybe he actually left a while back and is just making it official now."

"And how are the kids reacting?"

"They're kind of into their own lives and don't seem all that concerned. Maybe they just think he's not around. They haven't said much. But as I think about it, it seems like Steve has been disengaged for so long that none of us miss him that much."

"Or," Paul again brought it back, "you just haven't yet absorbed it all and are repressing your response. At the beginning of the session, you seemed distraught. Can you go inward and think about that more?"

Pausing and reflecting, I ventured, "I liked Steve a lot when we first met. He was different from anyone I had known. But we have grown apart. He's very much into the business world, and that's very materialistic and superficial. I'm more into the therapy world, which has meaning and depth. We seem to be on different planets, like from Venus and Mars.

"What's your anger at him?" Paul again guided me into my feelings.

"Ah, yes, I do have trouble with anger," I admitted, taking a deep sigh. "Okay, let me try talking directly to him as if he were here." I turned to the nearby empty chair and began, trying to make my voice loud and steady, "Steve, I am furious at you for disrupting our lives, for not trying to work on our relationship, for running out when the going got tough. I thought I knew you, but you have changed over the years. What happened to the idealistic young man you were when I first met you?"

"Good," Paul prompted, gently but firmly. "Now go over to the other chair and see what Steve might say in return."

I moved to the other chair and sat quietly for a minute to put myself in Steve's shoes. I spoke as if Steve were talking to me, "You've changed, too. I sense contempt on your part, as if I'm not good enough for you. I don't want to express my feelings all the time or work on our relationship endlessly. I meet people at work who think I walk on water. I feel more attracted to them than to you. It's just gone—whatever I once felt for you. There's nothing left."

"Move back to your chair," Paul pointed.

I moved and then sat quietly crying, "I can't believe you can give up on us so easily. I wonder if I ever knew you. I feel so sad. It feels like a death."

"Anything else you want to say to him?" Paul asked softly.

"Goodbye," I whispered.

"I'm interested that you said *goodbye*."

"It just seems like it's over."

"Any thoughts about what's going on?" Paul pushed. "I'm also struck by the word you used—*contempt*."

"Well," I hesitated. "I have to wonder if my fear of men is playing out here. We talked about that with my seeing you as a male therapist and worrying about whether you liked me. It brings up the old issues related to my father and distancing myself from him."

"But *contempt*," Paul again pressed. "What about that? *Contempt* is a strong word. Are men contemptible?"

"You're right. It's too much of a generalization. There are certainly a few good men, but maybe they're all in the Marines," I said jokingly.

Paul sidestepped my poor attempt at humor and went directly to the conflict. "Could you be feeling some contempt for him?"

"Hmm. He certainly has less education than I do. And it is hard for him to talk about his feelings. And he is avoiding talking about all this. Yeah, maybe there is some contempt there."

"And, go inside. How are you feeling right now?"

"Kind of gobsmacked, all over the place. Just within this single session I sob uncontrollably, I'm okay, I'm contemptuous, I'm moving on, I'm joking. Kind of a roller coaster ride. I want off."

"You're a human being, and a major crisis has just occurred. It will take a while to process and come to terms with what's happened. But first you need to grieve. And I guess I must ask, do you want the marriage to be over?"

"That's a good question," I pondered. "What do *I* want? I don't know. He walked out, so I just automatically assumed it was over. He made the decision for us. Do I want to fight for the relationship or let him go?"

"I can't help but notice, in the chair exercise, that all the blame was on Steve. I wonder what your part in this whole thing has been?"

"Oh, ouch."

"What's ouchy?"

"It feels like you're taking Steve's side. What's that about? I guess I feel angry at you."

"Okay, sorry, I can see that. Let me rephrase. There are always two sides to a relationship. I wonder if you've had anything to do with the problems?"

"Oh, yeah, I see what you're saying. Yes. I'm sure I do. Hmm, I guess I withdrew and took over everything, not trusting that Steve would step up. I quit confiding in him. I see what you're saying. Yes, I have played a role."

"What advice would you give a client?" Paul asked with a kind expression on his face.

"Oh, you're good," I exclaimed. "What advice would I give," I muttered to myself. "Let's see, I would come back to the idea of communication. I haven't been communicating as well as I could. It may be too late, but I need to work on better communication. I also need to work on the contempt thing. I guess I have to take more responsibility."

"*Have* to?" Paul challenged. "Can you change the word to *choose* to?"

"Good point. I *choose* to take more responsibility. That certainly gives a different meaning, doesn't it? Again, what do *I* want?"

"You might need to sleep on that. I'm sure you will have interesting dreams this week."

"Thanks for being here. It's so helpful to talk this out and not feel pressured to go one way or the other," I said on the way out.

I felt sad. Life sure throws some punches.

CHRISTINA:
DEATH

I got an email from Christina saying she needed to miss a session because her grandmother died. She said she'd be in touch as soon as she knew when they'd be back from Wisconsin. I sent a message expressing my condolences and urging her to take care of herself.

When we met after the break, Christina was subdued, "I have so much to talk about. Death puts things in perspective! I sat in a coffee shop after the funeral thinking that the world had stopped, and I needed to reevaluate everything. I'm glad I got a chance to talk to Grandma before she died. And it was terrific to meet so many relatives at the wake and funeral. It was kind of like a big party. Everyone had stories about Grandma."

Wanting to bring it back to her earlier expressed fears, I asked, "What was it like to see her dead?"

Christina eyes widened as she recalled, "It was the first time I had seen anyone in a casket. It seemed a little barbaric seeing a dead body all fixed up for burial; it reminded me of the TV series *Six Feet Under*. It didn't look like her. They put on too much make-up, and her mouth looked odd, kind of straight across instead of how the corners were always turned down. But I'm relieved that they showed the body because then I truly knew she was dead. I stood in front of her body and said a little prayer, thanking her for being my grandmother."

"What feelings did it bring up for you?"

"Hearing the preacher give this long sermon about getting saved so that you could go to heaven made me angry and guilty and scared. I don't think I believe in heaven. But then I felt anxious, like a bolt of lightning was going to come down and strike me dead. What does happen to us after death? What is the meaning of life? My grandmother was a good person. Is that enough? I had a dream the night after the funeral,

> I lay down next to my grandmother as she was dying. We went into that tunnel of light I've heard people talk about. We got to the end, and she kept going across the abyss, but I stayed back. I cried because I was so sad to see her go over to the other side without me. It's funny because I was not able to cry at the funeral or after, but I did cry in the dream. And then a couple nights later, I had a dream where she came to the foot of my bed and said that everything would be all right. I choked up when I saw her. But I was glad she came to say goodbye.

"What thoughts come to your mind as you tell me these dreams?"

"I feel like crying for not getting to know her earlier—the missed opportunities. People make so many mistakes in life. It scares me because I know I will make more mistakes, that I won't live life to the fullest, that I won't do all I *should* or could do. And the thought of just disintegrating into dust as if I never existed also scares me. Would anyone notice I was gone? And another point, I don't get the concept of heaven. What about all the people in the world who have never heard of God or were brought up in a different religion. Why should they go to hell? That doesn't sound right. And where are hell or heaven anyway? Like I said, I'm confused."

Wanting her to move into her feelings instead of just staying in her head, I coached, "You said you felt like crying, but then you ran away from it. Could you just take a minute and close your eyes. Imagine that you are in that coffee shop experiencing the feeling that the world stopped spinning and that nothing else mattered. Go inside your body. Describe what's going on in as much detail as you can."

Wiping away a tear, Christina sighed, "I'm having a hard time breathing. My heart feels heavy. I feel like a dark cloud is hanging over my head ready to rain on my parade."

"Be your heart. What would your heart say right now?"

As her heart, Christina said softly while crying, "I feel sad. I wish I had known Grandma better. I am afraid of death, and I am afraid of living. I haven't even started living yet."

After sitting quietly with Christina while she cried, I asked, "How are you feeling now?"

Wiping her eyes and blowing her nose on the tissue I offered, Chrisina whispered, "I feel relieved that I can cry and get it out. I miss my grandmother."

"What do you think your grandmother would say to you right now?"

Imagining herself as her grandmother, Christina said warmly, "Thank you for coming to visit me. I'm proud of you for being in therapy. You are the one who broke the cycle in the family."

Christina added, as herself, "I think she would hold out her arms and comfort me. I have an image of curling up in her lap like a baby. It's nice to be held. My parents were not all that affectionate, and I missed that. I think my mother missed it, too. My mother cried a lot before the funeral. I could hear her in the next bedroom. I can only imagine how bad she feels about all she missed out on. And probably beating herself up for not fixing things sooner. But then again, she said how glad she was that she repaired the relationship with her mother before she died. I think she found some peace."

Encouraging her to go deeper, I again gently coached, "What do you think your grandma would say about how to live your life from now on?"

Christina responded quickly, with a smile on her face. "She was very accepting. I think she would say that I need to find my own way, but that whatever I do is fine, and that she loves me unconditionally."

"How does it feel to hear that?"

"Relieving, like I don't have to do anything to get her love. That's how I want to live my life. I don't want to feel the weight of all the expectations that I used to feel from my parents. I feel a bit freer, like maybe I can begin to pursue what I want in life."

"That sounds lovely," I concurred. "Coming back to the feelings about death and what happens after, where are you at with that?"

"If you mean after my grandmother's death, I just don't know. And I'm not quite sure how to figure it out. I don't know the *right* way to grieve," she admitted with some discomfort.

"As if there is a *right* way!" I challenged.

"Yeah, you're probably right," Christina sighed. "But," she looked down, "it's hard having all these feelings and not knowing where to go with them."

"That makes sense. I don't think there's anywhere to go with them. It's good to just allow the feelings in and accept them. That's part of grieving, and it takes a while. You never *get over* the death of a loved one. You just learn to live with it and cherish your memories."

"Yeah," Christina said quietly, nodding her head.

Sensing that some difficult emotions had gotten stirred up, I offered, "Any more feelings about the experience that you want to talk about? You haven't mentioned anything about your father in all this."

"That's such a good question," Christina sounded relieved that I had let her off the hook by changing the topic. "It feels so much like these weeks were my mother's time. My father kind of faded into the background. But," Christina pushed back, "maybe we could shift to talking more about him in the next couple of sessions. I'm intrigued to think more about my fear of men. I want to get over that or at least try to understand it more. I do want to get into a relationship with someone at some point."

Wanting to reinforce and support her, I pulled back from more directly discussing the difficult emotions about death. "It's great seeing how energized you are talking about all these things. You seem so different from when you started therapy. You have lots of opinions. You stand up for yourself a lot more. And it's great to hear that you're feeling more ready to welcome a close relationship of some kind."

"Yeah," Christina immediately responded, giving more eye contact. "I feel as though I have more of a sense of who I am. At least when I'm in here with you, I feel better. I'm still unsure of how to act in a lot of social situations, but right now I have more confidence."

"I also want to check back with you about how you're feeling after our last session talking about your abortion?"

"Thanks for asking." Christina looked thoughtful, then said, "I have felt so relieved to get that out, and I appreciate your support. I have wondered how life might have been if that hadn't happened. I also wonder what I could have done differently. Did I learn anything? I don't know; what with my grandmother's death, everything feels a little turned upside down."

"You know," I said tentatively, "I keep thinking about the little ghosts over your mother's head and realizing that you also have a little ghost over your head."

"Oh wow, that's interesting. I guess I do."

"And maybe you need some time to grieve that loss?"

"Oh. Good point. I'm going to think about that. I do need to grieve that."

"Sounds like a good place to stop today. I'm glad things went well and you had a chance to be with your family. I'm eager to hear more about how you process these important feelings about life and death and meaning and relationships. These are certainly the core issues that all of us need to grapple with."

I felt so much empathy for Christina as she experienced her first death. It's so hard to experience all the emotions, yet so important to say goodbye. It reminded me of how fragile life is and the importance of living fully and resolving problems while there's time. Hearing about Christina's grief reminded me of my grief when my grandparents and father died. It's scary when the layer above you gets ripped off and you realize you're a step closer to death. It also brings up thoughts of the death of my relationship with Steve. I encouraged Christina to experience her feelings, and yet it's so hard for me to cope with all the anger and sadness I have.

32

ESTHER: ADJUSTMENT

"Well," I mumbled, feeling humbled and resigned. "I guess we're getting a divorce."

Paul listened patiently, encouraging me with his attentive silence to say more.

I studied the pattern in the carpet as if it held the answers, then looked up at the Monet print to calm myself. "After the last session, I went home and sobbed. A big chunk of my life has been with Steve. I felt a huge loss. Who am I without him?"

Again, Paul just listened and let me go deeper.

"At first, I thought I wanted to try to get back together with Steve. I had it worked out that it was all my responsibility and I just needed to communicate more. He's a good, kind person, and I was sure we could find common ground. And then," I faltered. "He sent an email saying he wants a divorce, that he's been having an affair for some time and wants to be with Henry. He has realized that he's gay. He said he still cares about me but not as a partner. He wished me all the best, but said our marriage is over."

"Keep going," Paul encouraged.

Sighing deeply, I said, "Of all the things I imagined, I never once imagined he might be gay. I feel stupid that I didn't pick up on any vibes, other than that we didn't have much of a sex life anymore. I mean I'm a therapist and have worked with many gay people. I thought he was having an affair but not with a man. I guess that's what all those meetings with Henry were about."

"Does it change your feelings that he's leaving you for a man rather than a woman?"

"Hmm, good question. I guess it seems more final. Sad. Hard to even say what I'm feeling. Maybe I'm just numb. It feels like rocks rolling around inside my head. It's hard to focus on work, but it's also a blessing to have something I can do and not dwell on myself."

"I feel so bad for you," Paul said quietly.

"Yeah, thanks. I think I'm in mourning."

"Yes, *mourning* is a good description. It's an adjustment."

"I had a dream about my relationship with Steve the night after our last session."

After a minute, Paul smiled and prompted, "And are you going to tell me the dream?"

"Sorry, my head is somewhere else," I admitted, coming back into the session.

> I'm in someone's house, and I'm hungry. I put together a brownie mix and cut up a mango and put it in. But then I cannot figure out how to turn the oven on, so I just leave the uncooked brownies on the counter and go to another room. Then I'm with a stranger having hot, steamy sex. I won't go into that scene in detail, but it was good. Then I'm with

a group of strangers in Japan, and everyone goes in separately for private audiences with the Buddha in a beautiful temple.

"Great dream, although you could give a little more detail about the sex scene," Paul grumbled mischievously and then shifted to more serious probing. "How do you know this dream is about your relationship with Steve?"

"It's the scene in the temple after engaging in hot, steamy sex with a stranger, like maybe I'm supposed to be asking for forgiveness. I was angry when I thought Steve could be having an affair, although at the time I didn't know for sure that he was. And here I was in bed with a stranger, like maybe I wanted to have an affair. True, yes, a dream, but obviously a part of me wanted to have an affair. Here I was having a dream about messing up someone's house, having sex with a stranger, and praying for forgiveness. It seems that maybe the message was what you were saying last week that I have some responsibility for the whole situation and I need to do penance."

"Sorry, but I'm confused with where you're getting this interpretation and why you're laying all this blame on yourself. And you're needing to ask for forgiveness from whom?"

"I just feel that I've messed everything up. I'm blaming myself."

"Maybe blaming is not such a good strategy. Maybe we need to work to understand and accept what is."

"Yeah, easier said than done."

"I can see and feel your distress. Take your time." After a few seconds, Paul continued, "Do a body scan, and tell me what you're feeling in your body."

I went inward to assess. "My eyes are burning, and I have to keep closing them to get some relief. My stomach hurts, as if I've eaten too much, but I haven't had anything to eat today. I'm experiencing an aura, similar to the sensation you get when a migraine is starting. My legs are tingling because I've been sitting for too long. I'm a mess and feel bummed out."

After another sympathetic pause, Paul suggested, "Close your eyes and take a few deep breaths." Then, he added slowly and meditatively, "In your mind, step onto the escalator you see in front of you. When I count down from ten to one, you will be completely relaxed. Ten, nine, eight, seven, feel the relaxation in your body, six, five, four, it feels like sand being poured into your head, three, two, one. You stroll off the escalator into a room that's totally peaceful. Notice how it smells, tastes, feels on your body. Look at the walls and notice something beautiful hanging there. Now, go out through the wide door in front of you. You enter a favorite quiet spot that gives you peace. Look around you and soak it all in. Notice how much calmer you feel. Your head feels better; you are relaxed. Savor for a minute, and then we'll go back up, keeping the relaxation with you. Step on the escalator and go up, breathing in the fresh, cool air. One, two, three, four, your headache has lifted, five, six, no tingling in your legs, seven, eight, your stomach is feeling pleasantly full, nine, ten." Giving me a few seconds to adjust, he brought me back into the room, "How are you feeling?"

I blinked and took a deep breath. "Better, more relaxed. Thanks. I needed that respite. You know, in the room I saw the Monet painting of the water-lily pond that you have over there on your wall. Steve and I went to see that painting on our honeymoon, and it's always been one of my favorites. So, it's both a painting that brings me joy and a connection to Steve. And then I pictured the quiet spot as this lovely beach on St. Johns where we went one time. So, Steve was kind of with me on the relaxation tour," I reflected nostalgically.

"Steve. Tell me your thoughts about Steve."

"I miss him. I feel so sad about throwing away everything we used to have, about no longer having a family."

"And how about him strangling you?" Paul reminded me, lifting his eyebrows.

"Oh, yeah, that. Or my strangling myself. You know, I come back to thinking about how my mother didn't leave my father even when she probably should have. If I am truly honest, things haven't been good for a while; maybe Steve and I were just never meant for each other."

"Let's rephrase that to 'not meant for each other right now.' And I'm not sure that anyone is *meant* for another. It takes a lot of work and communication, as you know, to pull off a relationship. And it cannot be all one-sided. It sounds as though Steve has had his foot out the door for some time," Paul suggested.

"That's what is so hard to grasp, how I didn't know. I just can't believe I never saw it coming. How can I compete with being gay?"

"But I would assert that a big part of you did know, and you just didn't want to deal with it. You kept saying how reluctant you were to talk about the problems with Steve."

"Hmm, there's some truth there. I guess I just didn't want to face the red flags that were waving frantically. Instead, I went off making mango brownies with no oven to cook them in."

"No oven to cook them in. No way to get your needs met!"

"Yeah. Good point."

"Well, what about this stranger and the good sex?" Paul wondered. "Maybe that's something to look forward to?"

"Or to ask forgiveness for," I countered.

"And maybe that's a choice. What comes next?"

"It will take some time to adjust and figure that all out."

"Your voice is already sounding a lot stronger. I think you're going to be able to pull through this okay. What resources do you have to turn to?"

"I called a friend from graduate school. It was good to talk it over with someone. Surprisingly, she wasn't shocked at all about Steve being gay. She said she had always wondered. Maybe I just didn't want to see it."

"Good to get that support. And how about your kids?"

"I just told them that their father and I were separating. Strangely enough, they were not surprised. Many of their friends' parents are divorced, and things have been tense for a while around the house, so maybe they were relieved. I don't know. I told Steve that he needs to be the one to tell them about being gay. It seems like his news to share."

"You might want to keep an eye on them and see if and when they want to talk about it."

"Good idea."

"You sound more confident as you talk now, which is terrific, but the mourning will take a while," Paul warned. Then he added, "I have to come back to challenge you, though, before we stop. What can you learn from this whole thing about yourself?"

"Good question," I nodded thoughtfully. "I am concerned about how I can be so reluctant to face difficult issues. His leaving has been a big wake-up call."

"And what are you waking up to?" Paul kept probing.

"I'm waking up to the idea that I want a good relationship. I want a partner, someone to share my life with, not just someone living in the house but not really being there.

I'm not going to rush into anything, but I can see that it's not enough just giving to clients and the kids. I want more from life than that."

"Good on you!" Paul agreed wholeheartedly. "And while we're at it, how's our relationship? How are we doing?" Paul asked.

"I'm so glad I came back to therapy with you. I like how we have a different relationship this time than before. More playful, more collegial. I'm beginning to trust you more," I said slowly, thinking through my feelings.

"I feel different with you, too. It's more fun working together, feels collaborative. But you seemed a bit put out with me a couple times today. Maybe I was pushing you too hard? What's up with that?"

I paused to reflect. "You are very confrontive. I need that, but I sometimes feel that you don't take my side enough."

"I can see that, and I apologize. Maybe you need to tell me to back off, so I know when I've gone too far? Good practice for communicating with others?"

"So right you are," I agreed.

"Sounds good to me." He paused and then added, "I'm aware that our time together is ending, and unfortunately this is not the best timing for you. Going through a separation and divorce is difficult. I'd like us to think about how I can be the most helpful to you in the limited time we have left. For example, you mentioned when you first came in about not wanting to find a new therapist, but there are a lot of practical issues to sort out in terms of ending your marriage, such as custody and financial details."

"Yeah, you're right, the timing sucks. And I can't even be angry about that because I am grateful that I have been able to have even a few sessions before you retire."

"Well, you can be both angry and grateful."

"True, feelings are so messy. Yes, I need to do more thinking about next steps. Maybe we can come back to that in the sessions we have left?"

"Okay. Let me know if you need anything from me during the week. And just a reminder that we have only three more sessions together."

"Thanks," I said feeling relief that I was not on my own in the muddy pit on this one. "I will let you know if I have a crisis before next week." I left the session, worrying that indeed I might be headed for a crisis when reality hits.

33

CHRISTINA:
FEAR OF COMPETING WITH MOTHER

I know I said I wanted to talk more about my father," Christina said as she sat down and petted Star. "But I've been thinking a lot more about my mother, and I would rather keep talking about my relationship with her." I nodded, and she continued, "It's funny; on the one hand she is supportive, but I also get a feeling she's upset with me," she said with a frown.

"What's that about?"

"I hate to say this," she winced, "but it's like she doesn't want me to get better because that reminds her of all the things she wanted to do in life and didn't."

"Maybe she feels jealous or competitive with you?" I offered tentatively.

"Something like that. It's weird to say that out loud. She should be happy for me that I'm working through my problems."

"There's that *should* word again," I challenged. "Let's try to unpack what's going on. What are you observing about her behavior?"

"At first, she wanted to hear all about therapy and was interested in what I might do in the future. But now she doesn't even want to talk."

"Let's try the two-chair thing we did before. Imagine your mother in that chair over there and tell her what you're feeling."

As if to her mother, Christina said, "Mom, is something going on? I feel shut out, like you don't want to talk to me since we got back from the funeral."

I noted to myself that she was now calling her "Mom" instead of "Mother." "Okay," I directed, "now go sit in the other chair and be your mom. What would she say back to you?"

Moving to the other chair and acting as her mother, Christina sighed and haltingly began. "I know I haven't been very communicative. I feel like I'm still grieving the death of my mother. I can't seem to get over that. I'm sorry. I just feel like crying all the time."

"Go back to the other chair and be yourself," I again suggested.

After moving back, Christina said to her mother, "I'm so sorry. I didn't know you felt so bad. Do you want to talk about it?"

I motioned for her to move to the "Mother" chair.

As her mother, Christina sat straight up with more energy and said, "It reminds me of other losses in my life that I never dealt with. Instead, I closed myself off from feeling. Then my mother died just as I began to repair the relationship with her. And I've retreated into myself again. It's funny, well not funny ha-ha but funny odd, but I kind of feel resentful and angry about how you seem to be just going on with life, almost like Grandma's death didn't happen. You're growing and changing, and I'm going backwards."

I motion Christina back to the "Self" chair.

After moving and thinking, Christina empathized, "I wondered what was going on with you. And I felt so distant from you. I don't know if it's okay to ask, but can you tell me about those other losses?"

I motion her back to the "Mother" chair.

After a long silence when I began to wonder if I was losing her, Christina, as her mother, haltingly deflected, "I want to at some point, but I just can't go there now. I feel bad telling you that I feel resentful and envious of you. I think I need to talk about that. I wish I could be as free as you seem to be. I feel so held back in life."

I motion back to the "Self" chair.

As herself, and again after a silence, Christina murmured, "Hmm. I don't want you to feel bad that I'm getting better. It doesn't mean that I'll leave you. I feel like we're just starting to have a relationship. I miss being able to talk to you."

"How did that feel?" I ask Christina to help her process her experience talking to her mother during the chair work.

"Wow," Christina said, with wide-open eyes. "I can't believe all that came out. I feel like she was right here in the room with me. That felt real."

I nodded in agreement. "What I noticed was that she seemed to be still grieving, and that sure makes sense given all she's gone through."

"It does make sense. I guess I wanted her to move on faster."

"It also seems to reflect your feeling that there's some competition between you and your mother, and that doesn't feel good."

"That blows my mind," Christina admitted. "I would think she would want me to get better. That makes me a little angry. How am I supposed to deal with her feelings?"

"You maybe feel some resentment?"

"Sure, but I also feel bad for her having felt so stuck in her life. I want her to start feeling better, too. I hope she has a lot of years left. It's not too late, right?"

"What would you like to say to her? You're in your 'Self' chair. Talk to your mother."

As herself, Christina earnestly asserted, "Mom. I love you. I want us both to be happy. I wonder if you'd consider going to therapy. It's really helped me. You could also start paying attention to your dreams. That's helped me learn about myself."

"Go to the other chair and be your mother. How would she respond?"

As her mother, Christina was more hesitant. "That scares me. It feels like there is so much inside me. Maybe it's better to let sleeping dogs lie."

"Go back and be yourself. How would you respond to that?"

As herself, Christina nodded in agreement with her mother, "It is terrifying, but it's also exciting. Besides, we're not sleeping dogs."

Ending the chair work for the moment, I asked Christina to process the event. "How was that, talking to your mother?"

"Good. I want to talk to her. I don't know how much is coming from her and how much from me, but there is a wall there that I want to push through. Now that I've seen what the relationship with my mother can be like, I want to keep it up." After a pause, she asked, "What's your advice on how I should go about this?"

"I could give you some advice," I said. "But honestly, you handled the situation terrifically in the chair work. I sense that you have some good ideas about how you might handle the situation."

"You're right," Christina allowed. "I guess I was looking for the *right* answer for what I *should* do. Maybe I do know, but maybe I'm not ready to talk to her about all this. If she is grieving, maybe I should just be there for her."

"That makes sense," I affirmed. "Good idea to move slowly and see what emerges. I just want to say that it's great that you're really pushing yourself to see what's going on with you and your mother. I know it's hard, but you did a great job with the chair work. I can see how much easier it is now for you to talk with her, at least in your imagination. And it's so interesting, the notion of the possible competitiveness between you. That certainly happens a lot between mothers and daughters."

"That's very interesting," Christina perked up. "What do you mean?"

"Well, as both a daughter and a mother myself, I know it's hard to have separate identities," I disclosed a little hesitantly because I didn't want her to think that I thought we were exactly alike. I felt a little vulnerable disclosing my personal life to her, but I also felt that hearing about my situation might validate her feelings.

"Sometimes I hear myself saying something that sounds just like my mother, and I freak out. And sometimes I hear my daughter saying something to me that sounds like what I said to my mother, and I chuckle in remembering. We get so bound up wondering where all these things come from. We want to be separate yet stay connected. It's hard to pull off, especially during adolescence when you're getting ready to leave home and trying to differentiate yourself from your mother. And clearly, your grandmother's death is bringing all this to the foreground."

"That's so true," Christina nodded fervently. "I think maybe for right now I'll just try to be a little more understanding of what my mother is going through. I might try to slip in a mention of therapy at some point. Could she see you?"

"No, that's not possible. My contract is with you in individual therapy. It would be better for her to have her own therapist. But I could give you some referrals if she's willing and interested in trying therapy. Doing marriage counseling would be even better since your father is involved in all this."

"That's really interesting. They do need to work on their relationship. That would be such a good way to both help my mother grieve and get them talking more about their relationship. There must be some way I can subtly bring it up."

"See what emerges and wait until the time feels right. I think you'll know. By the way, did you notice that a couple times you called her "Mom" instead of "Mother"? What do you suppose that's about?"

"Oh, interesting, I hadn't even noticed. I think I do feel closer to her now. She is more of a mom now."

"We need to stop now. See you next week."

Christina has been courageous about expressing her feelings. I'm especially aware of that now as I think about how much difficulty I've had in being open about my feelings about what's going on with Steve. I'm glad I've had these few sessions with Paul, but he was right that there are many more issues that need to be dealt with. Yikes!

34

ESTHER:
MY MOTHER

"As we've talked before," I said to Paul after sitting down, "many of my issues with Steve go back to my parents. I was reminded of this last week when Christina talked about her parents. I thought it might help to dig deeper into my relationship with my parents as I try to sort out what's going on with Steve."

"Yep, relationship issues usually go back to childhood," Paul affirmed. "Tell me more about what you're thinking."

"I've laid a lot of the blame on my father, particularly his alcoholism and anger. But today I want to focus on my mother. When Christina talked about her mother in her most recent session, it sparked a lot of thoughts about my mother. I think I told you that my mother hadn't worked until after my father died, and then she got a job as a secretary in a federal agency and worked her way up to an administrative post. She was able to channel her dominating and controlling personality productively in the workplace."

"Impressive! How have you managed your feelings about her dominance?" Paul asked.

"My way of dealing with her has been not to deal. I shut down and shut up, and I lose myself in the process. Kind of like in my dream where I vanish. I want to learn to show up and talk back and not fear that she will annihilate me."

"Hmm. I wonder if that is what carried over to your not being able to stand up for yourself with Steve?"

"Ah, good point. I think my general reaction to confrontation in my world is not to stand up for myself. That fear of annihilation is so strong."

"*Annihilation* is a strong word!"

"Yes, it is, and I think it's what makes it hard for me to assert myself."

"And what would your rebuttal be, Dr. Esther, if one of your adult clients had a similar fear of annihilation?"

"Right, I see where you're going," I reluctantly agreed. "Yes, when I was small, she had a lot of power over me. But I am no longer small, and she no longer has physical control over me. But I've continued to avoid her. When you keep avoiding anything or anyone, you never learn to deal with the situation and avoidance becomes reinforcing..."

"Am I sensing a *but* there?" Paul teasingly queried.

"But it's hard," I conceded. Hearing that I sounded whiny, I paused to regroup. "I've avoided so long that I've perfected the art of deflecting attention from myself. Maybe if we did some role-playing where you were dominating, I could figure out how to respond to you and that would give me practice so that I could respond better to others."

"No way," Paul laughed. "Wouldn't that just exacerbate your fear of men being bullies? I'm not sure I want to be thrown under the bus like that."

"Good point, between a rock and a hard place, a dominating mother or a bullying father. No wonder I backed out of that game."

"But again," Paul channeled what I said earlier, "you're not a helpless infant, and you do have resilience and skills. Let's take another tack. How do you help your children stand up to you, assuming of course that you do, given what a good psychologist you are."

"I encourage them to speak their minds. I explicitly ask them what they think and listen when they talk. And I try not to dominate or bully them. On occasion, when I find myself getting unreasonably angry, I take a time out to regroup and then go back and apologize and talk it out with them. I'm proud they have learned to express themselves so well."

"Right. So, you help your children and your clients speak up and celebrate them when they do so. You obviously have the skills but shrink back in fear and avoidance when fighting your own battles. What can you say to yourself when your mother starts dominating you? Give me an example of when she tries to dominate you, so we can work on something specific."

"Okay, one of her favorites is telling me how to raise my kids. She often says I should make them eat more vegetables or watch less TV. We were never allowed to watch TV when I was a kid, so she had a real bug up her ass about that. Or she insists that I should make them go to synagogue or do more homework. She has a whole list of things I do wrong. Let's do the TV one."

"Role-play what she said to you. Be your mother."

"Esther," I exhorted in my mother's patronizing tone. "I don't know how many times I have told you the evidence about how bad it is for kids to have too much screen time. You know better. You must stand up to them and set limits."

"Take a deep breath, and think about what your goal is," Paul coached.

"My goal is for her to butt out," I almost yelled. "If I want help, I will ask her. I want to stand up to her."

"Okay," he said calmly, "let's use that goal but moderate the language so that you can be more effective. Try it again as if you're talking as a reasonable adult to another reasonable adult and maybe use the broken record technique of repeating yourself until she listens."

"Okay here we go," I take a deep breath and face my mother chair. "Thank you for your advice, Mother, but we're doing fine. We have a schedule set up for screen time that we worked out with the kids, and they are very good at following it. When I need your advice, though, I'll be sure to ask."

"How did that feel?"

"Like I gave too much information, which would leave the door open for her to argue back and suggest other strategies. I really want her to stop giving me unsolicited advice, and to respect that I know how to be a mother." Suddenly, I got in touch with my rage. "It's none of her goddamn business!"

"Wow. There's a powder keg in there! Hang on to that feeling, and we'll come back to it. But let's keep track of your goal right now. Try again talking to your mother, being very matter of fact and letting her know that you're the boss in dealing with your children. Maybe try to shift the topic so that you can take control of the conversation."

Breathing deeply, I looked at the empty chair and said forcefully, "Thanks for your advice, Mother, but I've got it covered. When I want your help, I'll be sure to ask. By the way, how is Aunt Trudy doing after her surgery? Did you go to see her?"

"That was terrific," Paul praised me. "I love how you made the statement and then changed the topic. Masterful. How did it feel?"

"I liked it a lot better that time. I let her know what I thought but also that it wasn't up for negotiation. I think changing the topic would work with her," I sighed with relief. "But the line where I said, 'When I want your help, I'll be sure to ask,' sounded a little mean and, overall, I felt a little more aggressive than I'd like. I think research shows that hostility begets hostility, so I want to try to keep calm and not arouse her defenses."

"Good points. And sometimes it helps to put in a little empathy to show that you can see her side of things. So, try it again," Paul encouraged.

I looked at the empty chair and centered myself. "Thanks for trying to be so helpful, Mother. I know you mean well, but I've got it covered. By the way, I wanted to ask about Aunt Trudy. How's she doing?"

"Nice job with being empathic! How did that feel?"

"I felt more like an adult. I think I'd like to try it with her. If I can act differently, I think she'll respond in a different way." I was pleased that I suddenly felt more confident.

"So, let's go back to the powder-keg feeling. Where was that coming from? What's your understanding of what was going on inside."

"Ah," I said, with sudden comprehension. "I keep all my feelings inside, and they build up and explode. I kept everything in with my parents and then with Steve, and even with clients I take on too much of a giving, loving role. I don't allow my negative feelings to surface, and then they fester. You know, interestingly, I was remembering that in the first session with Christina I felt a twinge of hostility and sadism that I quickly squashed because it was so uncomfortable."

"And, what made that negative feeling so uncomfortable?"

"I think I had a lot of countertransference with Christina, given that my own issues got triggered. I am so avoidant

ESTHER: MY MOTHER

and understated with my feelings, although I'm much better than I was when you and I first started therapy many years ago. I think I reacted to Christina's passivity—you know, the inclination to kick someone when they're down."

"Right. And understanding that you felt like kicking her can help you understand how other people react to her. So, you can use your feelings, without acting out on them, to help you better conceptualize and help Christina. And you can apply the same principles to yourself."

"Yes! It's so important to have the whole range of feelings. So interesting that in our culture we're afraid of negative emotions, and yet they leak out in war and aggression, and putting others down who don't believe the same way as we do."

"Right. We have to accept all sides of ourselves. Jung talked about allowing the shadow side in," Paul concurred. "So, your shadow side is coming out into the daylight."

"Oh, and I'm thinking about that phrase, 'laugh when you're happy, cry when you're sad'—let the whole range of feelings emerge and then you can decide what to do about them and live more fully. Thanks for the good psychology lesson today," I said, and we both laughed.

Paul brought us back to the present moment. "So, how are you adjusting to the separation with Steve? You've not talked about it much today."

I paused to reflect. "I'm sad and looking inward, thinking a lot about life, happiness, meaning, existence. What do I want? Who am I? Where am I going? I feel more open to possibilities, like the notion that when a crisis occurs, things open up and you get out of your rut. Isn't there some saying that crisis is both a danger and an opportunity? I feel kind of like an adolescent—oh, interesting!—kind of like where Christina is at, where there are lots of possibilities.

I'm unstuck from the routine and figuring out where to go next. I do love existential crises when I can get into them."

"You certainly sound eager. And, I must say, I love talking with you about existential issues. It resonates for me going into my next phase of life. So, interesting how things go along a single path, and then we are forced to think about the future. Maybe *allowed* is a better word than *forced* though, because obviously a lot of people put off or push away from thinking about these issues when it's too hard."

"Yeah, I can see how it would be hard to retire, after working at something you love your whole life. Suddenly, what do you do with yourself? What will give you meaning?" I loved hearing about Paul's reflections and was so glad that he had disclosed his thoughts to me.

"That's a work in progress. I'll know more when I get there. But back to you. What are some of the consequences of your reflections?"

"There I go again avoiding the hard stuff. Okay, going back to what you said last week: I need to find another therapist after we're done in a couple weeks. Hard as it is to start a new relationship, I have to think about the kids and my clients. And your idea of a mediator is good, given that Steve and I are going to need someone to help us work through all the details." All of a sudden it hit me, "Whew! I can see why I avoid, but the problems don't go away. I'm tired."

"Is there a way that you can take some time off for yourself? You have a lot on your plate right now. Sounds like a good time for some self-soothing."

"I don't schedule anything right after our sessions because I know I need time to regroup and think. So, I might take myself out for lunch."

"Good plan. See you next week."

35

CHRISTINA:
I WANT TO BE YOUR DAUGHTER

Christina hesitantly said, "I had a dream last night that I was your daughter."

I felt touched and imagined how good it would feel if she were my daughter, although I was also intrigued by her reluctance to reveal her wish. I probed, "Tell me your dream."

We were in your house at the dinner table. Everything was so lovely. You asked everyone to talk about their day. After dinner, everyone helped with cleaning up, and then we all played a game together.

"Sounds ideal. Tell me more about the house and dinner table."

"Big house, old, brick, nice neighborhood, big dining room. You are there and your husband, at least I assume he is your husband, and two almost-teenage kids, and me. Everyone sitting around, a lot of laughter, a lot of talking. It just seems fun. And everyone is in tune with each other. We had fun playing the game, maybe Rummikub or Monopoly. I don't even know who is winning. I think you said it was family game night or something like that. Your kids seem to get along, and everyone is very welcoming to me."

"How did it feel to be there?"

"I loved it. I've always wanted siblings. And I wanted our family to have fun dinners and lots of conversations. I always loved the idea of a game night. Kind of a loud, boisterous family with lots going on. I felt included, warm, and safe."

"What are your associations?"

"This is what families *should* be like, like descriptions in books I read as a kid. The friend I had in elementary school had a family like that, and I loved going there for dinner. It was kind of like that Norman Rockwell painting of Thanksgiving that my parents have hanging in their dining room, all-American.

"What would it mean to be my daughter?"

"I would get to see you all the time. I could talk to you more often and more casually. We could do things together. It wouldn't be just one hour a week."

"Sounds lovely. What do you suppose triggered this dream?"

"I think you said something last week about your being a mother and a daughter. You hardly ever say anything about yourself, so I was interested. I know the dream is not real, and it's an idealized image of a family. I'm sure everything is not perfect for you. I'm sure there are sometimes fights, but it felt good to be part of the family."

I flashed briefly to how ironic it was that Christina was having this dream now, given how my real family is changing, but then I reminded myself that this was her dream rather than mine. I said, "It sounds like a lot of longings for fitting in and being loved. Also, a real wish for your parents to be different, if only you could change them."

"That's for sure. It would be so nice for them magically to become the ideal parents, sweet and talkative, up for playing games, being involved."

"It's hard to accept them as they are and work on yourself rather than trying to fix them."

"That's for sure! If only *they* would change," she sighed with a hint of regret. "I do long to be part of that kind of lovely chaos. But I also know the limits of the therapy thing and that it is confined to this space. I guess I have to accept that," Christina said wistfully.

"In another life, I would like to have you as a daughter. I feel close to you," I assured her. "But, yes, of course, there are limits to our relationship. You will grow up and leave me, just as you will grow up and leave your parents. I will treasure the memories of our time together on this journey of growth."

"It has been quite a journey."

"How does it feel to think that we will eventually end therapy?"

"Sad," Christina replied promptly. "I will miss coming here. But we don't have to end anytime soon, do we? How will I know when it is time to stop?" She suddenly sounded clingy, which was so different from her initial reluctance to commit to therapy.

"You will probably be the one to say when you're ready to stop. Or I might say that I think we've come as far as we can. Hopefully, we will agree when the time is right."

"I'm not ready yet. I need to do so much more work on myself, and I need your help. In fact, I wanted to tell you that I looked at the catalog for courses at the community college, and I'm getting excited about going back to school."

"Yay, that's great! Let's go back a minute and talk about this fantasy that families are ideal and don't fight. What's your thinking about that?"

"I'd like to fight more with my parents. It's the coldness and walls and not talking that's so hard. At least with fighting, I could tell them what's going on and have disagreements."

Thinking it was an ideal time to come back to the anger issues that Paul had noted, I said, "It's interesting that you and I have never had a fight."

Christina quickly reacted, "I don't want to piss you off. And, in fact, I can't think of a time when I was angry at you." She sounded like she was trying to convince herself.

"Maybe I could figure out something to do to make you angry," I playfully suggested, and both of us laughed. "But seriously, if you were to feel angry at me, what do you suppose would be the outcome?"

She immediately said, "I think you'd reject me, maybe kick me out of therapy. It feels like anger is not allowed; at least it wasn't in my family."

"Let's just imagine a small thing that you could be angry about if it ever happened."

A long silence. "Maybe if I emailed you, and you didn't respond."

"Have you ever felt like you wanted to reach out but didn't?"

"Maybe. But then again, it didn't feel like it was a real crisis, and I didn't want to bother you. I wouldn't want to waste your time. I wouldn't want to intrude on your family life."

"So, you felt some resentment that I had this *perfect* family life, from which you're excluded? And you couldn't even contact me if you really needed me?"

"Yeah," Christina looked down guiltily. "But then I feel mad at myself because I can't ask to get my needs met."

"Can you change the word *can't* to *won't*?"

Tentatively, Christina tried, "I am mad at myself because I *won't* ask when I need help."

"How did that feel?"

"A little forced, but I get your point. I can make a choice. No one is stopping me from asking. I might not always get what I want, but I can ask."

"Yes," I confirmed. "If you are in a crisis, I want you to contact me. I want to be there for you. I can't promise you that I will always be immediately available, but I will get back to you as soon as I can to set up an additional meeting. We both know that I cannot replace your mother, but I can be here for you as a therapist."

"That's a relief to know," Christina said plaintively. "I promise I wouldn't contact you unless it was something big."

"I know that, and I trust you. I'm glad you told me this dream. It's important that we work on our relationship. If we can be open with each other, you will be better prepared to be open with others. How are you feeling right now?"

"I have more energy to try talking to my parents. They aren't perfect, but they are the people I randomly got as my parents. I don't want to wait as long as my mother did to fix the relationship with her mother. And I know I have to try harder with my father."

"*Have* to or *choose* to?"

"Yeah, yeah," she said, sounding a little annoyed. "*Choose* to."

"You sound irritated."

"Yeah, it feels picky and like *gotcha* again. But I hear you that I can make a choice."

"Yes, and maybe if you start speaking up and asserting more of your needs, your parents will reciprocate," I suggested.

"It's worth a try," Christina agreed with a smile.

"You sneaked in the comment about looking at courses. Tell me more about that."

"A new semester is starting soon, and I could start taking courses. I'm seeing so many I want to take. The latest thing I am excited about is climate change. I want to do something to make a difference."

"*Making a difference.* Can you talk about that more?"

"It seems important to do something that matters, that gives me a purpose. I see so many people who just work to get money, and that seems sad to me. I want to have some passion about what I do. There are many ways to do that, and I don't want to get stuck in what the *right* or *perfect* thing is."

"And of course you know that there is no right or perfect thing."

"Yeah, but I feel jealous of those people who have known since they were young that they wanted to be doctors or teachers. I just never had a specific thing. We used to have these projects at school where we had to write about what we wanted to be when we grew up. That assignment always felt tortuous to me."

"What were some of the things you wrote about?"

"I just kind of picked them at random. Once I chose being a landscape architect because I love flowers, but then when I researched it, I realized I didn't have the requisite talents, and it also sounded boring. For a while I wanted to be a computer programmer. I liked that book *Tomorrow, and Tomorrow, and Tomorrow* about these two friends who created video games."

"Sounds good. I look forward to hearing where you go with this. Again, there's no perfect career, and many jobs that will exist in the future haven't even been created yet, so it's good not to settle on anything too quickly. Preparing yourself broadly seems like a good idea, so that you can be poised to go wherever there are openings." I frowned, hearing myself sound so obnoxiously professorial again.

"Yeah, good point. I would like everything to be perfect."

Realizing it was the end of the session, I dragged myself back. "Before we stop today, I wanted to suggest that we take some time next week to talk about how we're doing. We agreed to take time to think about whether you want to continue, which fits in with what we were talking about today. So maybe you can think about that before we meet next."

"Okay. See you next week," she said heading for the door.

Interesting how Christina gets into the positive transference of idealizing me, especially when my life has been rather rocky lately. I think it's important to be real with her that I'm not perfect without disclosing too much about my own problems.

I kicked myself for drifting into academic-type rants (e.g., there are no perfect jobs or ideal families; there will be jobs in the future that don't yet exist) that Christina doesn't relate to. I want to pay attention to how she responds and target my interventions more responsively to her needs. I suspect my own need to be perfect and my latent wish to be academic generated these professorial comments. Or maybe there was something about Christina that stimulated my wanting to teach her things; maybe her idealization prompted some pompousness on my part. I'll have to think more about that.

36

ESTHER: OUT OF THE MUDDY PIT

"Steve and I went out for coffee last weekend to talk over our separation," I said, feeling relieved to be able to unload on Paul about the situation. "He's processed a lot about being gay. Turns out he went to therapy finally, and that really helped. He seemed more emotionally healthy than I've seen him in a long time. I could see what initially attracted me to him. He's a good person, just not hetero. Maybe at some point we can be friends again."

"And you're feeling?" Paul probed.

"Sad but okay. I think maybe we can work together as partners raising our kids. And I think we can separate without a lot of animosity. We talked about going to a mediator to help us separate amicably; neither of us wants nastiness and fighting. And we're going to sit down together to talk to the kids about the plans for the separation, divorce, and custody."

"Did you gain any more insight into why you had no idea what was going on with him in terms of sexuality?"

"I think I didn't *want* to see anything. I certainly have been around a lot of gay, trans, non-binary, asexual people as clients both during my doc program and in my practice, but I didn't have much exposure to the non-hetero world when I was growing up." I paused to reflect. "His parents are conservative and antigay, so it must have been something he resisted thinking about for a long time. I suspect he tried hard to be hetero. It was more common when we were younger for people not to consider other lifestyles, but there has been so much lately in the media that it kind of forces one to think about what you *choose* to be rather than just accepting the sex you were assigned at birth."

Paul studied me intently, "And what are your feelings about being married to a man who came out as gay?"

"Oh, wow, great question. Hmmm, I guess I feel a little resentful that he wasn't completely honest with me and used me to pretend that he was straight. It feels terrible to say that because I know he's going through a lot. But, yeah, I do feel a little angry."

"And how about your own sexuality? Does it make you question that?"

"I've been pondering that recently. I'm pretty solidly in the hetero camp right now, but I suppose that could change depending on circumstances."

"Such as?"

"I don't know. Availability. As women get older, there are fewer men. And it could be easier to be with someone like me. On the other hand, it probably depends more on the specific person. I can imagine being attracted to different people." I paused. "Right now, I'm not looking for anyone. I need some time on my own before rushing into any relationship. This whole thing is just a little too raw right now."

"A couple sessions ago, you described that dream of the hot sex scene with a stranger," Paul reminded me.

"True, so I obviously still have sexual needs. But I'm a little appalled that it was a stranger. That seems so out of character for me."

"A little judgmental, huh?"

"I'm always telling my kids and clients to be careful. I guess my wild side came out in my dream."

"Tell me more about your wild side. That hasn't come up in our work together."

"Yeah, that's interesting. It hasn't. Maybe I've repressed that side. I had a time during college where I was kind of wild, and it was fun at the time, but I've been pretty tamped down lately."

"What would it mean to let more of your wild side out now?"

"Hmm. I would be more spontaneous instead of having everything planned out, maybe letting loose a bit in terms of dating when I start doing that again."

"You perked up when you talked about being a little wild," Paul observed.

"Yeah, it does sound enticing. Maybe I've been too much on my best behavior, being a good mother, therapist, wife. Maybe I can let up on that some."

"You talked a couple sessions ago about losing yourself and not taking up space. How are you doing with that?"

I was glad he brought that image back. "I've been trying to insert myself into conversations more. I used to just ask questions and let other people talk. I'm consciously trying to bring up things, to be more of a presence. It's a real effort now because I'm such an introvert. But I'm going to keep trying to take up more space in relationships."

"Good. You're taking up more space in here, which is terrific," observed Paul. "I feel like I don't have to do as much of the work. To go back to your metaphor about my throwing a rope to you over the bridge, it feels like you've grabbed the rope and are climbing out of that muddy pit. I don't feel as much a need to rescue you."

"I agree. I feel that, too. I'm coming to you for a consultation rather than for a rescue or a complete personality restructuring."

"Agreed. I am delighted to work with you. I look forward to our sessions."

"And while we're on the topic of asserting my needs," I said. "I wonder if we could spend more time talking about Christina."

"Sure. But I can't help but notice how you phrased it. Rather than saying this is what you'd like to do, you asked permission."

"You are so right! I bring that up when Christina does it in her therapy, and here I am seeking your permission. Seems like the female condition."

"Hmm," Paul smiled. "So not a choice or something you can change?"

"Yeah, yeah," I nodded in agreement. "But to the work with Christina. She had a dream in which I was her mother. I disclosed that I would like it if she were my daughter. It was a close moment, but I felt like I was doing something wrong saying I would like her as a daughter."

"Why would that be bad?"

"It feels like a boundary violation because of the limits of the therapeutic relationship," I admitted, wondering how he felt.

"I think it's fine. After all, even Carl Rogers said something like that to a client in the *Gloria* film," he reminded me.

"Oh, that's true. That's where I remember if from. Yeah, that was a nice moment in the film." I hesitated but then added, "I'm thinking similarly that I feel kind of like your daughter."

"I feel close to you, too," Paul affirmed, both of us smiling. "I wonder how that fits with your fear of men?"

"It has been a corrective relational experience working with you. You are a man who listens and is gentle. I've never seen you angry. I was worried about your being bored when I saw you years ago, but this time around I feel like I see you more as you really are—a kind person who listens and gives of yourself."

"I want to acknowledge that I also grow from working with you. It reminds me of having to pay attention to my needs and boundaries, of having to be aware of getting my needs met elsewhere instead of with clients, of thinking intentionally about what I hope to accomplish in sessions. And it also reminds me that we are getting close to the retirement date. We have only one more session after today."

"OMG, that's right," I said, feeling suddenly abandoned. "You will not be here if, or more likely when, I fall back into that muddy pit."

"Right, I'm graduating and moving on," Paul confirmed quietly. "And obviously, even if I weren't retiring, I will die at some point. I am close to eighty, and there is less time in front of me than behind me."

"I know we talked about this, but I'm still taken aback," I said, aware that my voice was wobbling. "I've always thought of you as totally stable and ageless. It's terrifying to think of you dying. It's like losing my father all over again."

"What was it like for you when he died?"

"On the one hand, very sad. My world felt ripped apart. That layer separating or protecting me from death was ripped open. On the other hand, it was relieving that I didn't have to deal with him anymore. And on the third hand, however many hands there are," we both laughed, "disappointing that I never felt as close to him as I would have liked and didn't resolve all the problems between us."

"Lots of ambivalence. What do you think you might feel when I die?"

"Sadness. Loss. I'll miss you. But, at least in one corner of my heart, I know I will carry you with me. You're a part of me. I will hear your voice calming me down and giving me advice, pulling me out of the muddy pit, teasing me."

"You can carry me with you just as you carry the voices of your parents with you. We are all part of you. Your memories keep us all alive," Paul nodded.

"That's such a nice way of looking at it." I nodded. "I really don't know what happens after death. Sometimes that scares me. I can see why people become religious as a comfort and as a way of finding answers. That doesn't work for me, so I guess my strength is in keeping the awareness that I have to live the life I want."

"Which brings us back to making sure you *are* living the life you want."

"I'm working on it. I've made the choice to limit my practice to twenty hours a week. I haven't taken on any new clients for a while and won't until I get the hours lower than twenty. It feels freeing to have made that decision. I look forward more to working with the clients I have."

"And what about the financial cost of not seeing as many clients?"

"That's a good point since I see a lot of insurance and low-fee clients. I feel passionately about making psychotherapy accessible to low-income people, but it means I don't make a lot of money. I didn't get into doing psychotherapy, though, to get rich. I don't want to be less helpful because I'm doing too many client hours. I've thought about the impact of decreasing my client hours now, when we won't have a two-income household. Although Steve will continue to pay child support, we will have to cut some corners. But it's doable."

"You mentioned last time about finding a new therapist. How are you doing with that?"

"I have been gathering names, but I was waiting until we end. Maybe I will start calling this week."

"Sounds right. What are you looking for in terms of a new therapist?"

"Someone outside my social circle and not related to my doc program. I don't think it matters about male or female, but maybe someone around my age or a little older so that I have a mentor for the next stages of life."

"All good. And how will you fill the other time if you're not seeing as many clients?"

"Well, going to therapy and a mediator and working through all the issues related to the separation is going to take time. Other than that, I'm going to let myself have some free time and see what emerges. I don't want to rush into anything. I think in our society we're all way too busy and trying too hard to be important. I want a simpler life, one with more balance. A retired neighbor said that she does nothing and loves it. That's something I aspire to."

Paul nodded appreciatively. "Do it! And now about your work with Christina. What do you think the main issues are between you?"

"Working with Christina has opened up this whole bit about working too much and not knowing exactly what I want to be doing with my life. Maybe a midlife crisis is like adolescence when you're trying to figure out what you want to do with your life. The difference is that I'm already on a path and could easily stay here my whole life without really pondering options. The other thing is that I feel protective of her. I feel an urgency to get her to make up her mind. I hold myself back to give her space, but I worry that I push her too much because of my own insecurities."

"That's a good awareness to have so that you keep to the boundaries. I wonder if you could ask her if she feels you're pushing her too much?"

"Actually, it's funny, she's always worried about intruding on me!"

"You're both worried about crossing boundaries. I wonder if you're worried about making her angry at you."

"Interesting that you bring that up. We talked about how she's never felt angry at me. Maybe we're both too nice and afraid of stirring things up," I pondered. "That kind of resonates. I don't like to have people angry at me," I admitted.

"Good food for thought. Something to talk about with your next therapist," Paul suggested. "Anything else?"

"I don't think so right now."

"How are you feeling about our work?"

"I feel good. We've done a lot in a few sessions, probably because we had such a good foundation from our previous work. I'm grateful that you agreed to see me. I'm worried about sinking back into the muddy pit but more confident about seeking a new therapist," I summarized, aware that we were already a couple minutes overtime and not wanting to push limits. "And I wish you well trying to figure out your plans too. Retirement sounds like a big deal."

"Thanks. We can talk about that more next time if you like. It's good to be thinking ahead and planning because you never know what the future brings," Paul said.

CHRISTINA:
FIRED

Christina came in with tears streaming down her face. "I *am* so pissed off," she exclaimed angrily. "I can't believe it. I got fired from that stupid waitressing job!"

"Oh, my. Tell me what happened," I said.

"Do you remember I told you that I sometimes picked up packages for Joannie when she wasn't working that day? I put them in my locker to give her the next day. And do you remember that the cook guy said I was gullible and naïve, and I never understood what he was talking about? Well, Joannie got caught selling drugs. They searched everyone's lockers and found drugs in the packages I had stored in mine for Joannie. What a dummy I was! I said I didn't know what was in the packages, but the boss didn't care. He said I was fired, and that was it."

"What a shock!"

"Yeah," she slumped into the chair without even looking at the dog. "It's just hard to believe. It's not a world I know anything about. I *am* gullible and naïve."

"You're being pretty harsh with yourself."

Still crying, Christina said, "How stupid could I be?"

"How are you feeling toward Joannie?"

"I can't believe I was friends with her. She used me. I wanted a friend so badly, I couldn't see what was happening. My eyes have been opened to what the real world is like."

"I wonder if you're feeling relieved, too?"

"Maybe. I was having a hard time quitting, and this decided the issue. The good thing is they are not going to report me to the police. I think they know I didn't have anything to do with it, but they had to throw someone under the bus to save face. I can't believe Joannie would do that to me. Just scummy."

"Not a great way to treat a friend."

"Well, I keep remembering that guy's description of me—*gullible* and *naïve*. I guess this was a wake-up call. I won't be quite so trusting."

"Has this been a pattern in your life where you've been too trusting?"

"Well, there was the rape. I went to that guy's house to play video games. I had no idea that he would assault me. As I think back on it, I wonder if he slipped something into the wine he gave me. I've heard about date rape, where women get taken advantage of."

"That makes sense. And here again you were trusting, and it turned out badly. But you know, I'm remembering that you picked up on some vibes that something was going on with these packages, but you didn't check it out."

"You're right. Maybe I should trust my intuition more."

"Right. Take a deep breath. What now?"

"Classes start next week at the community college, so the timing isn't bad. I don't know what to say to my parents about being fired. I feel so embarrassed and stupid."

"How would it feel telling them the truth?"

"I hadn't considered that," Christina said, frowning. "I wonder how they'd react. On the one hand, they wouldn't understand. They don't know anything about drugs. Nor do I for that matter. On the other hand, I don't think they ever felt completely comfortable with my working at the restaurant and being friends with Joannie."

"Would it be worth it to try that out and see how they react?" I suggested mildly.

"I might have to since I need their financial support. Ideally, as I think about it, I'd rather take a full load of courses and not work so I could catch up for the lost semester."

"Can they afford to pay your way through?"

"Yes. My mother told me they put aside money for me for college. And community college is not expensive. Maybe it's for the best," she sighed.

"How are you feeling now?"

"I am still angry that it happened and disappointed in Joannie, but I know she has problems. I feel like I dodged a bullet. Things could have gone a lot worse."

"Good perspective. What have you learned?"

"Not to be so willing to trust others and to follow through on my instincts more. I've also learned I need to move on and get back to school." Christina wiped her eyes.

"Would you like to practice what you might say to your parents?"

"Hmm, no. I think I'm okay there. I'm sure my mother will be supportive, and I'm not really worried about my father's reactions."

I waited to see if Christina wanted to add anything and then said, "If you're ready to move on, I would like to talk about how you're feeling about being in therapy."

"I've thought about it since you brought it up last week. In a way, it feels like we just started. In another way, it feels like

I've been seeing you forever." Christina took a deep breath and reflected. "I don't want to stop now. I just stopped waitressing and am starting community college. Things are better with my parents, but it's all so new. So many things we haven't even gotten to yet—friends, romantic relationships, eating and weight, career. I guess it takes a lot longer to change than I thought it would."

"True. It took you a long time to get where you were, and it takes a while to change things. But how does that feel?"

"Well, initially I thought you could fix me quickly, but I'm realizing how hard it is to change. I look forward to our sessions. I *need to*, I mean, I *choose to* keep working right now."

"Good to hear. I certainly enjoy working with you," I agreed. "Are there specific things you'd like to change in our relationship?"

"Hmm. Harder to talk about, but I did think about two things. First, it feels like I still don't know a whole lot about you. It feels like you've been so helpful, but it does feel one-way. I guess I'd like to know more about you, but I don't know if that's okay to ask, or if that's intruding on your territory too much, or if it's allowed. And the second thing maybe is related. I was thinking about what you said about there not being much anger in our sessions, and I was wondering about that. I have a hard time with anger, and I just feel so grateful to you for what you're doing that I don't think I could allow myself to feel anger. And I have no idea if you've felt any anger toward me. I know you've said you're proud of me, but I don't know much more about your feelings about me."

"Good things to think about. And what a change that represents that you're able to tell me some negative things. You're right. It does feel like it's one-sided in that you're the client and I'm the therapist. I've been oriented to helping you open up. I certainly use my feelings to gauge where to go next, but I haven't told you as much about what's going on with me in our relationship. Is there anything specific you'd like to know?"

"Yeah, I worry about being boring. And I think it came up early on when I felt like maybe you were bored. I'd like to know how you feel."

"Honestly, I did feel somewhat bored, or maybe a better word is frustrated, in our early sessions. You were so quiet, and it felt like I really had to dig to help you open up. But I have to say that even those times were intriguing and made me work hard to conceptualize what was going on with you. I thought a lot about possible defenses and how you might have needed to hide and avoid closeness. But I admit that I was relieved when you started talking about your dreams, because you really came to life. And when you disclosed about the rape and abortion things began to fit together. Any reactions about how you might have been feeling during those initial sessions?"

"I was scared to death. I didn't know what to expect. I was afraid that you would be judgmental because my problems seemed so mundane. In many ways I have had a privileged life, and yet I wasn't happy. I *felt* boring and self-involved. On the other hand, I liked how you sometimes reinforced me and said you were proud of me. I especially liked it when you said you would like it if I were your daughter. That meant a lot to me."

"To me, too. But back to anger. You're right that we haven't had big anger, although we've had a few disagreements such as with how much advice and homework to give."

"That's true, and I appreciated that you did not force me to do homework."

"I think you've taken a big step in terms of talking about negative things. And if you ever feel even any slight annoyance, please be sure to bring it up because that will give us a good opportunity to deal with anger. Anything else you wanted to know?"

"I guess I'm just curious about your journey. You seem to have it all: a PhD, a marriage, two children, a fulfilling career. I'm curious about how you navigated that. Maybe a little jealous, since I imagine that everything went so smoothly for you, like you had a perfect relationship with your mother and your children love you unconditionally."

"Hmmm. Actually, I have felt somewhat competitive with you too, given that you're young and have your whole future ahead of you, whereas I feel like I'm getting old. I've had my ups and downs, and life has certainly thrown me some curves. I'm by no means perfect, and I've had my share of angst and therapy and have had to work hard to figure out what I wanted in life." I paused and looked at her. "Any reactions to my saying these things?"

"I'm surprised. It certainly makes you seem more human. Thank you for telling me. It makes me feel better to know that you've had anxieties, too."

"We're all on a journey, and each of us is dealt different good things and obstacles, and each of us must navigate our path without being able to clearly see all the possible consequences. Here we are focused on you because it's your therapy; I work on my own issues outside of here as much as possible so as not to have a negative influence on you."

"Oh, that's interesting. I didn't know that. Could I ask what you do?"

"I'm in a peer supervision group where we talk about cases, and I have been in my own therapy to talk about issues that get triggered when I see clients. Therapy is a wonderful profession because you get to be with people as they're changing, but it often triggers issues for each of us that we have to be aware of."

"Wow. I never thought of that. Maybe I should become a therapist so that I can keep working on myself."

"Theres's that old *should* again," I said, and we both laughed. "I have confidence that you're going to figure out your own way, but it may take time and exploration."

"I'm more confident now than before. I'm eager to start school again and see what's out there. And with all the changes in the world in terms of technology, I think you're right that new things will keep emerging."

"Any reactions to our disclosures about jealousy and competitiveness?"

"I feel closer to you."

"Great. Therapists disclosing is often a bit tricky, but I thought you were ready to hear that I'm not perfect. It is important, though, to check out your reactions."

"It really helps to hear about your feelings."

"If you have any more feelings over the week, please let me know."

"Will do."

"And how are you feeling about continuing in therapy at this point?"

"Oh, absolutely, I feel like I need it. It seems like we are just getting started."

"Okay. Let's keep talking about our relationship though to make sure we're on track." Knowing that we needed to end the session, I asked, "Any final thoughts about being fired?"

"I'm glad I could talk it out with you. And I'm sorry that we went overtime this session."

"No problem. I wanted to make sure that we talked out the feelings. Good luck talking with your parents. I can't wait to hear about your classes. See you next session."

I am impressed with how well Christina handled getting fired, thinking about talking with her parents, and talking about our relationship. She has grown so much. It's interesting that as I deal more effectively with my own problems related to Steve and the kids I don't feel as competitive with Christina. I feel like we're in a good place right now—I'm eager to see how our relationship changes and develops.

38

ESTHER:
FINAL SESSION WITH PAUL

Driving to the session, I am aware of the many feelings that have come up for me this week: upset about Paul's retirement/eventual death, pondering that I might be blocking Christina from being able to express her anger, worry about how things will work out with the divorce from Steve, fretting about the kids being happy, anxious about what to do with my time if I'm seeing fewer clients, and worrying about starting with a new therapist. And there's always death anxiety, feeling like a failure because I haven't achieved enough professionally, and not having dealt with all my concerns about religion and friends.

I take a few deep breaths and try to decide the most pressing topics to talk about in our final session. Better to do one thing in depth than to cover a bunch of things superficially. It feels like I'm at a turning point in my life. But working on my dreams always seems to get me unstuck, so maybe I'll start with the puzzling dream I had last night. Feeling relieved that I have a plan, I pull into the parking garage and walk into Paul's office.

"In my dream last night," I said, as I sat down and gazed at the Monet painting,

> I am on an expedition at the South Pole. It is unbelievably cold. I am bundled up in a huge parka. I am with a group being led by a renowned leader. All of a sudden, I'm totally alone, and I don't know where I'm going. I know that if I sit down and give up, I'll die from the cold, but I don't feel like I can go forward. I'm paralyzed and don't know what to do. I wake up scared, with my teeth chattering.

"Take a deep breath," Paul said, giving me a moment to regroup. "What comes to mind as you think about the dream."

"We just had this huge ice storm, and everything shut down. It was cold, and Star refused to go outside. We had to carry him out to a special spot to do his business. I felt alone, isolated, and abandoned. Now that I think of it, angry too, like why isn't anyone rescuing me?"

"Ah, the old someone else needs to rescue me." Paul smiled a gentle confrontation.

I made a face, "Yeah, interesting that pops up again."

"What comes to mind when you think about being abandoned?"

"Now that you mention it, Steve leaving me. And you retiring or dying. Just when I start relying on you again, you leave, and I'll probably never see you again," I whimpered.

"And that makes you feel . . . ?

"Angry, upset, hurt, little, left out in the cold, alone, like I can't handle life on my own."

"I can see why you'd be upset and angry. You looked shocked when I told you last week that I won't be around forever."

"Yeah, life sucks. It feels unfair that just as I start feeling good about our relationship and more like an equal with you, it's ending."

"Let's change the dream. If you could redo it any way you want, how would it go?"

"First, it wouldn't be at the South Pole. I hate cold. I like walking and hiking, though, so let's make it a hike in Spain, maybe walking the Camino on a spiritual journey. You're the guide, and we have great discussions about existence and life, and we solve all the world's problems."

"Sounds like therapy, doesn't it? And does this trip on the Camino end at some point?"

Sighing deeply, I muttered, "All good things come to an end, don't they? Yeah, it ends after a wonderful trip. But, then again, on any trip there are hurdles. We might even get angry about little things, and I may want to be the guide sometimes and make some of the decisions."

"Would either of us need to be the guide in this fantasy, or could we be equals?"

"I like that, and we are equals in many ways. We're both psychologists, but I am coming to you for help."

"Yes, you are coming to me for help, but you're not helpless. You are an active agent, and you have a say about how things operate in this room. I make decisions about how I run my practice and when I retire, but you make the decisions about your life."

"Good point. I can't force you to stay with me forever. Nor would I want to. I know on an intellectual level that you have a right to retire, but it's a big loss. I wish I had come back earlier so that we could have had more time together."

"I can hear how much you're grieving, like there's an empty space in your heart."

"Yes, we just got close and now you're leaving."

"I hear you. Perhaps there's that sense that it's hard to get close because it's painful to lose the closeness, especially at the same time as the loss of your marriage."

"So true. I guess it's better to have loved and lost than never to have loved at all, but that doesn't stop the pain."

"The pain lets you know what you had. It's an indicator that you're alive. Life is up and down, and sometimes all you can do is hang on and go with the flow."

After a big sigh, I said, "I did call and set up an appointment for next week with a new therapist. I got a referral from a friend from grad school. I am mourning that you're leaving but recognize that I need support going through this divorce."

"Good for you. And what else are you doing to take care of yourself?"

"Well, I have been back in touch with my friend from grad school. I have a peer supervision group that meets once a month. I might reach out and make some friends in the neighborhood. And I could get more involved professionally, start going to conferences and seeing old friends."

"That all sounds good." He smiled and wagged his eyebrows. "What's the probability of your doing those things?"

"Good challenge there! You mean instead of sitting out in the cold whining and being a martyr about not having support?"

"Yeah, that summarizes it well," Paul chuckled.

"I'm getting ready. Maybe I need to change the dream even more. Rather than you and I being on the Camino, I want to change it to being with a group of friends. Or I could see doing it with my kids, and maybe my siblings. Actually, going with my siblings sounds great. I have so few opportunities to hang out with them. But I also hear you. I am getting ready to make some changes. I've already turned down two possible clients, and one client, not Christina, recently terminated, so I am keeping my word about lowering my hours. I must clear the space before I have time to start anything new."

"That makes sense. Let's go back to the dream. I'm struck that you were passive. What do you make of that?"

"Hmmm, interesting, let me think." I stopped for a minute before continuing. "Maybe I'm scared of change. Yeah," I said checking inside, "that resonates. Things are moving fast, what with Steve leaving, lowering the numbers of clients, and stopping therapy with you and starting with a new therapist. It feels a bit like staring into the void, like what if this doesn't help? What if I'm destined to be unhappy?"

Paul waited for me to stew in that.

I went on, "But even more, I think the discussion of death is scary, like a sword is going to fall. You'll die. Steve will die. The kids will leave home. I'll be all on my own. I'll be the sad, lonely old cat lady. No one will visit me. I'll be parked in a nursing home. And then I'll die. Will anyone remember me? Once I die, then what? Nothing? I am my world; if I don't exist, my world no longer exists. Things go on without me. That's terrifying."

"Where were you before you were born?"

"Nowhere. There was no me before I was conceived. Somehow that doesn't bother me, but not to exist afterwards does. Like, how can the world go on?"

"I haven't got any good answers for you. It's the existential reality that we all face. There are no easy answers. We live; we die. No matter whether you're special or not, you die. You come in alone, you go out alone."

"I agree. I just don't know what to do with it."

"You can live your life each moment as you choose. Live it like you might not have another chance."

"That's a lot of responsibility!" I protested feebly.

"True, and no one else can make the choices for you. You are adrift on the South Pole, stuck down in the muddy pit, hanging for dear life onto the rope thrown over for you, and you must figure out how to make your way in life. I was able to go with you on the journey for a while, but this is the end of the road for us."

"That sucks. I thought that if I was married and in therapy, I was doing all I needed to do. But here I am not quite able to cope on my own and wanting to be taken care of."

"Yes, it's the human condition. You know, the existentialists never said anyone would be happier when they stared into the existential realities. It's sobering to have to take responsibility."

"True. And opposite of that, religion and positive psychology make such promises. It's so seductive. They make it sound so easy. Just be positive. Yeah, well, lots of us feel even worse afterward when we realize that not everything is positive or secure or wrapped up."

"That's again the human condition," Paul confirmed. "In some ways it would be easier to be a plant or animal and just live and not be upset. When we developed these great thinking powers, it was also a curse. We can do critical thinking, we can run the world, but see where it's gotten us. We have climate change and dictators and wars. It's a pretty grim place. But you do have some choices—not complete control, but some."

"I remember a book I read one time that stayed with me. I don't remember the title, just the ideas. This woman and her dog go to some island in New England for the winter, and she begins every day by asking herself, 'What do I want to do today?' No *should*, just making decisions. Being alone for six months sounds terrifying to me, but learning how to live with oneself and make choices seems right."

"Any other thoughts?" Paul inquired gently.

"Thanks," I sighed. "It's been incredible to get a chance to talk in depth about all this existential stuff. I'm reminded of Yalom's *When Nietzsche Wept* and how much that book made me think. I remember back in high school thinking about all these existential issues. I love the idea of going off for six months and figuring out each moment what I want to do. I choose not to do that right now, but I can be more mindful of the choices I make. I can decide how I want to live my life. It's kind of exhilarating to think about making conscious decisions each moment. Do I want to be married? Do I want to spend more time with my kids, friends, siblings? Do I want to see clients? Do I—the list goes on. I made the right decision about cutting back on clients. The things beckoning to me now are friends and intellectual pursuits, like writing or research. I am going to think about how to make those things happen. And I'm energized for how all this translates to my work with my clients, including Christina. You are such a good role model. I'm sure you have your own issues, but you listen and give me good feedback."

"Let's look back. Have you gotten what you need out of this brief stint of therapy?"

"Yes. I had gone off the rails and was sinking into the muddy pit. You helped me get back on track. Funny, we didn't talk much about my children, but things are going better with them now that I'm back into feeling better about myself. But I'm going to need to focus on my relationship with them with my new therapist."

Paul smiled. "You're doing great. We must stop now. But I want to let you know how important this work has been for me too. And remember, you don't *get cured*. It's a lifelong journey to keep working on yourself."

"So true. Thank you," I said, giving him a hug before leaving. "Goodbye." I left with a heavy heart. Endings are painful.

PART III

TWO YEARS LATER

39

CHRISTINA:
GO WEST, YOUNG WOMAN

As Christina came in, I noted how much she had changed from the timid, nondescript person who knocked on my door three years ago. She was dressed in quirky thrift-store clothes, had a small butterfly tattoo on her wrist, sported a pink stripe in her hair, was slim and physically fit, and seemed self-assured. She looked like an artsy Gen-Zer. I realized how much I was going to miss her when we ended.

She began, "I can't believe we have only two more sessions after today. I have so much to tell you. I'm excited about going to Berkeley. It's always been a fantasy. When I went out there to visit with my parents, we stayed at this cool hotel where the key cards had pictures of famous graduates. Maybe I'll be a famous grad one day."

"I'm proud of you going off to explore the world," I agreed enthusiastically, thinking of how she had inspired me to do the same.

"And I'm so glad Chendu is transferring out there, too. She thought Harvard wasn't right for her, so we're going to room together off-campus with four other people. We've talked a bunch over Zoom, so I think we'll all get along."

"Could be great fun. Also," I added wanting to reinforce her changes, "it provides opportunities to negotiate and stand up for yourself and have some good fights."

"True that. After having a room to myself my whole life, living with others will be challenging. The others have lived together for a year and have house rules all set up. Chendu and I will be coming in as the new ones. They are all science majors and super smart. So, it's not as much a party scene as an academic place. And they all are into social justice and politics, and that's exciting too. It seems like the big bustling house I always dreamed of.

"Speaking of leaving home," I changed the topic so that we could reflect on how far she had come in therapy. "Catch me up on how things are going between you and your parents."

Christina stopped momentarily to think about it. "Much better. I like them now. I can communicate with them more openly. I'm glad I stayed home after high school and worked things out with them. They were stuck in unhappy lives, but now they are expanding and growing. I'm glad they went to couples counseling. They admitted to me that they had seriously considered divorce at one point but then they decided to work on the relationship. They also both quit their jobs and found better jobs where they are happier. They have encouraged me to find a career that I truly enjoy rather than just staying with a job for security. The atmosphere in the house is so much better now. There's more laughter, teasing, banter."

"You know, I'm remembering back to that dream you had early on of your mother sitting on her bed so unhappy, and there were these little ghost babies. Did you ever find out what that might have been all about?"

"I did. I asked my mom if anything had happened, given that there were so many years between when they got married and when I was born. My mother said she had several miscarriages, and they thought they would never be able to have a child. She said it just about destroyed their marriage because she was so sad, and my dad didn't know how to help her. They each withdrew into their own worlds. When they finally had me, they were scared and had a hard time attaching to me because they were sure I would die. My mom cried when she told me all this. She said that they talked about it a lot in couples counseling and were finally able to be honest with each other. They sat down together with me and apologized, and they thanked me for being a model for them by getting into therapy."

"Wow. That is so touching. Makes me feel like crying!"

"Yeah. It's so interesting how these things happen in families; lots of secrets, like I haven't told them about my rape and abortion, or like my mom dating the Black guy and then leaving home out of anger at her father. My father also opened up and talked about the dysfunction in his family. His father had been a minister, and his parents were rigid and didn't allow children to question their authority. There was also some abuse and hypocrisy. And he just shut down and gave up. He's actually a funny person. And they are making friends in the neighborhood. They have been playing pickleball and having people over for dinner. It's like, 'Wait, who are these people?' Again, it's funny how there can be an upward spiral when things go well, just like there can be a downward spiral when everything looks bleak."

"I noticed you said you hadn't told your parents about the rape and abortion. How are you feeling about that?"

"I don't have to tell them everything. I don't think it would help anything, and they would just feel bad they hadn't helped me."

"That makes sense. It's your choice."

"I might tell them later. I guess I'm still working through some feelings about it."

"Still some mourning to be done, figuring out about relationships and trust," I agreed.

"Yeah, something I will continue to work on."

"So, let's come back to having only two more sessions after today. One of the reasons we spend a few sessions talking about termination is to help you prepare because endings can be difficult. What memories do you have of other endings?"

"The big one that comes to mind is my grandmother's death. I was glad that I went with my mom on that road trip and got to know her. And it felt good connecting with my mom's family at the funeral. More recently, I've gotten to know some of my father's family too. But yeah, the ending with my grandma was sad. It brought on a lot of angst about death and what happens afterward. It helped me put life in perspective though and realize I want to live my life fully because time is limited. I also remember that my grandma loved life. She wasn't famous and hadn't done anything that would get her written up in the *Washington Post* obituaries, but she loved her family and was a good person."

"Other endings?"

"I am sad to be leaving the community college. It was a good experience. My classes were small, so I got to know my instructors and other students. I began to feel like I have some abilities. I am going to miss the friends I made there. There was so much diversity. Not the same people I went to high school with, and that gave me an appreciation of people who work hard to make something of themselves. We had a party with six of us who were all in the same classes and became good friends. I cried saying good-bye. Even if I see these people again, it won't be the same. We won't be hanging out in the same classes. Everyone will go their own way."

"I can feel the tears as you say that. It's hard to get close to people and then have to leave. What's coming ahead can look exciting, but it's hard to leave behind what you know is good."

"Oh, and I don't think I ever talked about this dog Snoopy we had when I was little. I told Snoopy everything. When I was a sophomore in high school, my parents put her down. But they didn't tell me they were going to do that. I came home from school one day and she was gone. I was upset with them because I didn't get to say goodbye. They apologized to me just a few weeks ago for not talking over that decision with me. I cried a bucket over that dog. I still feel sad thinking about it. I think that's why I love Star so much. He's such a good dog."

"And how about the ending of high school?"

"Oh, looking back, it was so painful. I had loved school before the rape, but then I just withdrew into myself. I didn't know where to turn. In a way, it was a relief for it to be over. But then it felt like I had nowhere to turn. Not a good ending, for sure."

"All the more reason for us to make sure this is a good ending," I affirmed. "What disappointments do you have, things you wished that we had talked about more, things you still need to resolve?"

"Probably the main thing is I'm not settled about my sexuality. But I know it's not something that I have to settle completely right away. As you know, I have experimented, seeing if I'm attracted to men or women, making sure now that I protect myself. I'm not sure, maybe I could go either way. I do feel comfortable being a woman, which I know is something a lot of people question. And maybe it's better to be going off across country when I'm not entangled with anyone, but I wish I had been in a longer-term relationship. I think living with my parents in a dysfunctional relationship put me off serious relationships. I'm wary of having the strength to stay true to myself."

"I can see that. Maybe you need to establish yourself more firmly before you can be in a relationship. I'm thinking of that old metaphor of two pillars. Each pillar needs to be strong enough to hold up the building. If the pillars are leaning on each other, the building will collapse because there's no foundation."

"Great metaphor! And with this move I'm feeling apprehensive about keeping a true sense of myself. And then there's the feeling that California is a different culture, more liberal, especially at Berkeley, and I'm not sure how I'll handle that."

"What kind of things can you do to keep a strong sense of self or to get back to a strong sense of self if you feel yourself slipping?"

"Oh, that's good. Be prepared in case or when I start feeling shaky and down. I can call my parents or talk to Chendu. She's become a good friend.

"There's a good counseling center at Berkeley. You could go there if you need help."

"Good to know about. I also wonder if I can come back and see you when I'm home on vacations?"

"At least as long as I'm practicing, I'm happy to see you when you're back in Maryland. Speaking of metaphors, I heard a person describe therapy as a lifelong journey. Kind of like you cannot cure the common cold but rather need to get treatment each time you catch a cold. Therapy can be kind of on an as-needed basis."

"Whoops, wait a minute, you said as long as you're practicing. Any plans to retire? You're not that old, are you? I guess you can hear the panic in my voice. I've relied on you so much, and there are already so many changes. The thought of your not being here and available scares me."

"In answer to your question, I'm forty-seven years old, so retirement is a long way away. But at some point, of course, I will retire."

"Whew, it's relieving that it's not now. But I do have to ask if I would be intruding if I wanted to come back over vacations."

"There's that word *intruding* again. Haven't heard that for a while." We both laugh, and I add, "I would be happy to see you over vacations, if that's what you want at the time. And I promise I will tell you if I feel you are intruding."

"That's a relief. I've tried so hard all my life not to be a bother to people. But I suppose it's hard to know from the outside if someone feels like they are being intruded on. A fear I have is that if I am too strong or abrupt, I will put people off and they won't like me or be able to handle me."

"And what could you do if that happened?"

"Ah, yes, I do have agency, I get it. I can ask how I came across. I can observe the other person's reactions. I can apologize and then try something different and see what happens."

"Yes," I affirmed. "It is good to check out how you come across to people, especially when you want to have a close relationship. Just as we have talked about our relationship a lot and you've talked with your parents, it's important to talk with others who are close to you. It can be hard to do. I imagine you remember some uncomfortable times in here when we talked about our relationship?"

"Yeah, I do. It felt really awk, like it was against the rules. Maybe I felt a little intruded upon or pushed to go beyond where I was ready to go at the time, even though now, when I look back on it, I'm glad you pushed a little on that."

"That's a good awareness. And I'm sorry if I pushed you more than you were ready. I couldn't always tell because you're good at hiding your feelings, and I cannot read your mind."

"Oh, that's funny," Christina laughed. "At first, I thought you could read my mind. But I know I hid things, especially things I didn't like about therapy and about the rape and abortion. I figured I was getting a lot out of therapy, so not everything had to be perfect."

"That is the way relationships work. They just have to be good enough. And it's important to speak up, so that others know what you need. I guess that's a good note on which to stop for this session. Just to repeat, we have two more sessions."

"Yeah, seems all of a sudden like there's so much more to do."

"There always will be more to do, but you will become increasingly able to do it on your own with support from friends and family. You're in a good place. See you next week."

40

ESTHER AND SUNDAY FAMILY DINNER

As Esther sat at one end of their long dining table, she rejoiced in how much she enjoyed the new tradition of Sunday family dinners, at once both chaotic and fun. Joel sat at the other end of the table entertaining the table with a funny story about a client who had sent a box of live lobsters after he missed a session. Jess and Josh sat on one side of the table along with Esther's mother. Joel's two children, Ed and Patty, about the same age as her kids, sat on the other side next to Steve and Henry.

Esther had met Joel, a family therapist with a wicked sense of humor, at a conference of the Maryland Psychological Association. His wife had died of pancreatic cancer after a brief but traumatic illness. Esther and Joel hit it off immediately when they met, laughing over one of the sessions where they had to role-play a therapist and client talking about therapist boundaries. During the next presentation, they had traded notes back and forth, giggling like middle schoolers. They shared interests in psychotherapy, biking, and dogs. After a year of dating, they moved the two families together into a big house in Silver Spring, each having a home office. After some tension, Esther and Steve had smoothed things out and were now friends, mutually involved in raising Jess and Josh. Esther had also reached a rapprochement with her mother and had begun including her in family events. They particularly enjoyed cooking the dinners as a way of spending time together.

"Mom, we're done eating. Can we go play video games?" asked Jess, bossy as ever.

"Uh, after you all finish your vegetables. But come back later because we made a special coconut cake."

"Ick, I hate coconut," Josh protested.

"There's plenty of ice cream to choose from in the freezer. Begone, you all."

Steve turned to Joel and asked, "How are you putting up with living with four kids?"

Joel good-humoredly said, "Easy—headphones and family meetings."

Sarah, Esther's mother, jumped up to clear the table. "Sit down, Mom," Esther said. Now that the kids are off, we can have a decent adult conversation. But no talk about politics."

Joel quickly jumped in. "What do you all think of green burials? We've been doing some investigation into them. It appears that the tradition of embalming and burials in big caskets and cremations are both equally bad for the environment."

"I've never heard of green burials," said Kristin. "Can't we talk about something more uplifting, like my upcoming cruise around the Greek islands?"

"Well, we all have to make decisions about what to do when we die, and it's better not to leave it all to the kids to try to guess what we might like," Esther added.

"Hey, that reminds me of a dream I had last night," Henry jumped in. "I think it was all of us together on Noah's ark. We each got to pick which animals we wanted to bring along."

"Oh, that's so funny," Esther said. "My dream last night was about taking flying lessons, and you all came to see me off."

Steve added, "Well, my dream was about salmon swimming upstream." We were all laughing loudly at this point. The kids edged back in to see what was going on.

Sarah jumped in, "Well, maybe this means that you all should go on the cruise with me. I'd love your company."

There was an enthusiastic clamor. "Let's do it!!!!"

Always the family therapist, Joel said, "Well, we have become a family. I treasure all of you, and I'm glad I've gotten to know you all."

We raised a toast. "To family."

CHRISTINA:
DREAMING ABOUT YOU

I had a dream last night," Christina said, sitting down next to Star. "I'm still not sure about it, but it seems like it might be related to my move to California."

"Go for it," I responded, loving how she spontaneously brings in her dreams.

"Okay," Christina said, looking down to pull her thoughts together.

> I'm walking with you up this dusty, rugged hiking trail. It's really hard work and takes a long time for us to get our footing. We get to the top, and it's a beautiful day. The sun is shining. There are fluffy clouds in the sky. There's a fork in the path, and we have to decide which way to go. To the left, there's a little stream going down the mountain. To the right, it's a dusty trail up with a sign that says there's a beautiful butterfly garden at the end. Then, suddenly, you disappear, and I'm with a group of strangers. We decide to go up the trail to the butterfly garden.

"Wow! What a great dream. I'm reminded of your dreams when you started therapy; you were all alone in the forest and the jungle. This time I'm with you on the way up, and a group of people are with you as you go farther. What a change!"

"Yeah, but then you disappear, which is a bummer, and I'm left with strangers. At least this dream isn't at night. I'm not scared, but I feel a little intimidated, like how are we supposed to make this decision? And where am I?"

"Not scared but intimidated. Can you talk about that more?" I probed encouraging her to experience the emotions.

"I guess I am confident that I can make it out. It's daylight. It's not a scary trail. It's just that we have to make this decision. I would like others to go with me, but it's not terrible if they don't. I just kind of wish I hadn't gone up this mountain. Maybe I should have stayed somewhere where I knew where I was. But, on the other hand, maybe I can make it. Kind of like in one of those extreme reality shows where you have to find your way out by yourself."

"I hear two major images: the tough trail and the separating ways. Which one do you want to focus on first?"

"Let's talk about the trail going up the mountain. In this dream we're on the trail together. Even though there are brambles and difficult things along the way, we can stop and figure out together what's going on and pick which direction to go."

"Yeah, it sounds like we're walking together. Neither of us is leading or following."

"Yeah, of course I know and respect that you are the therapist. But I appreciate that you regard me enough to make my own choices with your consultation."

"Thanks, that's important to me. It is your life after all, and I will not always be around. What are the feelings at this point of the dream?"

"It's hard work getting up the mountain, but the view at the top is great. I feel terrific that we made this trip."

"Any associations?"

"Lots. I'm thinking of the journey with my parents, how I believed I'd never be able to talk to them. I'm thinking about the first couple dreams I had when we started therapy of being lost in the forest and the jungle. In this dream, I don't feel lost. Another association is how I've begun to enjoy walking and hiking. I hear there are good trails to explore in California. I'm also thinking about how hiking is not always easy. Oh, and I'm remembering the owl in my first dream, thinking that, for me, the owl represents wisdom."

"And are you able to find that wisdom inside yourself?"

"Yeah. I am beginning to trust myself more than I did before."

"Anything you'd change in this part of the dream?"

"No, I like the journey upward, at least in retrospect," which sets us both laughing.

"So, let's go to the fork in the trail," I direct. "Tell me more about that."

"It feels painful that I had to make the decision to go off on my own. It is the right decision, but I'm going to miss your companionship."

"Interesting word, *companionship* rather than *guidance* or *therapy*, which reflects the changes in our relationship, that you're ready to go off on your own. What about the two paths?"

"Well, I do like butterflies," she commented, pointing to her butterfly tattoo, but a stream would provide water. As I think about it, the mountain I'm on looks a lot like the hills or mountains in California, a little barren but ruggedly appealing. So maybe this dream is about moving to California and being with new people. It's a strange terrain, certainly not the lush green of Maryland. I will have choices to make."

"Yeah, and maybe some fear that these new people will not support you."

"It will be a challenge to figure out how to relate to new people," Christina agreed.

"I notice that in some of your past dreams I was there to help you, but here I leave before the end. I wonder if maybe the dream is also about therapy ending?"

"Oh, I hadn't thought about that," she responded. "Yeah, here I have to make this major decision, and you won't be there. Can I make it on my own?"

"What are you feeling in your body?"

"All of a sudden, I am having a hard time breathing," she said looking down. "I can picture myself on that path wanting to call you, but you're not there."

"What would you want to say if you called?"

Softly, still looking down, Christina said, "Help me."

"Your voice was so quiet when you said that. Can you say it a little louder? Is there any anger there?"

"Okay, let me try. More loudly she cautiously demanded, "Why aren't you here when I need you?"

"Again, and louder."

Louder this time, she sounded more convincing, "I'm angry you're abandoning me. How could you let me go away when I'm not ready? Why did you encourage me to go to California? I'm leaving my parents and you. What support will I have there?" More softly, she added, "I'm scared."

"Yeah, I hear that you're angry about my abandoning you, although you're the one leaving. I wonder if you're also disappointed that you haven't gotten quite as far in therapy as you would have liked so that you could be completely self-sufficient?"

"Well yeah," Christina considered. "I guess there is a little disappointment that you haven't fixed me completely, even though I know I have to fix myself."

"Can you say directly that you are disappointed with me?"

Christina sighed and then looked at me more directly, trying to be assertive but not wanting to hurt my feelings, "I am disappointed. I expected to be fixed in just a few sessions, and here we have had almost two hundred sessions over three years, and I'm not *cured*. That sucks!"

"Where do you feel the anger and disappointment?"

"Again, I'm having trouble breathing, and I can feel that my face is red. I don't want to hurt you, because you've been so good for me. I've made so many changes, and I *should* be totally grateful. It's so hard to say negative things to you."

"You can feel both gratitude and disappointment or anger," I pointed out gently.

"Yeah," she nodded in agreement. "It is disappointing that life is not perfect and then you die. That existential stuff is so anxiety-provoking. Part of me still yearns for everything to be perfect, for me not to have to work for it, and to just have the answers handed to me on a platter."

"I wonder if you're disappointed that I wasn't the perfect therapist and that you're also not the perfect client."

"Yeah, it stinks to realize that we're both human and imperfect. But also relieving to know that I'm not the only one who struggles. In fact," she cocked her head to the side as she explored the thought, "that's kind of cool. I'm looking forward to taking some philosophy classes and maybe thinking about these things more."

"Great idea. Come back to your dream though," I said, focusing us. "Can you think how you'd change the dream if you could have it turn out any way you want?"

"Hmmm, yeah." Taking a minute to ponder possibilities, Christina reflected, "I think I'd like to go up the trail with a group of people I know, friends, maybe my new roommates. At the top, I want to stop and have the group discuss in which direction we should go. I want to be part of making the decision. And then we go down the mountain and hang out and have some craft beers at a local pub."

"That sounds lovely," I agreed, liking how she changed the dream into ways that we had discussed in therapy—making friends and making choices. "How could you make that happen in waking life?"

"I could invite people to go on a hike with me so that it's a planned thing. Or maybe I could join a hiking group and go with a group of people. Someone told me about this group called meetup.com where you can meet people, kind of a dating site, but it's for making friends and finding people who like similar activities. I could do that."

"Awesome. I think you could," I said wanting to support her fledgling self-efficacy. "You sound cool as you say it. Maybe you don't need me to help you make all your decisions."

"Hmm, but," she looked down, "I'll miss you."

"I'll miss you too."

"I'm sure I'll have issues as I adjust, given that I've never been away from home, but it's also exciting to make big changes."

"We all experience issues during transitions. And I know that you have the resources to figure out how to dig yourself out. See you next week."

"Thanks."

42

ESTHER AND HER MOTHER

Esther had started calling her mom every morning to check in. "How's it going?" she asked.

"Well, I had a hard time sleeping last night," Kristin said, sounding sleepy. "Our good friend Frank died yesterday. Remember all the family get-togethers we had with their family? He was your father's best friend. I can't believe that another one of our friends is gone."

"Oh, I'm so sorry. What are the arrangements for the funeral? I'd like to go with you."

"I'll let you know. It makes me think that I was rude when you and Joel brought up the idea of green burials last week at the family dinner. I apologize. It makes me anxious to talk about death," Kristin said.

"Sorry for bringing it up. I am concerned about what your wishes are, but I can see why it would be off-putting."

"I thought a lot about it when your father died. I do have a burial plot next to his, if you'll recall. I guess I need to think more about other details. It's just so difficult."

"How are you feeling about living alone? You've been healthy, thank goodness, but I worry about you."

"Well, I probably have too much time alone. I've been having a lot of regrets. I feel bad about the power struggles we've had; I didn't know any better. But I think we're doing better now, finally."

"Thanks Mom. We *have* had our difficulties getting along, and I'm glad we're at a better place together. Let's keep talking. I'd like to hear more about what it was like for you growing up. There's a lot I don't know about you."

"I'd like that."

43

CHRISTINA:
A LITTLE GIFT FOR YOU

Christina handed me a nicely wrapped package. "I brought you a gift."

"Oh, how nice. Thank you. I have a little something for you, too," smiling as I thought about how we both had brought gifts to the final session. "But before I open your gift, tell me about it and your thoughts as you were choosing it and while giving it to me now."

"I wanted something to remind you of me. And I wanted to get something to let you know how much I appreciated our work together. I thought about it for ages, and then suddenly it struck me that a dreamcatcher would be perfect. And you don't have one in your office. Since we have spent so much time talking about dreams, it seemed like the perfect thing. The myth behind it is that good dreams go through the big hole in the center and bad dreams get caught in the web around the edges. But if you can learn something from your dreams, I'm not sure they're ever really bad. I wasn't sure if it was okay to bring a gift. I asked a couple people who had been in therapy, but they didn't know. I figured you will let me know if there's a problem."

"Generally, it's considered okay to give a small gift," I noted reassuringly. "Most therapists want to know, though, what's behind giving the gift to make sure it's not crossing boundaries or would make either of us feel uncomfortable. Your reasoning sounds fine to me." Taking the gift from her, I asked, "Is it okay to open it?"

"Please do," she nodded eagerly.

I untied the bow and opened the package carefully so as not to tear the paper. I saw the dreamcatcher. "Oh, this is lovely! The feathers are so beautiful. I love dreamcatchers, and I like the idea that it filters out the bad dreams and lets the good ones go through. Thank you. It is touching because of how important dreams have been in our work."

"I pictured you hanging it right there," Christina pointed to a spot on my window.

"Perfect," I said, getting up and hanging it there, relieved that I liked it. "Thanks again. And here's a little something to remind you of our work," I said handing Christina a package.

Christina opened the gift bag and pulled out a small but heavy metal owl that fit easily in her hand. "Oh wow, the owl from my forest dream. I can play with it when I'm nervous and carry it in my pocket as a good-luck charm. The owl is like my spirit animal. I love it. Thank you!"

"I wanted you to have something to remind you of how wise you've become and how you can carry that wisdom with you."

"Yeah, I'll think of phrases you've said when I hold it in my hand. Like 'breathe,' 'shit on the shoulds,' 'make choices,' 'what do *you* want to do today,' 'live fully,' 'process your dreams,' 'communicate,' 'people cannot read your mind,' 'you need two pillars to hold up a building,' 'you don't have to be perfect,' 'you only live once and then you die,' 'enjoy the angst.' I've learned so much from you. I'll take with me these Esther's sayings."

"For our last session I'd like to spend the time looking back, looking forward, and saying goodbye to help bring us some closure on what we've done and what you have left to do. So, to look back, can you think about what brought you to therapy and how you felt about starting therapy?"

"I was totally stuck. I felt dead inside, like a frozen statue. I couldn't even cry. Looking back, I had no idea about emotions. I just didn't feel anything. I was beyond being an introvert. It sounds melodramatic, but I was desperate. I finally realized I needed help, but it was so hard to make the effort. It was hard to call. It was hard for me to trust you or anyone."

"You look so sad, thinking about your former self."

"I'm also angry that no one reached out to help me. Well, there was the guidance counselor who suggested I go to therapy. I'm grateful for that. It just seems so easy to fall through the cracks in our society."

"The anger is good. And good to remember back to what it felt like," I affirmed. "Let's talk about the goals you set early on. How are you doing on those?"

"In general, I'm doing much better, but of course there's always room to grow. I'm nervous about this big transition, and I'm feeling a little queasy. When I came here today, I thought how this might be the last time I'll see you for a while. Like sitting here in your office. I'll miss looking at your O'Keefe pictures and seeing Star."

"Yes, the losses pile up," I said.

"But starting with my relationship with my mother, so much better. We're becoming really close, and I can confide in her—not everything, of course. I think we turned a corner when we visited Grandma, and then when she told me about the miscarriages, and then again when she and my dad went to couples counseling."

"Yeah, you have all changed. To follow up, though, you said you don't confide everything in her. You mentioned a couple weeks ago not telling her about the rape and abortion. Anything else you're keeping back?"

"Mostly about my sexuality. I am still trying to decide about where I am with that, and I don't want her anxiety to get in my head. I think it's good to have some boundaries with them."

"Okay, makes sense. How about career issues?"

"A million times better. As I said last week, going to community college was the best decision. I feel more confident academically. I'm on track."

"And how about the eating and weight?"

"I'm doing better. I've lost ten pounds since we started. What you said early on about obsessing about weight and eating instead of focusing on more basic concerns like death anxiety and relationships helped. As we've tackled those issues, I've been able to control my eating more. I exercise more and don't snack between meals. Interestingly, I don't obsess about it as much. I'm more compassionate with myself too if I happen to have a bad day and overeat. So, pretty good, but I guess it's something I will need to keep working on."

"Right," I agreed, "It's a life-long project to keep track of exercise and eating, especially for women in our culture."

"Romantic relationships," she continued. "I'm still working on that too, but I've lagged behind. Well, maybe not behind. I'm just being cautious."

"Say more about being cautious."

"Again, I still feel hesitant because of my parents' relationship. They are getting along better now, but it wasn't good while I was growing up. I would rather be on my own than to be stuck in a dysfunctional relationship. And I don't want anyone telling me what to do. You know I have issues with being controlled. I'm afraid of falling into a traditional lifestyle. I heard a new term, *trad wives*, women who think they have to be perfect housewives, like back to the 1950s. OMG, I shuddered when I heard that term. I want to do something meaningful in my life, and it certainly doesn't involve cleaning toilets and being subservient to some man."

"Makes sense. And I sense that's something you could think about and ponder where all those feelings come from."

"They came from being around my father when he flew into rages," Christina said emphatically. "Let's see, next is self-understanding. Wow, I've changed a lot in that, too. At the beginning of therapy, I was despairing and didn't know why. I was stuck in a big block of ice. Now I feel like I am more into the kind of person I want to be. Again, I have work to do, but I'm on the journey instead of sitting on the sidelines watching. I sometimes think it might be fun to go into psychology as a field, like you. Seems like it gives you a chance to keep working on self-understanding."

"It does," I concurred wholeheartedly, thinking of all the work I've done that has been triggered by what clients talk about. "It is a privilege to be around people who are changing and growing, and it definitely helps keep me in touch with trying to grow and change."

"Next is Father. Better, but not as close as I am to my mother. He's just so much more reserved, and I have a hard time getting through to him. I still have some fear of men. It doesn't come through as often, but his anger and contempt are scary. I just retreat."

"A work in progress. And finally, friends."

"I'm feeling better about that, having made friends at the community college and moving in with roommates, but it will be challenging living with other people. Hopefully, I'm ready. At least, I think I have space in my life for new people. I'll try to think of you sitting on my shoulder, telling me to communicate," she chuckled.

"Sounds good," I smiled too. "I'm proud of you and the changes you've made. You've already started, but let's look back over what has been particularly helpful and not so helpful in our therapy. Maybe start with the helpful."

Christina looked down to reflect. "Well, I'll start with the dreams. I never knew I could get so much out of them. And particularly having dreams about you was wild and unexpected and revealed so much about what I was feeling. The dreams helped me bring up thoughts about our relationship that I might not have been aware of or otherwise would have had difficulty saying out loud."

"Yes, I love how open you are to your dreams. We both had dreams about each other. It certainly helped me think about what was going on between us. Anything else?"

"I remember your saying you would like it if I were your daughter. I love that statement. I feel as though you reparented me, and that helped me have a better relationship with my parents. So safe and trustworthy. I think you're the first person who ever listened to me this well and remembered things I said. I feel like I thawed after feeling so frozen inside."

"You have opened up. I can hear the difference in your tone of voice. Your voice was so timid and halting at first. I had to strain to hear you, but you have so much energy and vibrancy in your voice now. You have so many ideas, and it's fun talking with you about philosophy and life. I've learned a lot from you, too, about life as a Gen-Zer, your community college, biology, and waitressing. It's not all one-sided by any means. Speaking of which, I also want to thank you for giving me the impetus to keep growing. I made some big changes in my life, cutting back on the number of clients I see, getting more active and exercising more, and spending more time with family and friends. Watching you change and grow helped me too."

"That's cool to hear," Christina commented. "I thought at first that you had it all together, so I was surprised to learn you weren't perfect and had gone to therapy. I guess working on yourself is a lifelong process."

"As I mentioned to you before, it's a side benefit of being a therapist. Not only are you helping others. but you constantly have an opportunity to examine yourself and what's going on with you."

"Sounds intriguing, but a lot of work." We both laughed at that.

"I am also so grateful for our discussions about the rape and abortion. I have a new understanding of what happened and how I have to be more cautious and trust my instincts. I feel like my consciousness has also been raised about women's issues, and I want to do something about it. I don't quite know what that will look like yet, but I want to do something to make things better for women around the world."

"Great idea. There is so much need, especially in this current political climate." I continued. "What was not so helpful? What could have made this experience better?"

"It's hard to think of anything negative. I guess, though, I wish I had resolved more issues related to my sexuality. I'm still feeling a little lost there."

"That makes sense. I wish we had resolved more there, too. That's a growth edge for you. And it could be that if you seek out therapy with someone later who is queer or bisexual, you'll feel more comfortable talking about it."

"That could be true. No judgment, but you are married and have kids, and I have felt a little unsure about bringing up much related to feelings about sexuality."

"That makes sense. No one therapist can be everything for you."

"I'm not sure I'll go right away, but I'll keep that in mind."

"Let's look to the future now. What goals, in addition to sexuality, do you have for yourself to keep working on?"

"The big one is career. I'll need to declare a major within a semester of starting at Berkeley. I want to do something related to women's reproductive rights, so I'll have to discover what the best major is for that. And like we talked about before, living with roommates is going to be a challenge that I'm looking forward to. And continuing to work on my relationship with my parents, since I won't be living at home."

"To go along with *shitting on the shoulds*, you've got a lot of *fucking growth opportunities*, or *fgos*." We laughed together.

"I love that phrase. I'll definitely use it."

"Anything else?"

"I'm still worried about death. I feel so out of control not knowing when and how I will die. Someone recently said that people of my generation could live to 120 or 150. On the one hand, it sounds relieving that I won't be dying anytime soon. On the other hand, it seems like forever. If I worked until seventy-five, that would leave fifty years of retirement. What do people do with that kind of time?"

"Take a minute and close your eyes. What feelings come up when you think right now about dying?"

After opening her eyes, Christina said tentatively, "I feel claustrophobic, as if something is choking me. My chest hurts," she said slowly and quietly, her teeth clenched. "I want to run away. I don't want to think about it." She shook her head thoughtfully, "I think I'm most fearful about being sick and having a lot of pain, like with bone cancer."

"I'm noticing how hard it is to let yourself experience the feelings," I observed.

"Yeah, the feelings are there, but I don't know what to do with them. I'd like for them to go away."

"There might not be anything you can *do* with the feelings, but it's good not to avoid them. It is a fact of life."

"Yeah, I can't figure out if it makes me feel like I want to live my life to the fullest, that feels like a *should*, or whether I want to run away and hide and quit trying."

"Those are the two extremes. What's the *should* in there?"

"I *should* have meaning. I *should* do wonderful things in my life. But on the other hand, if I'm going to die, what difference does it make? Who will remember me fifty years after I die? Why run on a treadmill just to keep busy and get ahead if there's nothing to get to?"

"And what's the feeling as you say that?"

"Despair, like all of a sudden, I feel dependent on you, like you've kept me sane for the last few years, and how am I going to do this by myself?"

"I hear you. It's scary leaving therapy."

"Yeah, this is all I know. What if Berkeley is horrible? What if I don't make friends? What if I never find a partner or have kids? What if I'm not remembered?"

"You've mentioned being remembered a couple times. What is scary about not being remembered?"

"If you're not remembered, it feels like you're really dead. But then again, why would anyone fifty years on remember me?"

CHRISTINA: A LITTLE GIFT FOR YOU

"I'm thinking of that metaphor of ripple effects. That maybe you have an effect on one person, who has an effect on another and another, and it's the ripple that is remembered fifty years after death," I offered.

"I like that idea. Maybe it's enough to have one or two good relationships and live here and now and not worry about the future."

"Sounds good if you can pull it off. But then again, it sounds like you'd be living without awareness, and maybe that's worse. That could really be like being on the treadmill with blinders on, and then you die. It sounds like you'd like a guarantee of happiness."

"Yeah, that would be nice," she said, and we both laughed. "Can you give me a guarantee?

"Wouldn't we all like a guarantee of happiness forever? It's like the price of awareness is angst. Does it help to talk about your angst with me?"

"Yes, absolutely; the worst is when I keep it all to myself, like when I ruminate during the middle of the night. At least if I can share it and know that others feel the same, I know that it's maybe just the human condition. Yeah, I agree, we could be unaware of mortality, but if I have to choose, I'd rather have the existential angst than to be unaware."

"Yes, it comes back to making choices, right? We might not always know what choices to make. But we can do our best to figure out what we want to do. Each day you can say, 'What do I want to do today?'"

"Making choices seems both liberating and such a huge responsibility. It would be easier to blame someone else. But I don't want anyone else telling me how to live."

"You're dealing with the big issues that philosophers have dealt with since the beginning of time. We each come up with our own conclusions about how to live our lives. What works for me won't necessarily work for you. It's exciting to hear you grappling with these issues. Anything else?"

"That might be it for now. Except maybe talking about leaving my parents. They're going to fly out with me and stay for a couple days. I don't know how much contact I want to have with them. Some of my friends call their mothers every day, some talk once a month."

"What sounds right for you?"

"I think I might like to check in with my mother every day, especially at first. Parting will seem weird, since I've spent almost every day of my life with her. Maybe just a quick check-in, like 'What did you have for breakfast? What are you doing today?' Except there's a three-hour time difference, so it will be more mid-day for her."

"How would that feel?"

"Good. I want to stay in touch with her. Less with my dad, but I know she'll tell him everything. It's going to feel odd not to come home until Christmas, but the plane fares are high and it's far away, so I can't rush home every weekend, which is why I chose California."

"Speaking of finances, I know we talked towards the beginning of treatment about your financial concerns for college. What's that like for you?"

"I got some scholarship money, which will help. My parents will pay tuition and give me a monthly allowance, for which I'm grateful. I know it will be a stretch for them. I plan to be careful with my money and hopefully won't have to take out loans. I plan to pay my parents back after graduation, but I don't know how long that will take. Maybe I'll find a part-time job. If I'm careful, it should be okay."

"I'm glad that worked out for you. Having to work for your education can be good and make you realize what it's worth."

"The cost of college has gotten crazy expensive. It makes me question whether it's worth it, but I think it is. All the job ads say 'college degree required.' Unless you're incredible at technology and can start your own start-up, but that's not my talent."

"And now it's time to say goodbye. I am going to miss you. It's been such a pleasure working with you." I could feel my eyes tearing up and noticed Christina wiping away a tear.

"I will miss you too, Doctor Esther. I've grown so much here. I'm glad we took the time to reflect about our relationship for the past few sessions. It's funny, I feel like I'm fundamentally the same person but also different and better. I'm me but not me. I feel alive rather than dead and frozen inside. Is it okay to give you a hug?"

"I would like that." We stood and hugged, wiping our eyes. "Goodbye and good luck," I said.

"Oh," Christina said, backing away and petting the dog. "I have to say goodbye to Star, too. He has been such a good therapy dog, always sitting by me and encouraging me."

"He will miss you. He always perks up when he hears you come to the door and jumps right up next to you."

"Goodbye again." She waved on her way out the door.

"Good luck, Christina," I said, feeling the loss of ending.

I listen to Christina's footsteps fading down the hallway. I will remember her fondly. As usual, I reflect on the work we've done. On the one hand, she has changed a lot. On the other, she still has some problems, as we all do.

I think about the owl and the dreamcatcher. The children's nursery rhyme plays in my head: "The Owl and the

Pussycat went to sea in a beautiful pea-green boat." I smiled that we picked gifts that reflected the therapy so well.

I am grateful that she triggered me to get to work on my own issues. When I look back over the three years working with Christina, it feels like a lifetime. It took a long time to adjust to the ending of my marriage with Steve, but working with Paul for a few sessions and seeing my new therapist helped me get back on my feet. I feel more solid now, like I have myself back, and I feel fortunate to have this great new relationship with Joel and to have worked out things with my mother. I feel I'm more of an active agent in my own life and look forward to all the future challenges.

ACKNOWLEDGEMENTS

For ten years, people asked what I was going to do when I retired from the university as a psychology professor. When I responded that I was going to write a novel about dreams and psychotherapy, my friends and colleagues offered enthusiastic support, giving me confidence that I had a good idea. I learned a lot about shifting from writing academically from Kathryn Johnson in her course with the Bethesda Writer's Center on "The Extreme Novelist." Many friends read early versions of this book and gave me great feedback: Barry Farber, Jim Gormally, Sarah Knox, Carol Mishler, Kathy O'Brien, Kristen Pinto-Coelho, Pat Spangler, and Barbara Thompson.

I am grateful to Christine Kessides for educating me about the publishing process and referring me to Bold Story Press. Thanks to Emily Barrosse at Bold Story Press for taking a chance on a new author, Nedah Rose for her incredible help in editing and refining the story, Jocelyn Kwiatkowski for managing the process, Harlan James for copyediting, Kelly Schumacher for her help with marketing, and Karen Polaski for designing the cover and interior of the book.

ABOUT THE AUTHOR

Clara E. Hill retired from the University of Maryland as a full professor of psychology. She has been the president of two psychology organizations, editor of two psychology journals, and the recipient of international academic awards. She started and directed a low-fee psychotherapy clinic, had a small private practice of psychotherapy, and lectured around the world. She has published eighteen books, including books on dreams and helping skills, and about 300 empirical studies. She is now involved in several research projects as well as writing novels, including this debut novel about dreams and psychotherapy. Clara is married with two children, four grandchildren, and a cavachon dog. Her hobbies are reading, walking, and solitaire.

ABOUT BOLD STORY PRESS

Bold Story Press is a curated, woman-owned hybrid publishing company with a mission of publishing well-written stories by women. If your book is chosen for publication, our team of expert editors and designers will work with you to publish a professionally edited and designed book. Every woman has a story to tell. If you have written yours and want to explore publishing with Bold Story Press, contact us at https://boldstorypress.com.

BOLD STORY PRESS

The Bold Story Press logo, designed by Grace Arsenault, was inspired by the nom de plume, or pen name, a sad necessity at one time for female authors who wanted to publish. The woman's face hidden in the quill is the profile of Virginia Woolf, who, in addition to being an early feminist writer, founded and ran her own publishing company, Hogarth Press.

Thank you for reading my book!
If you enjoyed it, please tell a friend
and consider leaving a review on
Amazon or Goodreads—it really helps.